"A top-class, high-tech thriller. Emily is a true heroine: warm, funny, brilliant and more human than a lot of humans. You'll be cheering for her to the end."

DAILY MAIL

"Remarkably clever and engrossing . . . explores weighty questions of self and soul."

FINANCIAL TIMES

"The most fascinating AI character in recent memory."

ENTERTAINMENT WEEKLY

"A quirky mix of melancholy, irreverence, and romance. Wheaton renders a new twist on humanity's survival in this bittersweet post-apocalyptic novel."

KIRKUS REVIEWS

Praise for *The Quake Cities*

"A fast-paced adventure . . . this post-apocalyptic novel will appeal to fans across genres, and the resoundingly hopeful conclusion is a welcome message."

BOOKLIST

WRAITH

MARK WHEATON

ISBN 978-0-578-95289-5

The Half-Sisters LeClercq
Countess Sandrine LeClercq (1910-1956)
/ \

Marguerite LeClercq* (1938 -) Countess Aline LeClercq (1937 -)
m. Hubert Varennes (1928-1989)

|

Louis LeClercq-Varennes (1959-1992)
m. to Constance Moati (1960-1992)

|

Sandrine LeClercq-Varennes (1979 –)
m. to Kenneth Underwood (1975-2002)

|

Cecily LeClercq (2002 -)

*birth parents Georges Manzanarès (1916 – 1940) m. Colette
Manzanarès née Dutoit (1917 – 1979)

PROLOGUE

"**WAKE UP, WAKE** up," a voice whispered in her dream.

Cecily opened her eyes to a room of dancing shadows. The cypress trees outside the mobile home she shared with her mother oscillated in the dim light. Rain drummed across the roof as loud as gravel poured from a bucket. The outer bands of the hurricane they had spent the last two days preparing for were making landfall.

"What is it, Mama?" Cecily asked. "The storm?"

Cecily's mother, Sandrine, stood over her daughter's bed in a threadbare cotton nightgown. Her eyes were ringed with gray. She hadn't slept for days.

"*Oui*, the storm," Sandrine whispered, glancing to the window as if noticing the wind and rain for the first time. "It's not safe. We have to hide. Come."

Cecily pulled herself out of bed and shoved her feet into her pink kitty slippers before being hustled down the hall toward the bathroom. The narrow mobile home didn't have an innermost room. For storm purposes, the bathroom, with but a small window and the back wall facing inland, had to do.

The house shivered and groaned. Cecily and her mother lived half a mile inland from the famed strip of oceanfront Myrtle Beach resorts and hotels where Sandrine worked nights in the laundry room under the Hilton. It was a lonely job. Sandrine's only contact with others came when housekeepers or waitstaff pushed baskets of dirty linen through the door or rolled carts of clean ones out.

Even then, Cecily thought her mother would've preferred even fewer interactions.

Cecily would often walk with her mother to the beach, though the ocean and sand didn't do much for the eleven-year-old. She favored the longleaf pines, palmettos, and cypress trees of the forests and swamps she'd discovered along the nearby Waccamaw River when they'd arrived a few months back. They moved often. Sandrine led them on a near-constant migration up and down the Atlantic coast, stopping as far south as the Florida Panhandle, as north as Virginia Beach. Though the names of the towns changed, Cecily always found a nearby patch of woods to call her own.

Those trees, so inviting in the daytime, now felt like an extension of the storm as their branches battered the side of her home. Given their size, if even one fell onto the house, it could push straight through their thin aluminum roof and crush them inside.

Cecily hadn't minded the mobile home up until that point. She liked how close it was to the swamp and away from other people. But right now, she wished they were back in the apartment with the blue walls up in Newport News or in the upstairs rooms they'd rented from the old lady with the Burmese cats in Savannah.

Ours is a life in constant motion, Sandrine once told her, you and me against the world. Did I ever tell you I haven't stayed in one place longer than a few months since I left France?

2

Running away, Cecily called it. From what, she hadn't figured out yet.

"Stand there," Sandrine said, ushering Cecily into the bathroom's tiny shower stall so that she could squeeze into the room behind her and close the door.

In the instant before it latched, Cecily thought she saw the silhouette of a woman standing in their kitchen. The silhouette had long, matted hair. Her fingers were splayed apart and tapered down into sharp points. Cecily almost screamed.

"Mama!" Cecily whispered as Sandrine turned back to her. "There's a woman—"

Sandrine clapped her daughter's mouth shut so fast that it felt like a slap. She raised a finger to her lips and leaned in so close that Cecily could feel her trembling lips grazing her ear.

"I know, *petite*," Sandrine whispered. "She's been here since yesterday. In the darkness, in the shadows. I don't know how she found me. But after tonight, she will never find us again. Do you understand?"

Cecily stared at her mother through the darkness, unsure she'd heard right. Her mother knew there was someone in their house? Someone who meant them harm? Her mother's hand found hers and stroked it gently.

"I love you, *petite*," Sandrine said. "Forever and ever."

"I love you, too, Mama," Cecily replied, confused by what sounded like finality in her mother's words.

Her mother kissed her on the cheek but was back on her feet before Cecily could ask what was happening. Dim light flooded the bathroom as Sandrine hurled the door open and raced from the room. Cecily leaped up to follow her but was knocked back by the long-haired woman flying past the door after Sandrine. The woman's skin was an odd color, like slate.

She wore an old-fashioned dress. And the toes of her bare feet appeared whittled into sharp spikes, the same as her fingers.

It was her eyes that sent tremors of terror through Cecily. They were like black orbs with slivers of deep red running through them, the color of blood the moment it rises from pinpricked skin.

Cecily screamed. The wraithlike figure turned. Cecily slammed the bathroom door shut and ran to the window. She tried to open it, but it was stuck. She was trapped.

Lightning strobed outside. Cecily saw the wraith's feet through the gap at the bottom of the bathroom door. If she opened the door, she'd be face-to-face with that ghost. But her mother was out there, too. Cecily had to protect her.

She lowered herself to the floor and inched toward the door. She peered through the half centimeter of space between the floor and the bottom of the door but saw only shadow. She angled her head to look down the narrow hall that ran from the kitchen back to the two small bedrooms. There was no of the phantom or her mother.

That was why her mother ran out the draw. To draw the monster away. *No.* She couldn't let her mother do this alone. It had been them against the world for so long.

She opened the bathroom door and peered out. Nothing moved. The only sound was the rain. She gingerly stepped into the hall. Something passed the window. Cecily ducked. When she looked again, there was nothing. Probably a wind-blown tree.

Then she saw the movement and realized it wasn't outside. It was a reflection.

She whirled around. The wraith was tucked up in the hallway ceiling like a spider, staring down at her. Cecily shrieked and ran. The specter unfolded herself and swooped down at her like a bird of prey. Cecily leaped aside as the wraith passed, landing somewhere in the living room. Cecily didn't see where. She was already out the door.

The LeClercq's mobile home was in the back of a small trailer park surrounded on almost all sides by wetlands. Rather than side by side, the mobile homes were scattered across several mostly overgrown lots along a one-lane dirt road that formed a large horseshoe. Cecily hesitated when she reached the road. She wasn't sure if her mother had gone deeper into the park or out toward the nearby subdivision.

But then she spied several bare footprints in the mud heading toward the entrance, spaced widely apart as if their owner was running. They could belong to only one person.

Cecily followed them, the heavy rain soaking her hair and drenching her nightgown. It was so cold that it felt as if she'd been dunked in an icy lake rather than run through a downpour. All that mattered was finding her mother.

There were no streetlights along the dirt road but plenty when she reached the subdivision. She scanned the empty sidewalks but saw no one. The houses were dark, and the windows boarded up. Most residents had evacuated the day before. Sandrine had insisted she and Cecily would be safer if they stayed put.

"We don't want to be trapped for hours on a highway surrounded by thousands of people," Sandrine had said. "That would be worse than the storm itself."

Cecily couldn't tell if she was joking.

She glanced back toward her house, fearing the wraith was right behind her. There was no one there. Only trees being throttled by the high winds. She'd heard the storm called a

Category 2 on her mother's radio the morning before, only to be labeled a Category 5 right before she'd gone to bed, though she couldn't remember which was more severe.

The footprints led through the subdivision all the way to the four-lane interstate that divided Myrtle Beach's residential areas from the chaos of the hotel-lined Strand. Sandrine forbade Cecily from crossing the highway on her own. There wasn't a vehicle in sight. Cecily took a deep breath and bolted across.

As soon as she was on the other side, she spied the lone figure of a woman striding across the wide, empty hotel parking lot. She passed a light pole and the dim illumination revealed Sandrine's shoulder-length hair now plastered to her back. Despite the lashing hurricane winds, she strode on not to the hotel but around the side toward the beach.

"Mama!" Cecily yelled, though her voice was drowned out by the wind.

Cecily chanced a look back. The wraith was there this time. The ghostly specter slipped through the shadows, seeming to disappear into the dark water pooling on the highway before emerging on the other side. Her long, matted hair trailed behind her like the tentacles of a great squid. The skin on her face was pulled so tight over her skull that it looked like she had no skin at all.

She didn't seem to notice Cecily. Her dark crimson eyes stared straight ahead toward Sandrine. Cecily ran. She had to reach her mother first.

Her feet went out from under her, oil had mixed with rainwater and the parking lot was slick. She scraped her knees on the asphalt. Blood trickled down both legs. Cecily wiped aside the tears that had burst from her eyes, got up, and limped forward.

She wished her father were here. He'd died soon after her birth, a tragedy her mother had never completely recovered from. Cecily's memories of him were few and mostly augmented by her mother's stories and the handful of photos she'd seen over the years. If he were here, he'd know what to do.

She imagined him almost as her mother's opposite. He'd be the one who socialized easily with the other parents at all her new schools. He wouldn't avoid neighbors with quick waves and dismissive smiles. He wouldn't force them to do their grocery shopping at five in the morning when was still waking up.

He wouldn't elicit pitying looks from Cecily's aunts, cousins, and grandmother who probably hoped the quirky, occasionally irksome, often irritating Sandrine would be little more than a passing fling.

But Cecily loved her mother. Needed her mother. She had to keep going.

The Grand Strand at Myrtle Beach extended for sixty miles. What had made this stretch of the Atlantic coast so appealing to tourists and developers over the decades was the seemingly endless, gradually sloping beach extending from the water's edge several dozen yards up the sand to the grassy dunes that formed a natural breakwater. This meant the beach was broad enough to allow literally thousands of people to spread out up and down the shore with room to spare.

The hurricane had caused the beach to all but disappear. The storm surge, great waves of black water driven forward by the high winds, had consumed it whole. Even the dunes were submerged, the sea sluicing through the boardwalk's guardrails to drag anything not locked down back to the ocean.

Eyes adjusting to the darkness, Cecily could just make

out the white froth of the receding tide. She crept along the guardrail like a mountaineer traversing a cliffside. Each wave arrived with enough force to launch her backward. Still, she held firm despite her weakening arms and a feeling of numbness coursing through her body.

She caught sight of a flash of white maybe a hundred yards down the boardwalk. Mama! She lifted herself over the guardrail and dropped onto the waterlogged dunes, legs sinking into the wet sand. She struggled to free herself as the next wall of water slammed over her, as if determined to drag her out to sea. When it finally ebbed, Cecily spotted her mother again, now motionless on the sand.

"Get up, Mama!" Cecily yelled.

As if in answer to her cries, her mother rose to her feet. Instead of going to her daughter, she followed the tide down the beach. The waves rose to strike again. She stiffened as the waves thundered toward her, striking with such force that was lifted off the sand, carried backward, and slammed onto the dunes. When the water receded this time, she was carried with it.

From where she watched, Cecily let out a piercing scream. She thought her mother was dead. But Sandrine got up again and scanned the boardwalk. Cecily waved.

"Up here, Mama!" she yelled. "Up here!"

Sandrine's gaze fell not on her daughter but on a spot next to her. The wraith stood only a few yards up the boardwalk from Cecily. The little girl's eyes went wide in terror. She gripped the guardrail and turned away, unable to look at the phantom any longer. Sandrine stared at it a moment more and then turned back toward the ocean. With renewed determination, she strode in the direction of the oncoming storm. She made it to the water's edge and kept marching until she was waist-deep.

The white crests of the next wave rose in front of her like a cobra preparing to strike.

"Mama!" Cecily yelled one last time.

Sandrine turned her head again. She smiled in the direction of the boardwalk, though Cecily couldn't tell if she was looking at her or the wraith. The waves swelled. Their caps glowed white from the sudden appearance of starlight. The clouds had parted. The rain and wind lessened.

Cecily thought this was another figment of her imagination until she saw her mother staring up into the stars as well. Even the wall of water aimed at the beach seemed to hesitate to take in the sight. But that part was an illusion.

The wave careened forward like a bulldozer out of control. It extinguished Cecily's mother like a candle flame. She was there one minute, then gone. The water raced up the beach, over the dunes, and across the boardwalk with such force that it lifted Cecily off her feet and knocked her over the rear guard-rail. She landed on the dunes below, gasping for air while the water kept coming as if through a broken dam.

More and more and more saltwater surged past her, invading her lungs. She struggled to keep her head above water. Its temperature was so cold, as if dredged up from the very bottom of the sea, that her muscles tensed and grew numb.

The tide finally receded, dragging Cecily with it. She struck and was pushed under. She clawed at the underside of the planks but found nothing to hold on to. At the last second, her arm bounced against one of the boardwalk's support pylons. She wrapped herself around it, hugging it with all her strength.

All at once, the water released its hold. Cecily let go,

rolled down the dune, then limped around to the wooden stairs leading up to the boardwalk before the next wave hit. The gap in the clouds closed overhead as the hurricane's eye moved inland. The wind and rain picked up again, but Cecily stayed at the guardrail, staring at the incoming waters, praying her mother would be carried back with them.

She searched up and down the boardwalk for the woman with the long, matted hair, slate-gray skin, and talons for fingers, but she was gone, as if satisfied by Sandrine's sacrifice. Cecily knelt on the boards, all alone in the howling storm, terrified of a future without her mother.

You and me against the world.

1

CECILY STARED IN disbelief. What she'd stumbled across wasn't supposed to exist. Well, it was *supposed* to exist, especially in South Carolina and even more so along the winding Edisto River as it crept through Four Hole Swamp; it just hadn't for decades.

The base of the single-stemmed plant was surrounded by a rosette of lance-shaped leaves that were green with traces of red along their edges. Its narrow stem rose a foot in the air before it was topped by a large, pinecone-shaped explosion of tiny pink flowers. These flowers, so numerous it made an herb look like a dandelion, gave the plant its name. Swamp pink.

Or, in more refined company, *Helonias bullata.*

Cecily had seen photographs of juvenile swamp pink in a botany textbook she'd checked out from the campus library (and never returned) during her one, ill-starred attempt at college. If she remembered correctly, the red tint of its leaves meant it was a juvenile.

The book also said that swamp pink was highly prized by plant collectors who employed poachers to extract it from Carolina swamps, paying big bucks online. This wouldn't be such a problem if quirks of evolution hadn't resulted in swamp pink's tendencies toward accidental self-fertilization and low seed dispersal.

I still think you're cool, Cecily thought, using her cell phone's camera as a magnifying glass to zoom in on the tiny pink flowers' blue and white stamens.

She snapped a couple of photos to show her boss. Ina Anolik was one of Charleston's most highly regarded garden planners and landscape designers. She was also the one person Cecily had ever met who loved plants as much as she did. Still, she was careful to crop out any identifiable landmarks from the photo's background and to take a screenshot to eliminate location data so as not to tempt Ina or anyone she might forward the pictures to into retrieving a sample themselves.

Not that anyone besides Cecily trekked this far into the wetlands. It was off-limits to hunters and had few hiker-friendly trails. Cecily typically had miles of undeveloped shoreline along the Edisto and Wadmalaw Rivers to herself, save for a few game wardens. As long as she stayed out of the state parks and wildlife refuges, she was free to hunt down and remove as many cuttings and samples of nonendangered plants and flowers as she wanted to take back to Ina's shop in Old Charleston. As Ina's elite customers were among the most monied and politically connected people in the state, should Cecily accidentally remove a plant she wasn't meant to, a couple of phone calls from Ina always convinced the state to turn a blind eye.

It was August. For any of Ina's clients who wished their vast properties and plantations to be awash in wildflowers come spring, the seeds needed to be planted in the next couple of months before the winter chill set in. Cecily's task for the day was to track down wild spider lilies, bergamots, tulips, trilliums, and various species of violet to gently harvest their seeds or to take cuttings that could be transplanted, all with minimal impact to the existing ecosystem.

Once she'd filled three of her sample bags, she hiked back to where she'd left her bicycle, walked it through another mile of mud to the nearest access road, and cycled back to the city.

Charleston wore many faces. There was Military Charleston, which really meant North Charleston where the bases were. This included the air force base where her aunt Olivia worked in the PX. There was West Ashley, separated from Old Charleston by the Ashley River, where all the suburban normies lived. There were the Charleston islands—John's, Sullivan's, Kiawah, and a handful of others—where the wealthiest families in the region maintained palatial estates.

Finally, there was Old Charleston, the tourist mecca and birthplace of the town with its endless historical sites, dusty antique shops, and enterprising residents who renovated teetering old teardowns into overpriced bed-and-breakfasts for the out-of-town trade. Ina's showroom and greenhouse were in Old Charleston. Due to the amount of people out and about at almost any given time of day or night, Cecily ventured in only during the early-morning weekday hours when the population load was lightest.

She'd inherited her mother's avoidance of other people. But whereas Sandrine had regarded others as a half step above plague carriers, Cecily's conditioned reaction was somewhere between an allergy and a phobia depending on the situation. She avoided buses, large crowds, stores, and restaurants and lived alone out by the river in an old camper, though she spent most nights sleeping under the stars.

An outside observer might've judged Cecily as antisocial or worse. Anyone who knew her, like Ina or her assistant gardeners, the folks at the city's Night Market, or the vendors at the Marion Square Farmers Market, thought she was living her best life. Particularly given the tragic circumstances under which she lost her parents.

She was alone but happy. Isolated from the human world but constantly surrounded by the living.

"Hey, Cece!" a young woman cried, waving to Cecily as she set out sweetgrass baskets made from sturdy bulrush at the farmers market.

Cecily waved back, reminding herself to swing by later and pick up one of the vegan, pickle-brined fried chicken sandwiches the woman's brother sold at the market. She'd tried one the previous Saturday and was blown away.

She and her mother had lived in Charleston twice, once in Avondale and once in North Charleston back when her father was alive. Her mother, who'd whisper "*l'hommes*" like a curse when more than two people appeared on a sidewalk in front of them, had assiduously avoided oft-crowded Old Charleston. Cecily thought this too bad. There were certain things about the town—from its architecture to its troubled history—that she believed her mother would have found fascinating.

It had been ten years since her mother's passing. Cecily missed her every day.

A taxi cut across two lanes, almost sending Cecily into a parked city bus.

"Watch it, asshole!" Cecily said, kicking the driver's side door hard enough to leave a muddy scuff mark as it pulled to the curb in front of the farmers market.

She glanced back as she cycled on to see if there was any response from the driver. Instead, she spied a peculiarly dressed man emerge from the back seat and glance around. He had a shock of silver hair rising a full inch and a half off his head as if to try to add some height to his diminutive frame. His outlandish mode of dress fell somewhere between early Qing dynasty empress dowager and *Real Housewives of Beverly Hills*, with a white satin pantsuit that resembled pajamas, a silk cape embroidered with gold and scarlet thread, and a half dozen silk scarves around his neck in such a clash of patterns and color it was as if he'd gotten tangled up in the flags of competing nations.

He hovered a gold-tipped, slip-on loafer over a spot of mud before stepping onto the sidewalk. It looked like it had been fashioned from snakeskin then gilded over with rainbow-colored metallic leaf.

A snake in nature could only *hope* to look so chic.

The man glanced toward Cecily, but she couldn't hang around to people-watch. It was time for her to get to work.

Ina's Florals occupied two of three floors in a century-old building in the heart of Old Charleston. It was boxy and plain on the outside. Tourists could be excused for thinking it was just another antique store when they passed only to find no front door should they choose to wander in. There was a service entrance in the back alley, then one narrow, unmarked door around front that looked more like the entryway to an apartment than a shop.

If they stopped to look closer, they would see a buzzer and a small handwritten yet laminated note that read, *Appointments Only. Ring Bell But Wait As Proprietress May Be Upstairs.*

This, for a business whose minimum retainer for charity galas or weddings was in the low six figures, was considered charming by its clientele.

Cecily whizzed by the first-floor windows, waving to a

couple of the planners already stationed at their desks for the day's appointments. The showrooms, divided between gardens and landscapes, then weddings and other events, weren't that impressive to her. The latter used cut flowers, which Cecily thought a waste. The former, well, the hypercompetitive home-owners who had the money to burn on palatial gardens lacked creativity and tended to favor unsustainable, uninspired bursts of color. This weakened the soil from year to year, adding a zero or two to Ina's invoices when her landscapers had to build it back up.

No, for Cecily, the third floor was the garden spot. It was where Ina had her seemingly endless growhouses and planter boxes that sustained, at any given time, literally thousands of plants. For Ina, it was a stockroom. For Cecily, Wonderland.

She chained up her bike in the alley and headed up the fire escape. Though the building had an elevator—the second floor was a multiroom residence where Ina lived with her three daughters—Cecily had been trapped in the slow-moving car with other people a few too many times. Now she took the stairs and enjoyed the view of the city and the ocean beyond as she ascended.

"You need to use a Q-tip," Ina was instructing her assistant, Hideo, as they worked over a box of fledgling zucchini plants in one of three rooftop greenhouses. "The male flowers have the short stems. Insert the Q-tip to gather the pollen, then rub it over the stigma of the female flower. This is bee's work, so gentle as a bee."

"Hope I'm not interrupting anything," Cecily said as she stepped over the fire escape with her sample bags.

"The city council still refuses to hear the appeal," Ina said, nodding exasperatedly to four empty beehive boxes on the nearby balcony. "One tourist—*one*—gets stung and the city decides I'm the culprit. Now poor Hideo has to hand-pollinate the zucchini."

There was more to the story. It had been several people, including locals, stung over the years. Ina had been warned many times, but as there was no real way to keep bees from ranging wherever they pleased, she'd ignored the citations. Cecily had helped her move the bees to a home on James Island. She wondered if any ever flew across the river to visit.

"I found some swamp pink," Cecily said, passing over her phone.

"My goodness!" Ina said, scrolling through the pictures. "Look at those colors. How many did you bring me?"

"Zilch," Cecily said. "Wouldn't have survived the ride here anyway."

"Oh, look, Hideo," Ina said, showing her assistant one of the snaps. "Cecily's even cropped the pictures so we can't tell where they've been taken. She doesn't trust me."

"Would you trust you?" Cecily asked.

Ina barked out a laugh and was about to reply when an arcane but still functioning intercom buzzed nearby. She pushed its red button and called back, "Niko? Are you looking for us?"

"Maybe Cece," the voice of Ina's front room receptionist said back. "There's someone here looking for Cecily Underwood?"

Cecily frowned. Her father's last name was on her birth certificate, but she'd grown up using LeClercq. How any of Ina's clients, who she only met with if her boss insisted, might know this was a mystery.

"Are you sure?" Ina asked.

"He says he flew in from Paris to see her," Niko replied.

"I thought he had the name wrong until he said it's about her great-grandmother, Marguerite LeClercq."

Cecily's heart leaped. Her mother hadn't told her much about the reasons she'd put an ocean between herself and France at a young age, but Marguerite LeClercq was a large part of it. Like Cecily herself, Sandrine had lost both her parents when she was a teenager. Newly orphaned, she turned to her beloved grandmother. But rather than take her in, Marguerite turned her back on her granddaughter, depositing her in a series of distant boarding schools before Sandrine finally ran away to America.

Cecily walked to the edge of the roof. A taxi pulled away downstairs. The scuff mark she'd made with her shoe earlier was still on the driver's side door.

"Be right back," Cecily said.

Niko had installed the flamboyantly dressed Frenchman in the Magnolia Suite, a space filled with fall florals in rich reds, oranges, and browns. Cecily would have preferred to meet the stranger outside—or not at all—but figured she could handle it for a few minutes. When she entered, she found him snapping photos around the room with his phone.

"Hello?" Cecily asked.

"Eh, pardon," the Frenchman said, raising a finger. "I send these to my partner. It will entertain him."

There was a whooshing sound of a sent email. The Frenchman grinned in self-satisfaction, pocketed his phone, and extended a hand bejeweled with rings and several metal bracelets.

"My name is René Chaumière," he said. "Your great-grandmother greets you."

Cecily eyed the proffered hand warily. "She's still alive?"

"*Alors*, she is," René said, awkwardly lowering his hand.

"But this I must tell you. She is old and terribly ill. She wishes to speak to you before she passes on."

"Are you her lawyer or something?" Cecily asked.

"Neighbor, friend, confidant, and admirer," René said, spinning a hand in the air as if to summon his many roles. "Marguerite is an accomplished woman. You do not know this? There are surprising things you have in common."

He indicated the plants around the room. Missing the reference, Cecily scrunched her brow.

"I know next to nothing about her," Cecily replied honestly. "And I've never heard from her. Even when my mom died. I'd thought maybe she didn't know I existed or where I was. Seeing as how you're here, well. I guess that's not true."

René held Cecily's gaze for a moment as if taking her measure before he glanced out the window and took a breath. "I did not know her so well then," he admitted. "The deaths of her son and daughter-in-law were very hard on her."

"Like, say, the death of one's mother?" Cecily asked.

"*Entre nous*—between us—I am sorry for you about that," René said, raising his hands defensively as his tone darkened. "Marguerite shut out the world for so long. Only in recent years has she allowed herself to emerge in limited fashion. She had been such a famed personality before—"

"Famed personality?" Cecily asked.

"Did I say that wrong? She was notable. An artist."

This was a surprise. "An artist? I've never heard of her."

"You have heard of all artists? Good for you," René said caustically. "She worked, how do you say, behind the scenes. A textile designer creating patterns and prints for the most famous ateliers in France. Even a few whose lesser efforts might be worn in such a place as South Carolina."

Cecily scoffed. René shrugged. "Believe me or do not believe me. She but asked me to locate and accompany you back to France in order that you see her at her hospice before she dies."

"To France?" Cecily asked. "She can't pick up the phone?"

"It is my understanding that what she wishes to say to you is personal, confidential, and of the utmost importance," René explained.

Cecily stared at him before shaking her head. "I don't know you, and I certainly don't know Marguerite," she said. "I'm sorry you came all this way, but I won't be returning to Paris with you."

The flamboyance left René's manner, leaving him looking grave and severe. "It is a monstrous, great tragedy to lose those you love," he said. "I know Marguerite has regrets. I think she wants only the chance to make amends."

"Then tell her to write a letter."

René looked askance before continuing. "I was not meant to mention it, but I understand there is something of an inheritance to discuss as well."

Cecily's face flushed. Her body temperature rose a couple of degrees. "I want nothing from her. My mother warned me about her side of the family. As far as I'm concerned, there is nothing linking me to your neighbor and friend."

René eyed her for a moment before stiffening. "As you wish," he said, offering a curt nod before heading for the door. "Adieu."

2

CECILY RETURNED TO the third floor, then realized she couldn't stay.

"I need to take the rest of the day off," she told Ina.

"Take all the time you need," Ina said, the somber look on her face telling Cecily her boss must have gotten the lowdown on her visitor from an eavesdropping Niko.

Once back on the street, Cecily jumped on her bike and rode through the city to the Battery at the tip of the peninsula. For once, the park was empty. She settled under one of the grand southern live oaks, let her bike fall to the ground, and broke into tears.

So many memories of her mother flooded back at once. Images of the two of them driving over the Talmadge Bridge outside Savannah. Of walking to their Wilmington apartment with groceries. Of her mother leading them on a hike outside Raleigh. Cecily had taken such care to banish or bury all thoughts of her mother. Having someone appear out of the blue, someone who seemed to know a lot about her past, burst her mental dams like a wrecking ball.

She remembered her mother's smile. Her wry sense of humor. How she rolled her eyes at almost all TV shows and movies, only to sob heavily at the most melodramatic soap operas. How she'd loved to dance, sometimes even breaking out a couple of old French cassettes she'd brought over with her to play as she and Cecily executed disco moves in the living room.

She also remembered how rarely she spoke of her French upbringing, so much so that it had taken a moment to realize when René said the name Marguerite, he was referring to her great-grandmother, her mother's neglectful *mémé*. She wasn't sure her mother had ever told her the name. She'd seen a few photographs. Sandrine with her mother and father and grandmother at the beach. With a barge in the background near a river. Outside a church. But little more.

The great-grandmother, this Marguerite, was in a couple of them, she thought, but she couldn't quite remember. Were they smiling? Did they look happy?

A few years after her mother's death, when Cecily was living alternately at her paternal grandmother's and aunt's houses, she'd searched for her family history online. LeClercq turned out to be a common French name. There'd been a ballerina. An ambassador. A famous monk. But no Sandrine. No story of a couple who'd died.

But now she had another name.

She took out her phone and searched for Marguerite LeClercq. Two came back. One who'd died in the 1600s. Then another who'd been born in 1938 but who also went by her married name, Marguerite Varennes.

It was under this name that she found a few old photographs. Marguerite wasn't the focus of the pictures. But there she was in the background, listed in the French captions generally by her name, as an *assistante*, or in a couple of cases, *designer* or *couturière*.

In most, she looked happy. The designs were obviously

Marguerite's creations. There were dazzling colors, subtle patterns, and occasionally brash prints as if she'd taken on the dress or blouse as a canvas on which to paint.

To Cecily's surprise, in almost every case, the designs were botanical. Broad leaves across skirts. Vines of golden thread weaving up a seam. Bright floral prints splashed across a raincoat as if from buckets of spilled paint.

But then she came to a black-and-white image of Marguerite, sunglasses on, head low, being hurried into a building. She clicked on the picture, which took her to an old French newspaper article. She waited for her phone's browser to translate it into English, then gasped.

The headline read: *Inquest Begins in LeClercq Murder-Suicide.*

She scanned the piece quickly. There'd been a killing in a small town outside Paris. A brutal slaying late at night. A husband gone mad, accused of tearing through the town, ranting and raving. A wife murdered. The husband went missing and then was found dead, hanging from a tree, a day later.

Their names were Constance and Louis Varennes.

They left behind a daughter, Sandrine.

Cecily felt lightheaded. Her phone slipped through her fingers and clattered onto the tree roots below. She understood that trauma beget trauma. She'd been counseled about this following her own mother's death. That the children of suicide victims committed suicide at a higher rate than the rest of the population. Some even used the same method.

She'd absorbed this as a way of processing her own pain. While she'd considered that her mother's suffering and suicide were the result of her parents' deaths, she'd never known how brutal the ordeal must've been. Her mother didn't talk about her parents. Ever. Cecily realized that she'd never known how they'd died. She'd known it had happened at the same time, and in her memory, she'd filled this in with a car crash or some other disaster. She wondered if her mother had ever fed her that lie or never filled in the blank at all.

She picked up her phone and stared at the picture of Marguerite. She looked drawn. Distraught. Pained. And why not? This was a woman whose son murdered his wife. The guilt she must've felt. The shame.

Cecily walked to the seawall at the edge of the park to look out over the Atlantic. She wondered, if Marguerite had been there for her mother through all of this, might she have lived? Landed fabulous friends like René, discovered passions of her own, and even thrived? Or had she turned her back on Sandrine hoping, in some way, to give her the clean break and fresh start her granddaughter would spend the rest of her life seeking but never quite finding?

Cecily opened a new window on her phone and searched for a number.

"*Allô?*" said a sleepy voice as if roused from slumber.

"Is this Mr. Chaumière?"

"If you are determined to mutilate the pronunciation of my name, use Monsieur instead of Mister to perfect the insult."

"Did you know my grandfather murdered my grand-mother?" Cecily asked.

There was a pause. "I am to assume you did not?" René asked.

"No."

He sighed. "It is a terrible, terrible thing," René said. "A scandal made worse by Marguerite's maiden name of LeClercq, which your mother reclaimed when she left France."

Cecily realized though the article in the French paper used the name Varennes throughout, the headline screamed LeClercq. "Why is that worse?"

"The LeClercqs can trace their wealth and notoriety back several generations," René explained. "They have been the favorites of the aristocracy. Survived calamity, war, and plague. But, similar to your Kennedy family, they have had their share of misadventure and tragedy over the years, which gave rise to a belief in, how should I say this, a *malediction* bedeviling the family. A curse."

"A curse?" Cecily echoed, now slightly amused.

"It is ridiculous, yes. Yet for a time, it was a popular folk story for the papers to exploit. The current Count LeClercq dies under mysterious circumstances? Must be the curse. His laundress or chauffeur becomes injured? Also, the curse. A murder-suicide of a LeClercq descendant? *Definitely* the curse and something the newspapers can profit from for days and days. But do not let this swell your imagination about your inheritance. Marguerite was adopted into the LeClercq family and never in line for a title or piece of the fortune."

"Meaning I'm not suddenly going to be a wealthy French countess?"

"A tragedy for France, but no," René said.

Cecily nodded, understanding more and more why Marguerite, in a moment of grief, might have wanted Sandrine to be as far away from that as possible.

"I've never been on an airplane," Cecily admitted. "I'm not good around people."

"Meaning what?" René asked.

"Do you ever get claustrophobia on a crowded elevator?" she asked.

"No, because I am a functioning human adult, but I take your meaning," René said. "I have no enjoyment of plane travel, so I have magic pills that knock me unconscious for the duration. If you ask nicely, you may have as many as you like."

"OK. I also don't have a passport."

"Marguerite accounted for this," René said. "Your mother was born in France and never renounced her citizenship. With Marguerite ailing, her former assistant, Thérèse, tugged at a few of her old, well-placed contacts in government to acquire an emergency passport. Any further questions?"

"When do we leave?"

"Given Marguerite's condition, right away. If you give me your location, I will arrive within the hour."

Cecily hurried back to her camper to pack. She didn't have very many clothes, and what she did have was strictly functional. Her job involved spending time in the woods. Her wardrobe reflected this. She stuffed a few pairs of jeans in a backpack as well as any clean shirts and underwear. She put on one of her pairs of sneakers and laced the second one to her backpack's straps. She added toiletries, her phone cord, and the tablet she used for work.

She hunted through the bins tucked around her camper, trying to think of anything else she might need, and realized she had nothing else. This would have to do.

"We meet again," René said, climbing out of a taxi alongside the camper but then taking in the rural surroundings. "*Un moment.* You . . . live in that?"

"You don't approve?" Cecily asked, shouldering her backpack.

"It is not my place to approve or disapprove," René admitted. "As your traveling companion, I only hope any odor you bring with you is not seen as a fault of my own."

Cecily was about to retort, but the Frenchman had already ducked back into the taxi.

"Should be less than an hour to the airport," the driver said once Cecily was settled in as well. "When's your flight?"

"An hour from now," René replied.

"International?" the driver asked, incredulous. "Not sure you're gonna make it."

"Will you entertain me by trying?" René asked, exasperated.

The driver shrugged and pulled away from Cecily's camper. Cecily immediately felt the acute closeness of both René and the driver. It reminded her of why she hated cars. She opened her window to get some air. It did little.

"Are you all right?" René asked.

Cecily nodded but she wasn't. She closed her eyes, remembering a visualization technique she learned from one of her therapists. Like reciting a mantra, it relied on so-called one-pointed attention to push everything else from her mind. The image she'd chosen long ago was a surprise to her therapist. It was the inside of a hollowed-out oak tree.

"Are you certain?" the therapist had asked her. "Is that a completely positive image?"

Cecily had known even then why her therapist had cautioned her about it. After her mother vanished into the sea, Cecily hadn't returned home. For the rest of the night and into the next day, including for several hours after the storm moved inland, Cecily went missing. Her paternal relatives, already worried about the safety of mother and daughter, descended on Myrtle Beach. They found their mobile home destroyed. A search party was quickly formed with local law enforcement. Moments after sunset, Cecily was discovered deep in the swamps along the Waccamaw River.

She'd hiked in while the storm raged around her and found shelter in the hollow trunk of a swamp laurel. She eventually fell asleep, only to be woken by the baying of a sheriff's bloodhound.

She imagined herself in that hollow now, the process calming and easing her mind. As René spent the ride fiddling with his phone, Cecily concentrated on the sight, smell, and feel of a hollow oak in the deep woods.

Forty-five minutes later, the travelers emerged from the cab to a crowded departures terminal. Cecily hadn't been around so many people at once in years. She felt dizzy and took René's arm. If the Frenchman noticed, he gave no indication as he raised his hand to signal a gate agent.

"Welcome back, Monsieur Chaumière," the agent said, indicating for a porter to collect their luggage. "This way, please."

René handed the agent a transparent plastic folder filled with a thin stack of documents. The man gave them a cursory glance, then led the pair through a side door, past a nodding security guard, and to a waiting cart that whisked them directly to their gate.

"Have a pleasant flight," the agent said as a flight attendant ushered them down the jetway.

"Merci," René replied, as if unaccustomed to anything less.

They were met at the plane's cabin door by a flight attendant who greeted them before leading them to a pair of large seats up front. As soon as they were settled, a second attendant came by with two flutes of champagne.

"Oh, thank you," Cecily said, surprised.

But René shook his head. "In a wineglass, s'il vous plaît," he said. "Flutes are for wedding photos."

The attendant forced a smile and returned with a champagne-filled wineglass. René smiled, took a sip, and nodded to Cecily. "*Parfait.*"

An announcement came over the PA system telling passengers to turn off their phones. As Cecily did, René spied the images of Marguerite on her screen that she'd recently found.

"May I?" he asked.

She handed him the phone, and he quickly scanned through them, delighted. "I have seen some of these but not all," he said, marveling at the images. "You should show these to her when we visit with her. She will be charmed, I am sure."

A flight attendant raised an eyebrow at René's continued use of the phone. He ignored her and searched for something new.

"What're you doing?" Cecily asked.

"Looking for this," he said before handing the phone back to her.

On the screen was a photo of Marguerite, Constance, and a noticeably young Sandrine all in bright-white summer dresses decorated by a single large green palm leaf that swept diagonally down from the right shoulder to the hem of the skirt on the left leg like a great sash. It was dramatic and beautiful. All three women weren't simply smiling; they seemed to be laughing at the same joke.

"Have you seen this before?" René asked.

"No. It's wonderful," Cecily said.

"Marguerite painted the leaf from palms she saw on Tahiti," René explained. "Pierre Cardin used it in one of his collections. Your mother is probably ten years old here."

Cecily stared at the image, absorbing their happiness. Even though Sandrine was young in the picture, she recognized her mother's smile and its echo on the faces of Constance and Marguerite.

"Can I have one of your magic pills now?" she asked.

When the flight from Charleston landed at Newark two hours later, Cecily barely registered that she had to transfer planes. Newark's airport was filled with a hundred times more people than Charleston's. In a drug-induced haze, Cecily hardly noticed as she was whisked through on the back of a cart and then helped to her new seat on an Air France jet.

If the lighting hadn't been so different or the seats now in small, cubicle-like pods that allowed them to be stretched into beds, she might've thought she was back on the same plane. René appeared in what felt like a waking dream wearing some sort of airline-provided pajamas as he quaffed another glass of champagne.

"*Bon nuit*," he said. "Thank God we awaken in Paris."

Cecily went back to sleep only to wake what felt like seconds later to screams of terror.

The plane pitched to one side, rocked by turbulence. The engine whined as the lights in the cabin flickered to life.

"Ladies and gentlemen, please return to your seats, buckle your safety belts, and place your tray tables in their locked, upright position," a male, French-accented voice said over the passenger address system before repeating the message in French.

The passengers in the first-class cabin, some in a bewildered haze, some waking in terror, gripped their armrests and stared out their windows into darkness. A flight attendant stumbled down the aisle, gathering trays. She could barely stand up straight.

"René? What's happening?" Cecily turned to the seat next to her, but it was empty.

Her muscles tensed. Dread wormed through her body. She'd heard of planes encountering turbulence before but didn't realize it was so violent. The plane bucked upward, sending the hairs on Cecily's arms skyward and her stomach churning. She could feel the change in air pressure within her chest. Ceiling panels burst open. Masks dropped and dangled over the passengers like a hangman's noose. More people screamed.

Cecily tried to remember the safety demonstration at the beginning of the flight but couldn't. How could a day that began with her peacefully traipsing through the South Carolina swamp end with her death twenty thousand feet above the Atlantic Ocean?

The plane dropped suddenly. The flight attendant was hurled face-first into a bulkhead, sinking to the floor where she lay motionless. Cecily glanced at the passengers nearest her. They were all more concerned with their own safety. She unbuckled her seat belt and slid out of her seat, crawling to the attendant as the floor tilted below her.

"Are you OK?" she asked, putting a hand on the woman's shoulder.

The flight attendant's body shuddered. When she turned around, her eyes were dark red. Cecily feared she'd split open her forehead or fractured her skull. She touched the woman's hand, but it wasn't soft like flesh. It was as hard as marble and as cold. Cecily looked down, wondering if she'd touched a part of the aircraft but instead saw bone in place of fingers. Bone whittled into sharp, talon-like points.

Cecily leaped backward. A distant memory, long buried, crept forward from the dark reaches of her mind. The flight attendant's hair, brown moments before, was now black and clumped together with mud. As she got to her feet, it flowed downward like black snakes slithering from Medusa's head. Her mouth opened to reveal jagged rows of blackened teeth. Her pale skin turned silver and then lost its shine, becoming slate gray. It tightened over her skull like a death mask.

It was the wraith. The monster from Cecily's childhood that had stolen away her mother. She'd long dismissed it as a product of her youthful imagination. A crisis apparition that had attached itself to the memory of her mother's death as a coping mechanism to convince herself that her mother had been in danger, had been protecting her, when she died. Not succumbing to her mental illness. Nothing so ordinary as that.

"Help . . . help me, René!" Cecily begged as the cabin lights flickered and faltered. "René!"

No one answered. She crawled backward as the ghost or monster or flight attendant approached, its eyes black and unreadable. Its matted hair grew longer by the minute, sweeping across the aisle like dark water. Cecily's head bumped against another passenger's hand gripping an armrest.

"Help me!" she yelled, grabbing at the hand.

But it was as hard and cold as the wraith's. Cecily pushed herself away as the skin of the passenger's face flaked away, becoming a mirror of the monster. Her pupils expanded, drowning the whites of her eyes in a layer of black mucus as the bones of her fingers pierced the skin and her mouth dropped open, revealing black teeth and a blue tongue.

Cecily thought she might hyperventilate. The other passengers turned to her, their skin darkening into slate grays and earthy browns as it tightened around the bones. Their fingernails popped off as sharpened bones stabbed through their flesh. Blood filled their eyes, revolving around the socket like a living creature, as they turned toward Cecily.

She crawled backward as everyone in the cabin moved toward her, a wolf pack cornering its terrified quarry. The flight attendant led the way, her bony fingers arching toward Cecily's chest as if preparing to drive them through her breastbone and skewer her still-beating heart.

The plane lurched forward. Cecily's head snapped back and was caught by the wraith. She grabbed Cecily's face in her claws, sharpened thumb and forefinger pressing into her features as she wrenched her closer to her maw. Cecily's lungs burned as she tried to breathe. The pressure weighing down on her chest was too great. She felt like she was having a heart attack.

The monster's eyes were so close that Cecily could see her own distorted reflection in the slick darkness. She blinked involuntarily in time with her pounding heart rate as the plane tipped into a dive. The world swam around her as if she were drowning. Color faded into blacks and whites. The wraith's grip tightened. Cecily drifted in and out of consciousness, the echo of terrified screams drowning out all other sounds.

"Miss LeClercq? Miss LeClercq? Can you hear us?"

Cecily's eyes shot open. The flight attendant was inches from her face, but her eyes were her own again. The jagged teeth were also gone. The long, matted hair now brown again and neatly pulled back. She held an oxygen mask in her hands with clean, manicured fingernails, not bony talons.

"Miss LeClercq?" the flight attendant repeated. "Are you with us?"

Cecily nodded groggily. "I think so."

The flight attendant held the mask over Cecily's nose and mouth. "Breathe in slowly but deeply."

Cecily did as she was asked. Two other passengers down the aisle were also receiving oxygen while a third was being attended to by a young man holding a medical kit.

"We passed through turbulence," the flight attendant explained. "Easy to understand why you might have had a panic attack waking up to that. You're not alone."

A panic attack?

"What're you talking about?" Cecily asked. "The plane was out of control. The cabin pressure dropped. You fell. You hit your head."

She trailed off, noticing that the gash on the flight attendant's forehead was gone.

"No, cabin pressure remained stable," the attendant said, a hint of worry in her voice as she glanced back to the man with the medical kit. "Did you hit your own head? Are you experiencing any pain or problems with your vision?"

Cecily glanced around for René. His seat was still empty.

"I'm sorry," Cecily said. "I'm a little disoriented. That's all. Do you know where the man who was sitting here went? Mr. Chaumière?"

"Yes, he is back at the bar," the attendant said.

She pointed down the aisle to a small in-flight bar complete with bartender. René, still in his pajamas, leaned against the bar staring at his phone. Cecily thanked the flight attendant and made her way back. Still dizzy, she had to grab onto the nearest seats to keep from tipping over.

"Pardon, the charger at my seat did not work," René said, holding up his plugged-in cell phone. "You are all right, *non*?

You thrashed like a cat chasing a mouse in her dream. The attendant said you had a panic attack."

"And you left me alone?" Cecily asked, incredulous.

René's phone vibrated. He left the question unanswered as he accepted a video call. Cecily was surprised. She didn't think people could make calls on planes. The bartender pushed two small bottles over to Cecily, one of vodka, one of orange juice.

"I was sorry to hear about your great-grandmother," he said. "My condolences."

Cecily shot a look to René, wondering if he'd lied to the bartender to get free drinks or to explain away her attack. He looked grave, as did the two people on the video call. One, an older woman with a gold nose ring and a thin chain that ran to her ear, appeared to have been crying. Cecily reached for the vodka.

"Marguerite?" Cecily asked when René finished his call and stepped back over.

"*Oui*, she is gone," he said quietly, as if speaking too loudly would give the word unwanted permanence. "My partner, Auberon, sent me the news as the plane's troubles began."

"I'm so sorry," Cecily said. "You had said we needed to hurry. I didn't realize how bad off she was."

"With Marguerite, there is always a surprise," René said sadly. "After convincing her cancer she'd go quietly, she slipped from her hospice bed late this night, made her way to the forests of her youth, and, *alors*, sliced open her own throat with a dagger. What a trickster, eh?"

3

René excused himself to take another call. Though he spoke in French, Cecily understood he was speaking of funeral arrangements and notifying others. She left him to it and returned to her seat.

A dagger? Through her own throat?

It was horrifying. So brutal and sad.

It also didn't make sense. If she were at death's door waiting for her great-granddaughter to race across the ocean for some final confession, what would drive her to take her own life? She must've known René was on his way. What had she wanted to tell her?

She stared at the dark window, the comparison to her own mother's death impossible to ignore. She'd taken her own life under duress, imagined or otherwise. She wondered if her own impending arrival had brought back too many painful memories of Marguerite's son and grandchildren. Hadn't she herself just suffered a hallucinatory panic attack, one so strong it reanimated a long-forgotten, childhood boogeyman?

She replayed the attack, turning it over piece by piece. It felt like a nightmare, justifying her mother's paranoia of being around other people. *L'hommes*. Her mother's whispered curse echoed in her mind. Cecily seldom remembered her dreams. This one was fresh in her mind like a newly minted memory. Probably, she decided, because she'd been abruptly snapped out of it by the worried flight attendant.

Dawn broke as the plane entered French airspace. Cecily had tried to get back to sleep but couldn't. René, sweaty with alcohol, had passed out the moment he'd returned, then woke the second the plane came to a halt at the jetway.

"Shall we?" he asked, turning to Cecily as if they'd been mid-conversation.

He said little as they made their way through Charles de Gaulle Airport. His phone updated with countless voice mails and texts that he attempted to return as they made their way to the baggage claim. This left Cecily to marvel at her new surroundings.

She hadn't known what to expect of arriving in a foreign country, particularly in an airport packed with thousands of people. There was no agent to whisk them through customs here or a cart waiting to carry them to the entrance. She had to stand in long lines, push past other travelers, and try not to panic again.

Whether it was the novelty of being in a new place or the lingering results of René's pills, Cecily found the effects of the nearness of others minimized. She read the various signage—helpfully all written in French, English, and what she thought were Chinese characters—and glanced in the numerous stores. While some were familiar, such as a McDonalds, she also saw outlets for extremely high-end brands like Chanel, Bulgari, and Hermès.

She wondered if these were some of the ateliers Marguerite had worked with.

What also stood out were the people. Though they didn't look so different from folks she saw in Charleston, everyone was slightly more fashionable. Except for a few younger people, this wasn't a T-shirt and jeans crowd. Men wore suits or sweater and trouser combinations that made them look like billionaire CEOs about to step from one yacht to another. Women dressed similarly, almost formally in some cases, in the kind of expensive blazers, blouses, skirts, or pants Cecily couldn't fathom ever having the occasion to wear.

There was also cultural- or regional-specific dress that Cecily had seldom encountered before. Women in flowing saris and colorful hijabs and niqabs. Men in bright kente cloth or long kurtas. It was as if everyone, *everyone*, had gotten the memo to dress well when passing through France's premiere airport except for her.

Though nothing could've screamed American tourist louder than her sneakers, jeans, and faded hoodie, no one looked at her or seemed to care. She didn't either.

René waggled his cell phone her way after they picked up their bags. "I was afraid of this," he said. "Marguerite always threatened she would make me the executor of her estate. This, she has done."

"That means a lot of work for you?" Cecily asked.

"*Oui*," he agreed. "Also, you."

"Me?"

"You are her sole heir," René said. "You will inherit her house and all her possessions. There is some money but hardly a great fortune, particularly after tax. We should find you a lawyer to take you through it."

Cecily balked. She thought she was coming to Paris to meet an elderly relative. Not to receive a hasty education in

French inheritance law. Part of her wanted to turn around and return to Charleston on the next plane.

"This way," René said, leading her out a sliding glass door toward a parking lot packed with cars.

For whatever reason, Cecily thought she'd emerge into the French sunshine and be able to see the Eiffel Tower, Notre-Dame, or some other grand Parisian landmark. But beyond the airport, there were farm fields, a few warehouses, and a large Holiday Inn. She resisted the urge to say something, knowing René would make fun of her.

They tromped past several BMWs, Mercedes, and Porsches as well as French-made vehicles like Peugeots, Citroëns, and Renaults. Cecily was picturing René in some stylish French convertible when he stopped behind a bright-purple Toyota Prius and opened the back. He placed their bags inside and circled to the driver's side door.

"It will be a long drive into Paris," René said as he got behind the wheel.

Though she shared the car with only him, the euphoria Cecily experienced in the airport waned. She was trapped in a small space with another person. She tried to visualize the hollow oak, but her mind felt too scrambled. She rolled down the window as they entered the highway. It didn't do much good.

"You are sick?" René asked.

Hearing the judgment in his voice, Cecily shook her head. "I'll be fine," she said.

She focused her gaze on the passing farm fields and numerous tiny villages, the tallest structure in each the church steeple in the center of town. These pastoral scenes soon gave way to warehouses and chemical plants. The two-lane highway became four. As Paris loomed ahead, the villages and most signs of nature receded to be replaced by large buildings and endlessly paved roads and sidewalks.

She wasn't sure when they entered Paris itself. The buildings on either side of the highway had simply grown taller. Overpasses soared above them. Commuter trains with double-decker orange cars whizzed along bridges. Columns of towering apartment blocks blotted out the gray sky to the west. Traffic increased until they were surrounded by cars, tractor trailers, and work trucks, the Prius inching along at a crawl.

"Merde," René muttered.

He flipped on a turn signal and headed for the next exit. The neighborhood they descended into was filled with vast apartment blocks, businesses with signage painted in both Arabic script and French, and dozens of people on the sidewalks. There were plenty of cars, but many walked, seeming to run into acquaintances, and waving at neighbors as if they resided in one of the smallest cities in the world rather than in one of the largest.

"Much better," René said, pulling up to a red light.

They continued on toward the interior of the city. Apartment blocks gave way to older buildings, many of which looked as if they'd been constructed in the nineteenth century or before. There were gorgeous old row houses by the hundreds with businesses at street level and residences above. The pedestrians were as fashionable as the travelers at Charles de Gaulle, convincing Cecily it wasn't the airport that people dressed for but being in France itself.

"Where is Marguerite's house?" Cecily asked.

"Ah, you like what you see, *non*?" René asked. "Maybe inheriting a house here is not such a *horreur*?"

"That part sounded OK, but didn't you say you were Marguerite's neighbor?" Cecily retorted. "How close a neighbor exactly? Two blocks? Three?"

René laughed. "You arrived an hour ago and are already an asshole. You will fit in well."

They reached the Seine, the river that bisected the city, and drove alongside it. The water was kept a few dozen feet below street level as if in a canal, Cecily presumed, to keep any potential flooding at bay. A glass-topped boat filled with sightseers idled past a long barge before ducking under one of several stone bridges marked with ornate statues and bronze art nouveau lampposts.

"It's all so beautiful," Cecily said as magnificent, sprawling palaces appeared on either side of the river, repurposed now as museums and the Paris City Hall.

"It may look so," René said. "Live here long enough and you find that every street in Paris, no matter how beautiful, has borne witness to some grisly horror. Whether during the Terror, the Paris Uprising, even way back during the student revolt in the thirteenth century. The cobblestones are lacquered with blood."

Cecily was still trying to absorb this when they reached a neighborhood of smaller buildings, quaint houses, and narrower streets. There were bakeries and shops as well as a few museums not housed in palaces, along with churches and even a couple of synagogues. It was quieter and less trafficked.

"These streets are also lacquered with blood?"

René snorted. "This is the Marais," René said. "Where your great-grandmother lived for the last several decades. Too fashionable these days to run with blood."

They wove their way through the narrow streets, some

buildings so close to the road that there was hardly a sidewalk. René slowed as they turned the next corner. A middle-aged man with thinning orange hair huddled next to a tall older woman in a black dress with exotic jewelry cascading from around her neck, wrists, and ears. Cecily recognized them from René's video call on the plane.

"This will be your great-grandmother's former assistant who is now a jewelry designer in her own right, Thérèse Derrien," René explained as he pulled up alongside them. "As well as the saint who endures me night and day, Auberon Gaulé."

He parked and jumped out of the car, kissing both on each cheek before embracing Auberon with a ferocity that suggested they'd been apart for months rather than a day or two. Thérèse made her way to the side of the car and forced a smile.

"*Bienvenue à Paris*," she said, opening the door for Cecily. "My English, it is wobbly, so you will forgive it."

"Your English is elegant," Cecily said.

Thérèse stiffened as if insulted by such a transparent lie. "I was your great-grandmother's assistant for several years, while she was a designer and after," she explained. "I am sorry for your loss."

"Thank you," Cecily said. "I am sorry for yours."

"She was an extraordinary woman," Thérèse said, bracelets jangling. "For her to have survived all she did and yet find a way to carry on and even discover more joys of life is *incroyable*."

These words stung. Cecily knew Thérèse didn't mean it this way, but she thought of her mother. Was her mother somehow less than because she endured so much and couldn't carry on?

"I pray my husband was not incorrigible to you," Auberon said, interrupting Cecily's train of thought as he came over to introduce himself. His French accent was different from

René's. More elliptical and less crisp. "He is a pussycat but hates traveling alone and believes Marguerite was trying to get rid of him."

"It seems she was," René added.

"'Seems?'" Auberon asked as if unsure of the translation.

"*Semble*," René said.

"Ah," Auberon said, then smiled at Cecily. "My English is not as good as these Parisian sophisticates. I am only a miner's son from Lorraine."

This made Thérèse and René laugh. It sounded as if they needed it. It made Cecily like Auberon even more.

"As much as it pains me for you to see Marguerite's house unlit by her presence, I think you will like it," René said to Cecily, gesturing up the block. "Given your profession."

He led the small group up the street. Their path was shaded by tall horse chestnut trees, the edges of their leaves reddening with the coming of autumn. The buildings on either side of the road were less adorned here than elsewhere, windowless walls rising two and three stories like the ramparts of a fortress.

The house at the end of the block was different. Though it had red brick walls and few windows, the exterior was obscured by zigzagging wisteria vines that began at street level and rose all the way to the top. Olive trees, horsetails, climbing ivy, and great ferns hung over the side of the roof to complete the effect. It was as if the neighborhood had suddenly come to an end to allow an entrance to a great forest.

"This is Marguerite's house?" Cecily asked, amazed.

"Beautiful, *non*?" René said.

"Very," Cecily agreed.

She didn't even see the front door, hidden as it was beneath the vines, until Thérèse unlocked it and ushered everyone inside. The interior was equally florid. There were pots of snake plants and ficus, bird's nest ferns, and even palms. A lanky bird of paradise stood alongside a rubber tree in a dining room. Basil, rosemary, and other herbs overflowed from the kitchen. Even the walls were covered in sketches, paintings, and vintage anatomical drawings of plants and trees.

"Did Marguerite do any of those?" Cecily asked.

"The best ones," Thérèse said. "But she wasn't one to display her work. Most are in boxes in her workroom. Look if you wish."

When Cecily balked, Thérèse shrugged. "They are now yours after all."

Cecily was going to ask about this when someone knocked on the front door. René answered it, finding an elderly couple on the stoop. He kissed them on the cheek in greeting and swept them inside where Auberon greeted them as well.

"There may be people coming over," Thérèse said. "Friends who have only now heard the news."

Conversations began in French, and Cecily took this as her cue to head upstairs.

The house looked large from the outside, but the interior was quite narrow. The second floor had four rooms, each barely larger than the camper Cecily crammed herself into on rainy nights. The first was a bedroom with a tiny bed and dresser. Any more furniture and the room would burst. The second, Cecily surmised given the worktable and closet as overflowing with boxes and files as the downstairs was with plants, was the workroom. There was a bathroom no larger than a closet beside this, followed by a library.

This captivated Cecily the most. Every inch of wall space was devoured by full, sagging bookshelves. There were works on art, fashion, plant life, French history, architecture, and every other topic in between. There was a single high-backed chair next to the window that suggested this library favored parties of one.

Cecily sat in the chair. It was incredibly comfortable. She recognized the names on several of the book spines as famous fashion designers. To her surprise, she saw her own last name staring back at her from a few at the bottom. She took these out and flipped through them. They cataloged her great-grand-mother's work showing her paintings and designs transformed not simply onto clothing but also jewelry, napkins, plates, even curtains. The photos were mostly of the work, but there were a couple of images of Marguerite alongside designers as well.

She went to replace them when she saw a small paperback that had fallen behind them. It also had the LeClercq name on the spine. There were several black-and-white photographs inside as well as reproduced paintings and even a tapestry or two. Inside the back cover was a family tree that folded out like a map.

The book was in French, but like most things, Cecily had an app for that. She opened it, held her camera over the first page of the introduction, and tapped the button. It took several seconds but then the translation appeared on her phone.

The story of the LeClercq family has several beginnings. The first LeClercq is believed to have come from the Loire Valley to the north of Paris over one thousand years ago. LeClercq means clerk but could refer to a scholar, member of the clergy, or scribe. Any of these positions suggests some education. At some point, these educated LeClercqs became traders. Merchants. How and why is lost to time.

The recorded history of the LeClercqs, therefore, begins in the

*late twelfth century when the first Count LeClercq, Sabastien,
was rewarded for services rendered in wartime by King Philip
Augustus. Whether against England's King Henry II or Philip I
of Alsace is also unknown.*

*What is known is that the service, possibly relating to the
supplying of French soldiers, was so great the merchant LeClercq
received not only the title of count but also several hundred acres
of royal lands north of Paris with the creation of the peerage.*

Cecily stared at the translation. These were the people her
great-grandmother had grown up with? Nothing could feel
farther removed from her own upbringing.

She flipped through the book looking for references to
Marguerite. She finally found a few toward the end. She held
her camera over and translated a few more paragraphs.

*Marguerite LeClercq, the younger half sister of Countess Aline
LeClercq, was adopted by the family after her father was killed
during the German invasion of France in 1940.*

Ah.

She unfolded the family tree in back. There was Marguerite, born in 1938 and married to Hubert Varennes in 1957.

Huh. *Married young back then, eh, Great-Grandma?*

It also listed a son, Louis, born in 1959. Cecily's grandfather.

Marguerite's sister, Countess Aline, was listed as having
been born in 1937. No death date was noted. When she flipped
back to the last chapter, she saw Aline's name and translated
a paragraph.

*Countess LeClercq retired from public life at an early age and
lives in seclusion at the Chateau LeClercq outside Félice, alongside
the ancient abbey constructed by the first of her noble line in the
early thirteenth century. She is known for her philanthropy.*

That was it. The beginning of a family and an end. There

46

were a few notes on the family tree—initials D. D. and G. D.—pencil marks made by, Cecily figured, Marguerite but nothing more. She wondered if they or Aline were still alive.

Someone laughed downstairs. The conversations grew louder. It made for an odd disconnect. The friends of the very real Marguerite who'd taken her own life hours before against the sentences in a book tying her to a storied family.

Cecily took the book upstairs with her to Marguerite's bedroom. Unlike the second floor, the third consisted of one room that was more like a glassed-in porch than anything like a rooftop garden. If Cecily could've designed a bedroom, it would've been a lot like this. There was a bed, dresser, chest of drawers, and wardrobe, but there weren't walls so much as windows, as if it were more of a greenhouse than living quarters. The ceiling was one large skylight, capable of being covered with retractable blinds. Cecily couldn't imagine why anyone would ever close them.

She put down her backpack and stepped through a pair of French doors to the garden. She recognized several of the plants as those that extended over the wall but there were so many more. She wasn't sure how long Marguerite had been in hospice care, but the plants needed attention. She picked up a small watering can, filled it at a nearby nozzle, and set to work.

As she watered, she took in the rooftop's views. One side revealed little more than a few blocks into the Marais. On the opposite side, Cecily could see all the way to the Seine, including buildings on the other side of the river and even the tiniest hint of one of Notre-Dame's famous rose windows.

It was a spectacular view. The kind people paid a lot of money for. For the first time, it occurred to her that this inheritance her great-grandmother had left her might not be a bad thing. She'd never had much money but had never needed much. Selling a house like this might be enough to set her up with real financial independence and also pay back her grandmother and aunt in America for their kindness and help over the years.

She still felt odd about accepting such a substantial gift from a distant relation she'd barely heard of. But in eyeing the plants around the garden, she recognized a kindred spirit in the absent Marguerite. How strange to discover oneself descended from someone who also had an affinity for all things botanical.

She moved to another pot and started in surprise. It contained a tree sapling maybe one or two years old at most. The leaves were oval, shiny, and dark green, with tiny, spiny lobes around their edges that tapered up to a sharp point. They were leathery in texture with a light underside. There was no mistaking what it was, an evergreen oak.

It was one of the oldest species of tree in Europe but also one of the rarest, their numbers having steadily declined over the years due to pollution and deforestation. What made it stand out even more was that it didn't belong in a rooftop garden at all. Oaks were social plants. They tended to live in large familial clusters in forests in which they acted as steward, organizing any number of aspects of its surrounding ecosystem.

An orphan like this was cut off. Though it was in a large pot, it was nowhere near big enough for its root systems, oaks having at one time been believed to be as large aboveground as they were below.

What're you doing here? Cecily thought, staring at it.

Her great-grandmother knew so much about plants. How could she not know that this one would die if it stayed here like this?

Something caught her eye. Tied lightly around the sapling's

top branches was a small antique necklace with a decorative, liquid-filled vial, like the kind used for perfume, hanging from the center. It was such an odd place to put a piece of jewelry. Like something a child might do. She tried to untangle it but had to undo the clasp to remove it.

"Where was that?" René stood in the doorway, eyeing her curiously.

"In the tree," Cecily said. "What is it?"

René took it from her, eyeing the vial closely. "It was Marguerite's. I never saw her take it off. She thought it was a lucky charm. Look at any photo of her and you will see it around her neck."

"Do you recognize this sapling?" Cecily asked, indicating the tree.

"No," René admitted with a shrug. "But I don't know a gardenia from a thistle, so it could have been here for years or arrived yesterday. Pourquoi? Is it special?"

"Marguerite took such care of her plants, I'm just surprised to see a tree that'll grow to such a great size here," Cecily said. "Also, it's endangered. Borderline extinct."

"Leave it to Marguerite to raise the dead," René said. "If I had to guess, I would say you will find many surprises in the relics of her life. I came up here to see if you wanted to join us. Many people have brought food. Even wine, though the hour is early."

"Is her half sister here? The Countess LeClercq?" Cecily asked. "I mean, I'm not even sure she's still alive."

"Ah, she very much is," René said. "But you will not find her here. The sisters have—*had*—not spoken for many, many years and were very much estranged. Countess Aline is quite eccentric, although there are those who say insane."

"How so?" Cecily asked.

"She has never married, never had children, lives all alone, and has dedicated her life to spending the LeClercq billions down to the last *sou* out of a mortal fear of eternal damnation."

4

THIS CAUGHT CECILY off guard. She stared incredulously at René and waited for him to admit it was a joke. He shrugged.

"In recent years, there had been attempts at rapprochement between the sisters, mostly due to the countess's ongoing legal affairs," René continued. "There was one lawyer Marguerite had suitable interactions with. One more understanding and competent than the others. When Countess Aline entered the picture again, however, peace and harmony fled. Marguerite withdrew. N'est-ce pas?"

Cecily wasn't sure she understood but nodded anyway.

"Do you know what they fell out over?" Cecily asked. "Was it money?"

"I do not think so," René explained. "When they were young, they were close. They survived the occupation together. These were dangerous times. There have always been rumors the LeClercqs hid Resistance members and their weapons caches in tunnels under their property the same as they once hid nuns and clergymen during the Terror. Marguerite used to tell us one of her earliest memories was of the gestapo raiding their house and she and Aline hiding in a closet."

"What changed?" Cecily asked.

"After their mother died, Marguerite left home and started a new life in Paris with her Monsieur Varennes," René said. "That her adoptive mother stipulated in her will that Marguerite was to receive no part of the LeClercq fortune and was not in line for the title of countess, this did not drive a wedge between sisters as it might in other families. Aline offered to split it with her, half and half. Offered this time and again. Marguerite always refused. Until she took her life there, I do not think she had been anywhere near the LeClercq estate in decades."

"That's where she died?"

"*Oui*, sadly," René replied. "In the forest."

"Why there? Was it a place she talked about?"

"Not at all," René admitted. "The only time she mentioned the estate at all was to say the countess's lawyer, Eglantine, told her that upon the countess's death, the woods, the chateau, and the old abbey would all be bequeathed to the *Fondation pour les arts français*. They mean to turn it into a non-profit arts colony. The countess stipulated in her will that no money should ever made off the land."

"Wait, then who is the next Countess LeClercq?"

"No one," René said. "She is determined that the title, the LeClercq line, and the curse will die with her. Crazy, *oui*? Now, will you come down?"

This was a lot to take in. Cecily considered making an attempt at sociability but envisioning being surrounded by strangers made her wince. René noticed.

"Ah, of course," he said gently. "Crowds are not your friend. Take your time."

Cecily smiled. "Merci," she said, proud of her pronunciation.

René shuddered. "I was going to ask if you had a girlfriend or boyfriend back home, but I realize I do not need more people to pity today."

He smiled and exited. The voices from downstairs grew louder. She felt her blood pressure rising. She didn't think it was a big deal, but after her panic attack on the flight, she decided not to risk it. She opened the map app on her phone, scanned around for a large patch of green, and found a cemetery, a botanical garden, and a park labeled Jardin du Luxembourg.

Not wanting to be among the dead or the living, she gambled on the park being the least populated and headed downstairs. She stopped in the library and grabbed the paperback on the LeClercq family in case she felt like reading. She doubted she would but what better to bring along than tales of her own fancy lineage?

There were about three dozen people now packed into the rooms on the first floor with several conversations going at once. She had to get out of there. She reached for the door. Auberon hurried to her side, slipping a piece of paper and a couple of Euros into her hand.

"My phone number, René's phone number, and Thérèse's phone number," he said. "Also, the address of this house and cab fare. A marvelous city to get lost in but perhaps not today."

Cecily smiled and pocketed the note. "Thank you."

The app made it easy to navigate Paris despite the streets, which could arrive at odd angles. She stayed on the rue de Archives as long as she could, passing several impressive-looking buildings, both modern and centuries old. She hooked a left on the wide rue de Rivoli, a right past a museum dedicated to European photography that was somehow currently honoring the work of an American, Gordon Parks, and passed an arts academy filled with high school age students. A sign near its front gate said that it was fully underwritten by the *Fondation pour les arts français*. She idly wondered how ubiquitous the organization had to be for her to encounter it twice in such a short amount of time.

The sidewalks and streets were filled with people, as were the shops, museums, and houses. As long as she kept walking, Cecily didn't feel crowded in. Her anonymity helped. Knowing she would not—could not—run into anyone she knew lessened the claustrophobic effect brought on by others.

She crossed the Seine at Notre-Dame. It was half-covered with scaffolding as workers rebuilt sections damaged by a recent fire. She admired the massive structure for a moment before continuing to what her map referred to as the Left Bank, even though, to her eyes, it appeared to be south. Something else to ask René.

The sidewalks on the other side of the Seine were filled with young people. Many appeared to be about Cecily's age. She thought they might be tourists or backpackers, then saw signs pointing to the nearby buildings of Paris's Sorbonne University. The students chatted with each other, passed around phones and tablets to view this or that. They seemed happy to be moving together into a future of their own making.

Cecily watched them for a while. Her eyes landed on a young woman and her friends. She didn't know what they were discussing. They could be making plans, talking classes or romance, or chatting current events. What Cecily noticed most was how easy their interchange went. How confident they were. How focused and interested.

When she saw people her age in Charleston, particularly college students from the Citadel or from other parts of South Carolina, she occasionally felt the odd pang of jealousy. If things had gone another way for her, she'd be on her way to some bright, smart future as well. But then she'd remind herself that she loved what she did. Loved being in the swamps, discovering something new every day, and working for Ina.

But it hit differently in Paris. She didn't want to do what these young women were doing, she wanted to *be* them. Wanted that self-assurance. That poise.

She turned away, refusing to be overwhelmed. She knew the tears weren't about who circumstances had allowed her to be or not be. They came from the sudden realization that a part of her might have believed her great-grandmother, far away in Paris, had answers she'd sought for much of her life.

The audacity. She scoffed at herself and kept going.

The Jardin du Luxembourg turned out to be a vast garden located behind—what else—a palace. In front of the building ran a long concrete pool. A child raced a sailboat down it watched over by a young woman in a well-tailored silver pant-suit. Men and women in fancy suits and skirts emerged from the palace doors like modern-dress versions of royal courtiers.

Cecily flashed back to the melting faces of her fellow passengers on the airplane and turned away. She went around to the back of the palace and found it populated by the statues of long-dead French dignitaries, an echo of the living courtiers she'd seen out front.

She picked an isolated spot near a linden tree-shaded fountain and sat. The fountain was oblong, with a square-shaped statue of a man rising over a rectangular pool of water no more than a foot wide. It was as if someone had been told to make the exact opposite of every other fountain in Paris—not circular, not topped by a cherubic statue—which might explain why it was now relegated to a spot under the trees.

She leaned against the tree trunk, inhaled its scents, and absorbed the sun's warmth as it trickled through the tree's branches and leaves. A calm came over her body and she relaxed into the grass. She closed her eyes for a moment. When she opened them again, she was looking at her great-grandmother.

Her photo was on the front page of a newspaper left behind on a nearby bench. Cecily recognized the picture. It was the one that accompanied the article about the inquest into her grandparents' deaths she'd found online. Marguerite had sunglasses on and her head low.

Cecily got up and hurried over to grab the paper. The headline referred to a *"dernière victime de la malédiction de LeClercq."* She translated it with her app. It came back, *Latest Victim of LeClercq Curse Found Dead in Forest.*

She took a deep breath and translated further. The article was salacious. It dripped with innuendo and felt like a recitation of plot points from a soap opera. It wrote about the LeClercq curse first, mentioning LeClercqs who'd died across the centuries in war, of disease, and in other mishaps that included a plane crash early in the twentieth century and a fall from a horse some two hundred years before that.

The stories were spotty and, at times, felt like intentional misreads of ordinary accidents or the prevalence of mortal illness in the days before antibiotics.

When it finally came to Marguerite, her death felt like an afterthought. It explained that onetime fashion designer Marguerite LeClercq had been found a few kilometers from the LeClercq estate near Félice. Her throat had been slashed in an apparent suicide. It then listed several of the famous couturiers Marguerite had worked with over the years as well as celebrities who had worn her designs.

The next paragraph covered the death of her son following the murder of her daughter-in-law. It related how she'd withdrawn from the public eye afterward. There was no mention of Sandrine or even that she had a granddaughter.

She was about to put the paper away when she saw there was one last short paragraph. She held her phone over the page and then gasped at the translation.

Marguerite LeClercq's suicide took place at the location where her mother hanged herself several decades before, an act witnessed by her late daughter.

What?

Cecily read the information over a few more times. René had mentioned that Marguerite's mother died but hadn't said it was a suicide. Maybe he hadn't known. She reached for the book on the LeClercq family only to realize she'd left it next to the fountain. She hurried over to retrieve it only to see she was no longer alone. The woman in the silver suit she'd thought was watching over the boy with the sailboat was reading from her phone a few yards away with no child in sight.

Cecily forced a smile toward the young woman, grabbed the paperback, and sat back down with the newspaper. She unfolded the family tree in the back, looked above Aline and Marguerite, and was surprised to see the name there.

Sandrine. Her mother's grandmother and namesake. *Né* 1910. *Mort* 1956.

She checked the index. There were but a couple of pages dedicated to Sandrine LeClercq. She flipped to the one with the listing of *mort* and translated the single sentence.

Sandrine LeClercq hanged herself in the LeClercq woods in 1956, an act tragically witnessed by her teenage daughter Marguerite.

Cecily put the book aside and stared out across the garden. Of all the things she should've known, of all the things she wished her mother had told her, this was up there. This she wished she could speak to Marguerite about. This shared horror. This shared pain. She felt a dull, hot throb behind her forehead.

She rose, unsure of where to go next, then realized she hadn't eaten since she'd left Charleston. She made her way back toward the Sorbonne. There were choices between greasy fast food or sit-down restaurants already filled to the brim with customers. Neither would do. She was about to check her map when she stumbled upon an alley of open-air food stalls. The smells emanating from each were so intoxicating she knew she'd found the right place. The signage was in French, Arabic, and a few other languages but not English. A few had helpfully put out small flags on their counters. There were ones from Turkey, India, Ethiopia, Indonesia, and Algeria.

The Ethiopian one smelled the best, so Cecily approached the counter. In broken French, she asked the man there what he recommended.

"How has your day been?" he asked back in English with a shrug.

"Challenging," Cecily admitted.

"Five minutes," the man replied, as if "challenging" was the house special.

She found a seat at one of the several empty tables set up in the alley. The sky had darkened as if it was soon to rain. She opened the LeClercq book again but wasn't interested in learning more. She knew too much. She flipped to the pictures in the center, held her phone over the captions of a few of them—*Artist's Rendering of Castle LeClercq, Portrait of Third Count LeClercq, Map of LeClercq Estate, Circa 1789*—then gave up. It was too much.

"Mademoiselle," the counterman said, placing a tray of aromatic food on the table in front of her.

"Merci," she replied.

She dug into a bowl of exotic-looking vegetables sautéed in an extremely spicy sauce with peppers before trying a stack of triangular pies filled with lentils, onions, and herbs. It was so delicious she almost cried all over again.

She glanced back to the counterman to thank him, but he was with another customer. Surreally, the young woman in the silver suit from the Jardin du Luxembourg was now a few tables away eating a bowl of curried chicken. Cecily stared at her for a moment, wondering if it was possible that she'd followed her to the alley. The woman caught her gaze, offered a quick smile and nod, then went back to her lunch.

Cecily decided she was being crazy.

Her phone vibrated. The display showed the +33 country code for France. She answered it, figuring it was René.

"Am I speaking to Cecily LeClercq?" a clipped, efficient-sounding voice asked in French-accented English.

"You are."

"My name is Gregoire Gens," he said. "I am the assistant forensic medical examiner in the Val d'Oise Department, coordinating with the National Police on the investigation into the death of Marguerite LeClercq. I am to understand you are her great-granddaughter and sole heir?"

"It seems so," Cecily admitted.

"I am sorry for your loss," the medical examiner continued. "We understand that this is a very difficult time for you, but we were hoping you might come to our facility in the morning."

His voice lilted up at the end as if making a request.

From her few experiences with law enforcement, however, she doubted it was.

"I'm not sure I can answer any questions," Cecily said, hoping to put the man off. "I never met Marguerite."

"Understandable," he said. "It is a formality only as it relates to the release of her remains for burial. They were to be transferred to a René Chaumière, but if there is a living relative, they must be engaged for the identification."

Cecily shuddered. She had no desire to see a dead body. She was about to voice as much when she remembered all that René, Auberon, and the others were likely already doing. If this were one responsibility she could take on herself, she figured she should do it.

"When and where?" she asked.

He gave her the address and suggested eight o'clock in the morning. Cecily reluctantly agreed.

"Merci," Gens said, then changed tack. "It is quite a remarkable something for me to be speaking to you, a LeClercq."

"Why is that?"

"Like anyone who grew up around here in the Val d'Oise region, LeClercq is a notable name," he admitted. "My friends and I spent many hours hiking, illegally, I admit and apologize, through the Forêt de LeClercq looking for the ruins of the old Castle LeClercq. We were hobbyists of it. Enthusiasts, if that is the word? Is this a strange thing to admit?"

"Not at all," Cecily lied.

"Ah, good," Gens replied. "I will see you tomorrow."

Cecily hung up, wondering if every person she met in France would be so eccentric.

"How is it?" the Ethiopian counterman asked, appearing at her side.

"Perfect," Cecily replied, then remembered the French. "*Parfait.* Merci."

"Good," he replied as if any other response would be criminal. "Be careful with yourself."

She watched him retreat to his counter, thinking on his admonition. Her eyes tracked over to where the young woman in the silver suit had been, but she was gone.

5

RAIN FELL IN a torrent as Cecily made her way back to the Marais. It had gone from sunny to cloudy to a thunderstorm in under an hour. Not that she minded. Weather was one of her favorite things and it had the secondary effect of driving away all other pedestrians. She tucked the LeClercq book under her shirt and hoodie and darted from awning to awning but was quickly drenched regardless. By the time she reached the Seine, the river had already risen a foot or two, almost cresting the lower pathway where barges and other boats tied up.

Cecily seldom got lost in forests, so even though she kept her phone dry in her pants pocket, she found she didn't need the map to backtrack to Marguerite's house. She crossed the Seine at Notre-Dame, passed the art school and the museum with the Gordon Parks exhibit, and was soon a block away. She followed the horse chestnut trees to the front door.

The guests had left by the time she arrived. Only René and Auberon remained. Auberon washed dishes while René dried.

"*Alors*, someone forgot to bring in the cat!" René said when she entered, sopping wet.

"*Pas fute-fute*," Auberon said, rolling his eyes.

He tossed Cecily a dry towel and walked to the stove where

he'd been boiling water in anticipation of her return. He poured her a steaming cup of tea as she took off her shoes and hoodie.

"Merci," Cecily said.

"I have some news," René said. "I am uncertain what to make of it, but Marguerite has left us a gift. We, the three of us, have a reservation tomorrow night at the most exclusive restaurant in all of Paris. It can also be said that it is the best. Their waiting list can be as long as a year or more. Somehow, she worked magic and arranged it for us."

"Did she make it for three? Or for four?" Cecily asked.

"You mean, did she think she was joining us?" René asked. "She did, it seems. Though the proprietress, Pauline, says Marguerite joked about her health and said she might not attend. Make of that what you will."

"Will there be lots of people there?" Cecily asked.

"In fact, *non*," René said. "It is as if Marguerite accounted for that peculiarity of yours as well."

"I have some news of my own," Cecily said, then recounted her conversation with the medical examiner. Auberon looked alarmed, but René nodded.

"I am sure it is as he says," René said. "The one thing worse than Parisian bureaucracy is the kind they practice outside of town. I can drive us if you wish."

"Thank you," Cecily said.

"There is enough food in the refrigerator to feed a squadron," René said, kissing Cecily's cheeks before audibly sniffing her mouth. "But you already ate. Ethiopian?"

"*Alors*," Cecily said, rolling her eyes.

René laughed. "Marguerite would be glad to know her house is occupied by one such as you."

The men exited into the pouring rain. Cecily headed

upstairs to get dry. Once she was in Marguerite's glass-enclosed bedroom, she lay down on the bed and watched the storm.

She was soon asleep.

The storm passed and night fell. Cecily awoke in darkness. She watched the fast-moving clouds overhead for a moment longer before padding downstairs to look for food. She found a container of cooked vegetables, heated them up, and poured herself a glass of red wine from a half-empty bottle on the counter. It made for a delicious combination.

She headed back upstairs after refilling her wineglass, stopping in Marguerite's workroom. The closet, with its piles of boxes tipped over and tumbling out, looked somewhere between daunting and dangerous. Cecily pulled down two of the highest boxes which set off a chain reaction that dumped the rest all over the floor.

Cecily stacked up what she could then opened the first two. They were filled with faded, sepia-toned photographs from decades earlier. Almost all were images of plants, some in the wild, others in the studio. There were close-ups of leaves, trees from every angle, blades of grass filmed from such a low angle they rose like Roman columns, and more pictures of flowers, several in bright, vivid colors, than anyone could need in a lifetime.

Some were artful, sure, but most had been taken to amplify the delicate botanical architecture on display in order to reproduce it in another medium. Cecily's favorite was a series of photos taken of purple cistus flowers, eight bunched together on a shrub, from various angles but also with a revolving light source that made the shadows thrown off by their crepe-textured petals long and dramatic.

The next box contained fabric swatches, some with floral

patterns on them, some in solid colors. She put it aside. The next three were filled with more of the same. It wasn't until she reached a cream-colored box with a faded Kodak logo on the side that she found what she was looking for.

There were people in these pictures. Luckily for Cecily, a few had names and dates scrawled on the back. She met Marguerite's husband, Hubert Varennes, this way. He was a tall, thin-faced man with an easy smile who seemed to be wearing a wool suit and tie in every image. He was older than Marguerite by maybe ten years or so. There were a few photos of them together where Marguerite looked younger than Cecily was now.

Though Marguerite smiled in some pictures, she looked reserved in others. Distant. Maybe a little unhappy to have her photo taken. René was right. Marguerite wore the necklace Cecily had found on the sapling in every photo. Her smiles returned a couple of years on in pictures where she was holding first a baby, then standing alongside or with her arms around a young boy. This had to be Cecily's grandfather, Louis.

He was a handsome child with black hair and a toothy grin. As he grew older, his hair grew longer until it was down past his shoulders. In photos with his mother from this time, she was always smiling. He was always affectionate. A hug. A kiss on the cheek. There was one with Hubert kissing Marguerite on the other cheek.

The portrait of a perfect family.

She checked the LeClercq book but saw no death dates for Hubert. Given that he wasn't in the photos with Marguerite for the inquest, she figured he must've died in the late seventies or early eighties. This was meted out by the next few pictures, which introduced Louis's wife, Constance, followed by several featuring their baby daughter, Sandrine.

It was obvious that Marguerite delighted in photographing Sandrine. There were pictures of her as a baby, as a toddler, and as a school-age student. There were others of her at parties, at the seaside, on a bicycle. Though she'd never seen these pictures before, they felt to Cecily like reclaimed memories. She recognized Sandrine's every smile and gesture as ones she'd seen in real life and had now inherited.

It wasn't as if she'd forgotten her mother's appearance, but memories fade. She remembered pictures of incidents rather than the incidents themselves. Whatever inheritance Marguerite had left for her, she wasn't sure any amount of money would be worth as much to her as these photos.

She sifted through more pictures but found only much older ones. Ones that showed Marguerite as a young girl next to someone who the backs of the pictures told Cecily was Aline. A matched set. Their mother dressed them the same.

There was just one with Sandrine, Marguerite and Aline's mother, in them. Cecily was just thinking how much the elder Sandrine resembled her own mother then remembered that Marguerite was adopted and not a blood relative.

A distinction the LeClercq curse didn't seem to make.

The last picture in the box wasn't a photo at all. It was one of Marguerite's botanical drawings, though this one was unusual. It was of a towering oak tree with a great, stag-headed crown and horizontal branches that looked like they must weigh a ton or more. What made it so strange was that Marguerite had taken the time to sketch in walls and a roof overhead, drawing the tree as if it were somehow growing indoors.

It made no logical sense but was an interesting image, nevertheless. She wondered if Marguerite ever used it in a design.

That's when she noticed the care Marguerite had taken

in creating a few of the leaves at the tips of the branches. The shading and details were so fine, Cecily wondered if she'd resharpened her pencil with every line. She took out her phone and used the camera as a microscope, zooming in to one tiny leaf. It was oval, shiny, and had spiny lobes around its edges that tapered up to a sharp point. The shading made it look leathery in texture.

It was the leaf of a rare, nearly extinct evergreen oak. The same species as the sapling in Marguerite's rooftop garden.

"Did Marguerite ever talk about her mother?" Cecily asked René as they drove to the medical examiner's office as the sun rose over the east side of Paris.

"Which?" René replied, yawning as if he'd tumbled out of bed right before picking her up. "Birth mother? Or Countess Sandrine?"

"Either?" Cecily offered.

"She did not meet her birth mother—was it Christine? Colette?" René said. "All she knew of her father, Georges Manzanarès, was that he was killed early in the war leaving his young wife destitute."

"How did she come to be adopted by Countess Sandrine?"

"Sandrine knew of the tragedy, the Manzanarès family living nearby, and suggested to them she bring young Marguerite into her own household, having recently given birth to a girl of her own, Aline. They would be raised as sisters."

"Did they get along? Marguerite and Sandrine, I mean."

"It sounded as if Marguerite and Aline loved their mother very much," René said. "The father was a mining boss and never around. The three of them spent all their time out of doors, making games for themselves and exploring the woods. One of their favorites, like your medical examiner, was looking for the lost Castle LeClercq."

"So that's a real thing? There really is some lost castle?"

"Eh, doubtful," René admitted, exiting the city to take the highway north to the Val d'Oise. "Possibly at one time, but Marguerite said they hunted for it for years but never found a brick."

"Did she believe in the LeClercq curse?"

René hesitated as if he either wasn't sure or didn't want to say.

"This I will say," René said finally. "The first time she spoke of it to me, she said her mother and later her sister's obsessions with the curse drove them both to madness. She feared this for herself."

"Feared what?"

"That it could become a self-fulfilling prophecy and whether it existed or not didn't matter," René replied. "What gives the curse its strength, its power to control you, is your belief in it. If you believe in it as fervently as Countess Aline does, you will live your entire life in abject fear. You will let it haunt you. Pursue you. Keep you from joy. This is why Marguerite severed herself from the LeClercq family and its fortune at a young age. She feared being consumed the same as the others. She wanted no part of it."

"But tragedy followed her anyway," Cecily said.

"*Oui*," René said, nodding absently as if ready to change the subject.

The drive up to the Val d'Oise took almost an hour. Along the way, Cecily received a history lesson on France, its ninety-four regional departments ("Paris is its own department, but I suppose they are like your counties maybe? Maybe not?") and how the Val d'Oise was so named as it was the valley alongside the Oise River. The LeClercq lands, including the forest that bore their name and the estate in the forest's southeast corner, were somewhere close by.

They arrived at a small white building that shared a parking lot with a rural hospital. A young man in a lab coat, thin tie, and patchy brown facial hair the same shade as his shoes, waited outside. When René pulled into a parking space, he straightened and walked over.

"You are Cecily LeClercq?" he asked as she stepped out of the car.

"I am."

"Gregoire Gens," he said, shaking hands with her and then René. "Again, my condolences for your loss. Please, follow me. We will attempt to make this as painless as possible."

We? Cecily wondered.

Gens led them into the building, offering a quick wave to an officious-looking receptionist before ushering them through swinging metal doors into a short hallway. A strong, sour scent of antiseptic filled Cecily's nose but did little to hide the scent of death and decay that hung in the air. Gens walked them into a small room with a large window on one wall, darkened with blinds on the other side.

To Cecily's surprise, there were already two men in the room. Gens nodded but didn't introduce them to Cecily or René. Given that they were both well dressed and pretending not to take her measure the moment she entered, she figured them for police detectives.

Gens took a clipboard off the wall and flipped through the pages. Cecily saw her own face looking back at her from one of them.

"Wait, what's that?" she asked.

"A copy of your emergency passport," Gens said as if it should be self-evident.

"How did you get it?" Cecily asked, concerned.

"From the Foreign Ministry," Gens said, sounding again as if curious why Cecily would want to know. "It establishes where you were when Marguerite passed away, *non*? Also, Monsieur Chaumière."

"Why would you need to—"

Cecily cut herself off, glancing to the two detectives listening intently behind them. "I thought we were here to identify Marguerite's body for burial."

"Is this not a formality?" René added. "A tragic suicide but a suicide nevertheless?"

Gens glanced at the detectives, then tapped a button next to the window. Something beeped. The blinds opened. The body of Marguerite LeClercq lay prone on a metal table.

Her throat looked as if it had been torn out by a wild animal.

The wound was so deep, her neck so elongated, it pitched her chin back at an inhuman angle. It was as if the one thing keeping her head attached was the remains of her spine and the last few intact inches of flesh, now stretched to their limit, at the back of her neck. She'd practically been decapitated.

Cecily's body went cold with fright. Growing dizzy, she grabbed René's arm to steady herself.

René yelled at Gens in French. Though a small man, he puffed up with the ferocity of a wolverine. Gens appeared apologetic in the face of the verbal onslaught. The detectives, if that's what they were, seemed bored.

"Could you close the blinds, please?" Cecily begged.

The detectives shook their heads. *Non.* One said something to Gens, who turned to Cecily.

"What kind of contact did you have with Marguerite or others of her family in recent years?" he asked.

"None at all," Cecily said, fixing her eyes on Gens.

"What did you know about your inheritance?" he asked. "What had your mother told you?"

"Nothing," Cecily repeated. "If you suspect me of something, should I have a lawyer present?"

Again, Gens glanced to the detectives. Their expressions didn't change. Cecily turned back to the assistant medical examiner only to have all the air sucked from her lungs at once.

Marguerite was sitting up and staring through the glass at her. Except, it wasn't Marguerite. It was the wraith from the airplane. Her eyes were a deep red. Her matted hair spilled over the table and onto the floor. The broken teeth in her mouth mirrored the jagged edges of the gash across her throat, opening and closing as she moved, a hellish, double maw.

Cecily gasped for air but couldn't fill her lungs. She turned to the others in the room, terrified their eyes would change next, their skin tightening over their bones as it turned slate gray.

But the detectives, Gens, and René didn't move. They stared at her as if fixed in space. She turned again to Marguerite. She was back on the slab. Her throat was still torn away, but Cecily forced herself to look at her face instead.

The corpse was so shriveled, so small, it seemed more like a cheap, drugstore-bought Halloween decoration than anything that had once been human. Marguerite's silver hair, thin and wiry, was flat against her head. Her face was inhumanly white, almost fluorescent. Her eyes weren't quite closed, the lids revealing enough of her unseeing pupils to make her look asleep rather than dead. Her mouth was open as if to gasp one last breath. Her teeth were stained with blood.

"If you would like a lawyer," Gens said carefully, "we can give you time to procure one. We wanted to speak informally as questions have arisen about whether this was a suicide given the severity of the wound."

"She was a very old woman," René said. "At the end of her life."

"Precisely," Gens replied. "The wound suggests someone with strength. Someone capable of that level of brutality."

"Also, we made contact with the hospice where she received her cancer treatments," one of the detectives said in flawless English. "They told us not only was the victim's cancer in remission but also she had been informed as much the day before."

René looked stunned. Cecily put her hand on his arm, but he waved her away as if to assure her he was fine.

"There have been many claims on the LeClercq fortune in the past," the detective continued. "You will understand why the sudden appearance of a previously unknown heiress mere hours after the victim's grisly death raises questions."

"I'm no heiress," Cecily said.

"Marguerite has nothing to do with the fortune," René said. "She renounced it years ago."

"This is what Countess LeClercq's solicitor assured us," the detective said. "But that hasn't stopped many, many claims from being made in the past."

"You have informed the countess?" René asked.

"Of course," the detective said. "It happened on her property."

"How did she take the news?"

"We did not see her," the detective said. "Only the lawyer."

"Eglantine Saintève," René said.

"The very one," the detective replied. "She said she would

communicate the information herself. She said that she had known Marguerite only a little, though liked her a great deal."

The detective nodded to Gens. The medical examiner tapped the button on the wall and an unseen someone closed the blinds. Cecily stared at the body until it wasn't visible anymore. One thought filled her mind. Whoever cut that throat, it wasn't Marguerite.

6

"**I am bringing** you straight back to Marguerite's house," René said, practically spitting with anger as he drove them out of the parking lot a few moments later. "We will pack your things, head to the airport, and put you on the next plane home. I am sorry. Marguerite would not have wanted you to endure this."

Cecily turned the business card the medical examiner had given her over in her hands before shoving it in her pocket. Gens had apologized when he walked them to the door, mentioning that the police had indeed found a second set of footprints near where Marguerite's body had been discovered.

"She was found due to an anonymous tip," Gens explained as he half-escorted, half-chased them to the parking lot. "The mysterious circumstances surrounding this began right away. That kind of wound suggests a knife with a curved blade. We have recovered no weapon from the scene and her nurses said she had no such thing among her personal effects."

Cecily had nodded numbly and followed René. She'd never needed to leave a space faster.

"People here, the detectives as well, are defensive about the old countess," Gens continued. "There are always reporters snooping around. The world sees her as a . . . kook. A lunatic. We know her as someone who has spent her life reclaiming and liquidating her family's fortune to donate to worthy causes. Again, pardon our suspicions, but I hope you can understand there are those who would take advantage of the countess. If there's anything I can—"

René slammed his car door and cut Gens off.

"That was not Marguerite," René continued as they drove. "Everything that made her who she was has vanished, leaving behind an untidy husk. There is something both ugly and absurd about it. And the police! They concern themselves more with their beloved countess than with Marguerite. As if it was she who died."

"It's OK," Cecily said.

"It is not," René said. "That was cruel."

As they headed back to Paris, Cecily's gaze traveled to the fields alongside the highway. After a few minutes, the road angled south and she saw the beginnings of a forest off to the right. Not just any forest, though. A broad swath of trees that went on for miles to some unseen horizon.

It wasn't the trees themselves that made it an unusual sight. It was their height and relative position to one another. This wasn't some carefully reforested timber range waiting to be harvested by future loggers or suburban woodland. This was old growth. Wildwood. Completely untouched.

"What's that?" Cecily asked.

"Ah, told you we would see it," René said. "That's the Forêt de LeClercq—the LeClercq Forest. Beautiful, *non*?"

Given the images still swirling in her head, it was a palliative.

"Can we go over there? To get a closer look?"

"*Absolument*," René said. "That was no way to say goodbye."

The road wound down to a small village much like the ones Cecily saw on the trip from the airport. A sign introduced it as

75

Félice. A raised platform and what looked like an ATM turned out to be a train stop, Cecily realized as they bounced over railroad tracks. When they drove into the village itself, they passed the usual small-town businesses, including a pharmacy, a repair shop, a couple of cafés and restaurants, and even a pizza delivery.

In the center of town stood an old church with a spire that rose several stories above the next highest structure. The entire village radiated around it like planets orbiting a star.

On what counted for the far side of town stood a modern-looking grocery store about the size of the produce section of a Walmart Supercenter back home as well as a lonely gas station. The road ended at a two-lane highway before continuing on the other side as little more than a dirt path leading into the LeClercq Forest.

"The family never let anyone in?" Cecily asked.

"No logging or building," René said. "I think maybe the local government impressed upon them to allow electrical and phone lines to pass through. Likely water lines, especially to connect with the Oise River. That is all."

The sky grew dark as they moved into the woods, the tree canopy blocking out the sun as the forest consumed everything else. The farm fields to the south vanished from sight. The village behind them a distant memory. The road itself was barely visible ahead.

Cecily rolled down her window and let the scents and feel of the forest wash over her. It was reinvigorating. She wanted nothing more than to get out of the car, high-step into the nearest grove, and never return. There were beeches and linden trees. Chestnuts and ashes. More than anything, there were a wide variety of oaks.

"It's perfect," Cecily said.

"In its way, I suppose," René said dismissively.

Though the road looked mostly untraveled, the mud on both shoulders had been churned and turned over as if by a road grader. René saw where Cecily was looking and grinned.

"How should I say this in English? The countess's closest neighbors are barbarous savages," he said. "They tear through here every night, dozens at a time, ripping up the earth and making a big mess, all in pure silence. Despite all the mayhem, their palate is so refined they simply want the finest truffles."

"Wild boar?" Cecily asked.

"Herds of them," René said. "Perfectly harmless, but according to Marguerite, some reach hundreds of pounds in weight. All those truffles, I guess."

Cecily eyed the nearby trees and the ground littered with broken oaknut husks and empty cupules. "All those acorns, too," she observed.

They drove another half mile down the road before René slowed the car and pointed into the nearest section of woods. "Look," he said.

At first, Cecily didn't know what she was meant to see. Beyond her open car window were dense trees, grasses, and the occasional shrub. Then she saw it. Something man made. A high stone wall. It was practically invisible, perfectly camouflaged amid the tall, similarly colored tree trunks.

The LeClercq estate.

"The wall surrounds the property," René said. "The abbey is toward the back. It is the oldest structure. A great pile of fieldstone built in gratitude to God for his good fortune. Farther down, I think you can make out the chimneys of the chateau where the countess lives."

They were hard to see, but sure enough, there appeared to be a quartet of chimneys rising above the wall.

Which begged the question—what kind of house needed four fireplaces?

"The chateau was built in the seventeenth century," René said, driving forward so Cecily could get a better look. "Marguerite said it was like growing up in a vast museum full of art, people, and furniture so fine it might have been stolen from Versailles. A palace."

René turned down a gravel path. They drove along next to the stone wall. René slowed when they reached a high iron front gate.

Cecily had expected some grand, well-manicured domain, but this was the opposite. The grounds were completely wild and overgrown. Shrubs had exploded their great stone pots and Grecian urns. Tree roots shattered up through the driveway and even the steps that led to the likely once regal chateau was covered in dying vines and ivy that appeared determined to tear it down. Grass grew in ill-managed tufts, some stalks three and four feet high.

"It's beautiful," Cecily said.

"You would say this," René said, scoffing. "Though it looks abandoned, the countess seldom leaves, or so it is claimed. That lawyer, Eglantine, looks after her. I think she has a gardener, though this view may prove me wrong."

Cecily peered past the garden to the chateau itself. It was built of limestone, was three stories high with a slanted roof, regal details along its lintels, and several tall windows all of which had been shuttered as if in anticipation of a winter storm. Two vehicles were parked in front, a gardener's work truck and a Renault with a red cross on the door.

"An on-call nursing service," René translated. "I imagine the countess has had a stressful twenty-four hours."

Cecily nodded, then spied a gardener watering a patch of sunflowers near the chateau's front steps. He was young, tall, dark haired, and broad shouldered. Also—

"*Très beau*," René said. "Handsome."

Indeed.

"This must have been a magical place to grow up," Cecily said.

"*Certainement*," René agreed, turning the car around to return to the dirt road.

René took a right turn onto a path so narrow Cecily was dubious whether his Prius would even fit. She reached out the window, letting branches and plant stalks slide through her fingers as they passed.

The road became less visible as the forest overtook it. Cecily tried to get a sense of the trees' ages, but it was difficult. Some had the thick bark and wide trunk of a centuries-old specimen while others looked at most forty or fifty years old.

Babies compared to the rest.

What stood out the most was that they appeared in harmony with one another. Trees, it was said, were forest managers. They cooperated for resources rather than competed like other species. They nurtured their young. Took care of their sick. Grew mushrooms up from their root systems when a neighboring tree died and needed to be broken down. They exhaled pheromones when under attack by certain insects to warn other trees and produced poisons to fight off invasive species.

Working together, trees were less like individual plants and more like a single superorganism. One of the few invasive species trees hadn't evolved a defense against was people. Cecily wasn't sure how many large-scale forests like this even still existed.

"*Merde.*"

René had spoken so quietly Cecily hadn't registered he'd said anything until he slowed the car to a stop. Up ahead, a long strip of yellow tape hung limp from a tree.

Barrage de police. Ne pas traverser, it read in black letters.

"According to Thérèse, this is near where they found her," René said softly.

He stopped the car and they both climbed out. Though the scent of the forest was everywhere, there were other lingering smells. Cigarette smoke. The oily scent of newly used plastics. Human sweat. Deodorant.

A second strip of crime scene tape led several yards into the woods, creating a thin trail carved out by many footprints and thin wheel tracks Cecily thought might belong to a gurney. It told a grim story.

"Marguerite drove all the way out here?" Cecily asked, picking her way forward.

"They say she 'borrowed' a bicycle from the hospice," René said. "A feat for someone her age."

Cecily thought she saw something out of the ordinary up ahead. A building or some other structure. Impossible. The area was too remote for there to be a house or even a work shed this far out unless it was something long abandoned. The path indicated by the crime scene tape led straight to it.

"What is that?" René asked quizzically. "It looks like a black hole."

Within the shadows, there was a dark shape. Cecily imagined for a moment it was the ruins of the Castle LeClercq the medical examiner had mentioned. But it wasn't the proper size for a turret or bulwark. There were no right angles. No foundation. Its base bulged like a fat cauldron sending up a towering plume of smoke that mushroomed wide enough overhead to blot out the sky.

"Oh," Cecily said. It was a tree. A vast, gigantic, ancient tree. The mother oak to the surrounding trees and easily the largest Cecily had ever laid eyes on.

"*Sacré tonnerre*," René whispered, a smile spreading across his face. "What on earth is this?"

"An evergreen oak," Cecily said.

"Are you serious?" René asked, dumbfounded. "Like Marguerite's sapling?"

Cecily nodded. It couldn't be a coincidence. Part of her wondered if Marguerite, knowing she might not live long enough to tell her great-granddaughter all she needed to, might've left clues behind for Cecily to follow. Placing a necklace she never took off around the trunk of a sapling might seem like a harmless eccentricity unless, like Cecily, one knew enough about trees to know it was the one plant that didn't belong there. More than that, for the tree to survive and thrive, it would need to be returned to its birthplace.

Could it have come from the very place Marguerite had died?

Cecily stepped into the clearing and stared up into the great oak's canopy. It was so thick she couldn't see how high it went, but it was clearly the dominant tree in this part of the forest. The lower branches were as wide around as the trunks of other oaks, spilling from the center like serpents. Its lateral roots spread away from the trunk like a great spider's web that extended dozens of yards in every direction. In several spots, mushrooms rose off the roots, suggesting that the tree could be in the early stages of death or decay.

"How old is this?" René asked.

"Probably one thousand years or more."

René scoffed. "A thousand years old? Nothing lives that long. Why not, say, ten thousand?"

"Because this was a glacier then?" Cecily replied.

René huffed and wandered around the clearing. Cecily eyed the neighboring oaks and wondered if the sapling from Marguerite's garden could've come from here. She took a step and crunched down on several acorns. Unlike the brittle snap of the empty shells she'd encountered earlier, these were like pebbles. Though they'd devoured plenty from the surrounding trees, the boar had left the ones beneath this great oak's crown alone.

"*Quel dommage,*" René said mournfully.

There were several footprints around a slight sunken spot in the mud. Strips of used medical tape and a couple of empty bandage wrappers were trapped under the dirt. René knelt, kissed his fingertips, and touched the ground with them before closing his eyes to pray.

Cecily understood. It was where Marguerite fell.

She turned away to give him privacy, focusing her attention on the tree. Still thinking about the sapling, she took out her phone to take a few pictures to send to Ina. Even if it wasn't the exact location of the sapling's birth, she thought Marguerite might like the idea of it being replanted out here. She hoped Ina would have an opinion as to where to plant the sapling amidst the crowded grove.

Her first photos were muddy. The shaded trunk was barely distinguishable from the dark background. She turned on the flash. These pictures didn't look much better. What they did show was how thick the oak's outer bark was with deep ridges and striations, some an inch or more in height. She was even more certain now that the tree was several centuries old.

How much it must have borne witness to over the years, she thought.

She took another picture. The flash bounced off the trunk like a strobe light, illuminating the entire clearing. When she checked the photo, she noticed a large oblong knot on one of the branches. It appeared to be hollowed out or decomposing. She zoomed in with the camera and took another picture.

It wasn't a knot. It was the slate-gray face of the wraith. Her hair wove around the tree's trunk. Her fingers, tapered into talons, gripped the bark.

Cecily blinked. She stared at the image on her phone, waiting for it to become something else. This time it didn't. She looked back to the tree itself, the dark knot perfectly still in the dim light. Cecily edged closer, her body quaking with fright. She needed to know the truth. This was no panic attack. No childhood flashback or crisis apparition appearing in a moment of stress.

The specter was real and had stalked her mother all the way to a watery grave.

Except, as Cecily leaned against the trunk to get a better view, she saw that it was a knot after all. Large and misshapen, a bulbous tumor swelling up from the branch, it was no more a wraith than she was.

She turned on her camera's flashlight to get a better look but sensed a presence beside her but knew right away it wasn't René. She felt the specter's hot breath on the side of her face. Her piercing gaze practically flaying the skin from her skull.

The wraith was beside her, tall and imposing. Her hand flew up, the talons extending as if to strike with the ferocity of some great monstrous bird. Cecily could already feel the jagged claws penetrating her soft flesh to pierce bone.

She shrieked and whirled around, her foot coming down not on root or rock or even earth but on thin air. It was as if with the arrival of the wraith, the ground around the tree had dissolved, opening a huge, deep chasm. Cecily tumbled down between the roots, through layers of damp earth and sinew, disappearing deep below the forest floor.

The air was sucked out of her lungs as she fell through darkness until her head struck something hard. A root maybe. Just when she thought she couldn't fall farther, she landed face-first on hard-packed earth.

"Oh my God," she sputtered, catching her breath even as she spit dirt. "Oh my *God*."

She tried to sit up but hit her head a second time. When she inched forward, her ankle throbbed. She hadn't even realized she'd hit it. There was an angry, stinging sensation from her forehead. She touched it lightly. Her fingers came away slicked with blood.

"René!" she rasped.

She rolled over but pain shot up her leg. Had she broken it?

"René!" she yelled again, looking skyward.

Still no answer.

She leaned onto her side only for pain to shoot up her wrist as well. Her eyes adjusting to the darkness, she could just make out the murky tangle of roots overhead. She'd fallen at least a dozen feet through hollowed-out space beneath the oak.

No wonder the boar left this oak's acorns alone. She wondered how many tumbled down here before the whole herd got the message.

She was about to call out René's name again when she blanched. The wraith. Oh, god, what if she'd attacked René? Could he be down here, too? Also injured? Maybe worse?

She felt around the loamy surface for another body, but the pit just kept going.

She wondered if the tree above her was stable. The mushrooms should've been a clue that it was in decline. If it were hanging on by its lateral roots and a few clumps of earth, it could collapse at any minute. She needed to put as little weight on its roots as possible.

She inched forward, waiting for the ground to fall out from under her. It remained solid. She might avoid a premature burial yet.

Something trickled past her face. She reached for her cheek, but there was nothing there. She tensed, a new fear electrifying her nervous system. When she looked up, she saw the wraith's dark silhouette picking its way spiderlike through the roots.

Cecily screamed and dug her elbows into the dirt to propel herself along. When she glanced up again, she could make out the oak's cauldron-shaped lower trunk and the taproot leading down. Could she climb it? When she took hold of a few lower root fibers, however, they broke off in her hand like dry twigs.

She tried a second root. Not only did it snap off but also she felt the root it was attached to sway and give. Though the oak's trunk didn't move, Cecily was sure it wouldn't take much to bring the multiton tree crashing down on top of her.

She had to find another way.

She glanced back toward the wraith but couldn't see her anymore. Somehow, this didn't make her feel any safer. She felt her way forward, and her fingertips touched rock rather than dirt.

No, not rock. Bricks. Hand-tooled. The broken remains of a wall or barrier rising next to the taproot. She ran her hand up them as high as she could reach, finding breaks in the molding and the bricks themselves. Potential hand- and toeholds.

Roots tearing at her face and body, Cecily lifted herself to her full height. She found a couple of holds and began to climb. Her wrist exploded with pain when she tried to lift herself up.

It wasn't easy, but she managed to climb up a few steps. Dust and dirt cascaded past her with every touch, seeming to threaten that the whole wall might collapse. Still, she climbed, inching her way back to the surface one step at a time.

Though scared, she controlled her breathing. Forced herself to calm down. Refused to give up. Demanded her numb muscles keep pushing her up to safety.

A hand, as strong as the jaws of a ferocious beast, grabbed her ankle. Adrenaline surged through her body as she tried to free herself, but it was like fighting against a machine. It was too dark to see the wraith even as her claws tore into her flesh. Warm blood trickled down her legs and into her shoes.

"No!" she yelled, pulling herself higher. "Stop!"

She forced herself up another few inches, but the wraith yanked her back down like a crocodile drowning its prey. She'd lost feeling in her foot. She was out of strength and out of time.

A second hand grabbed at her wrist, this time from above. Cecily shrieked and pulled away. The hand held tight. Cecily feared she was seconds from being torn apart.

"*C'est moi,* Cecily!" someone shouted. "Stop fighting me!"

It took Cecily a second to recognize René's voice. She kicked at the wraith one last time using all her strength. Her body erupted in pain, but the specter's grip slackened for an instant. Cecily launched herself up, clawing through the roots and mud as René hauled her up onto solid ground.

Cecily coughed and spit dirt. She wheeled around to the tree.

"She's there!" Cecily warned. "Did you see here? She's there!"

"*Qui?*" René asked, alarmed. "Who is?"

"The wraith! She tried to kill me. The one who killed my mother! She's real! She killed Marguerite! She's under the tree!"

"Listen to me," René said. "You had a bad fall. You hit your head. We have to get you out of here and cleaned up."

"It's not my head!" Cecily cried. "Just look! She tried to kill me!"

René eyed her with real concern, then moved back to the tree. "Right. Do I need a gun?" he asked, voice wavering toward sarcasm. "Maybe a big stick?"

"Be careful!"

René edged over to the tree trunk, balancing on the largest exposed roots to look back down into the darkness.

"I . . . I see nothing," he admitted.

"She was right there!" Cecily cried.

Something moved in the oak's upper branches. Cecily looked. It was the wraith. She was about twenty feet above René, her limbs tucked under like a hawk about to swoop down on a mouse.

"Look out!" Cecily screamed.

She tried to stand. The world spun around. The earth became the sky, and the oak inverted as if growing directly down into the earth. Cecily fell, digging her fingers into the dirt in a desperate attempt to hold on as the day's light flickered and vanished.

7

CECILY AWOKE SOMETIME later to the smell of dust and damp wood. It reminded her of the far-flung hunters' cabins she'd sheltered in while hiking in the Smoky Mountains. Except, instead of a sleeping bag, she was on a small, foldable cot in a room with a high, vaulted ceiling, an empty fireplace, and tall windows, their view blocked by heavy shutters.

The cot was the room's only furniture.

"Oh, bonjour," someone said from the doorway.

It was the gardener she and René had seen earlier. He sat in a chair, scrolling through his phone. She realized she must be in the Chateau LeClercq. Where was all the furniture?

"Hi," she replied, still groggy.

"How are you feeling?" he asked, in English now. His accent wasn't French, though Cecily couldn't place it.

"Not sure," she said.

She sat up straight. Her entire body ached, but it didn't feel like anything was broken. She had bandages on the various cuts along her legs, arm, and face.

"Your doing?" she asked.

"The countess's nurse," the young man said. "Your friend arrived at the gate in a panic. Said he saw the nurse's car and there had been an accident. She fixed you up."

"My friend? So, he's OK?" Cecily asked, suddenly remembering what had happened in the seconds before she'd passed out.

"Downstairs drinking tea with Eglantine," he said. "I'm Bashir Maleh, by the way, but everyone calls me Bash. I'm the head and, well, sole gardener for Countess LeClercq."

"Your English is very American," Cecily remarked.

"Eh, picked it up watching *Breaking Bad* and *Scrubs*."

"*Scrubs?*"

"Three of my four sisters are doctors; the fourth is a pharmacist," he said. "They all say *Scrubs* and *ER* are the only realistic American medical shows."

"I'm Cecily LeClercq."

"There's a coincidence."

"My great-grandmother was Marguerite LeClercq," Cecily explained. "She was the countess's sister."

Bash grimaced in recognition. "She's the woman they found in the woods."

"Yeah."

"I'm sorry," he said, picking up a bottle of orange juice next to his chair. "I'm supposed to give you this to drink. You were dehydrated when you got here. Your friend said you fell into a sinkhole or something?"

Did that mean René hadn't seen the wraith? The realization hit home. It took Cecily right back to her childhood in the months following her mother's death, when relatives, teachers, and therapists collectively convinced her that she'd seen only her mother, not some spectral monster.

Now, she knew the truth. There was something out there. Something dark and really dangerous, but only she knew about it.

No. She and one other.

"Is Countess LeClercq home?" Cecily asked, sitting upright.

"Always," Bash said. "Whether she is seeing anyone is a question for Eglantine."

Cecily got to her feet and tried to walk to the door. Her ankle buckled. Bash caught her by the arm.

"Let me help," he said.

Cecily, not exactly a fan of having anyone that close to her, was about to refuse when she noticed her other ankle felt rather numb, too.

"Thanks."

She limped out of the room with Bash's help. The hallway was as bare as the room. There was no furniture. No rugs. No wallpaper. No art on the walls. Not even any light fixtures. Only a couple of unlit bare bulbs marking where the sockets were. It looked like the house had been abandoned.

"Ah, it is your first time here," Bash said, catching her look. "All the furniture, except what's in use, has already been sold off."

"Why?" Cecily asked.

"It's part of the LeClercq fortune," Bash explained. "The countess means to die penniless. She's already legally handed over the house and grounds to an arts foundation with the stipulation that she's allowed to live here until her death."

"What does she have left to donate?" Cecily asked.

"Nothing, I believe," Bash said. "She spends her days going over and over the LeClercq family records to see if there's anything she missed, but there hasn't been anything new in years."

They reached the landing of a high, winding staircase with carved oak banisters that descended all the way down to the first floor. Cecily steadied herself on the guardrail, the feeling now returned to her legs.

"I saw your garden earlier," Cecily admitted. "It's beautifully wild."

"Thank you," Bash said. "In case they don't keep me on when the foundation opens their arts colony, I wanted to make sure it's spent a couple of years growing as wild as possible. Enrich the soil for whatever they plan for it."

"Smart," Cecily said. "I work with plants back in America."

"Ah, then if you get a chance later, you should look around," he said. "The garden is full of amazing specimens."

This sounded exactly like something she wanted to do. He helped her down the two flights of stairs to the foyer on the first floor, then nodded to the door.

"Find me if you want that tour," he said.

"Will do," she said. "And thanks."

He nodded and headed away. Cecily tested her legs and nosed around. The rooms on the first floor were as empty as the ones above. The walls had been whitewashed, covering over sconces, carvings, and all manner of detail. The floors were bare wood in places, some looking centuries old and worn away.

"René?" Cecily called out. "Are you here?"

"In here, *chérie*," he answered from a parlor off the foyer.

The shutters were open in this room. Bright sunlight streamed in, warming the air. Cecily hadn't even realized how cold she was. René was seated on a black ergonomic office chair that couldn't have looked more out of place. Opposite him on a threadbare barstool sat a well-dressed young woman with blond hair and green eyes. Cecily recognized her immediately. The woman in the silver suit from the Jardin du Luxembourg.

"Cecily LeClercq, meet Eglantine Saintève," René said, getting to his feet to make the introduction. "Eglantine, Cecily."

"Nice to meet you," Cecily said, unable to keep the surprise from her voice.

"And you," Eglantine said, shaking Cecily's hand. "Though we have seen each other before, *non*? In the Jardin du Luxembourg? Near the Sorbonne where I tracked you like a spy?"

Cecily glanced at René. He was amused. Eglantine sighed and smiled. "I am sorry about all the cloak-and-dagger silliness. I hope you did not think me a stalker."

"So, you were following me?" Cecily asked.

"Sadly, yes," Eglantine admitted. "In my defense, I was sent by Madame, the countess. I was meant to be discreet, but it felt ridiculous. I would have introduced myself, but again, I was forbidden."

Part of Cecily was relieved. Another part, disquieted. "Why did she want you to follow me?"

"You recall the police?" René asked. "It seems that the countess is as paranoid as they are. A new heiress appears out of thin air, and voilà, the mad old woman unleashes the hounds."

"It is me," Eglantine said. "*La chienne.*"

"For someone so focused on heirs and fortunes, it seems strange she didn't know I existed," Cecily suggested.

"Oh no, she knew Sandrine LeClercq's daughter, Cecily, lives in Charleston, America," Eglantine said. "What she did not know was whether you were that Cecily."

"Can I speak to her?" Cecily asked.

"You are sure?" René asked. "You have had a very rough day."

"If that would be all right," Cecily added, looking to Eglantine.

"Like you, she has had a very difficult past couple of days," Eglantine said carefully. "Though they were long estranged, she cared deeply for Marguerite. Seeing you might be nice for her. Shall I inquire?"

"Please," Cecily said.

Eglantine exited the parlor. Cecily turned to René, only to see that he'd been scrutinizing her the entire time.

"The countess is very old and, it seems, prone to outbursts," René cautioned. "She believes in this LeClercq curse like others believe in the religion of their childhood. What you said in the woods about this *wraith* I worry could enflame the old woman."

"You don't believe I saw anything?" Cecily asked.

"Ah, *non*," René said. "I believe you did. I also believe you had fallen and become injured first. This, directly after receiving a major shock at the medical examiner's office. The nurse said your blood pressure was extremely high and you had all the signs of fatigue. If tomorrow you wake up and recognize it as a fantasy, I would not want you to regret what you might have said to the countess today. Understand?"

Cecily didn't have the energy to persuade René. And anyway, Eglantine returned a moment later, forcing a smile. "She will see you. She is tired but anxious to meet."

"Thank you," Cecily said.

Eglantine led her to the stairs and indicated the countess's room on the second floor. "She asks me to send you up alone. If you need my help, do not hesitate to call out. Yes?"

"OK," Cecily said.

Cecily moved up the stairs, marveling all over again at the emptiness of the chateau. *How does anyone live like this?* she wondered. It was like a strange punishment or penance.

Which, she thought, maybe in the countess's mind it was.

She tried to imagine the two little girls from Marguerite's photographs gallivanting down the halls of this old house, roving from room to room under the watchful eye of their mother. How they'd emerge out onto the grounds to play in the garden or the woods beyond the wall. It was difficult to picture. The current dreariness of the place made anything merry hard to envision.

She took a deep breath when she reached the countess's bedroom, then stepped inside. The room was as empty as all the others except for a single bed and nearby chair. An elderly woman who seemed as nervous about meeting Cecily as Cecily did her stood by the window. She was very thin. Her long, gray hair was pinned back with tarnished silver combs atop her head. Her pale, arctic-blue eyes flitted up and down the newcomer like those of a child rather than someone in their mid-eighties.

"Bonjour, Madame," Cecily said.

"Bonjour, Comtesse," the woman corrected.

Cecily waited for her to smile as if this was a joke. She did not.

"Bonjour, Countess," Cecily repeated.

The countess indicated the chair. Cecily went to sit, expecting the old woman to join her. Instead, she stayed by the window.

"Cecily LeClercq," the countess pronounced, her English so tightly clipped no syllable hung in the air for longer than a second. "It has been a long time since I met anyone who shared my name."

"Me, too."

The countess started, as if this were the first time she'd considered such a thing. "I am sorry you never got to know Marguerite," she said. "She was strong. I looked up to her with reverence."

It was an interesting choice of words. Cecily wondered if it was what she meant, then saw from the look on the countess's face that it was.

"You resemble her," the countess said. "This is nice but unimportant. When she sent that man to bring you to her, did you understand then what inheritance awaited you?"

"I did not."

"But now, it seems, you do."

Cecily wasn't sure how to respond. "I don't know what you mean. If you think I want money—"

"Who did you see out there?" the countess asked. "Out in the woods? Who is coming to you in your dreams and waking nightmares?"

"I don't know," Cecily said, her voice a whisper.

"Tell me!" the countess insisted.

"Some kind of wraith," Cecily said.

"Go on."

"I don't know anything more. I saw her when my mother died, too."

"You are certain you did not imagine this?" the countess asked.

"I don't know. I really—"

"Yes, you do. Did you imagine it or not? Is this a response to trauma? It is no weakness to admit this."

"No," Cecily declared. "I know what I saw."

"A woman?"

"Yes."

"Dark matted hair down to her feet as if connecting her to the earth?"

"Y-yes."

"Black dress? Bright-white skin? Eyes of cobalt blue?"

"No," Cecily said, confused. "A woman, yes, but in a white dress. Skin like slate. Eyes a deep red, almost black."

The countess stared at her for a long moment, then darkened. "Fingers and toes that taper into points as if their tips had been whittled down to sharp, clawlike stakes?" she asked quietly. "Jagged teeth?"

"Yes," Cecily whispered, realizing the countess had been testing her.

"*Alors*," the countess said, voice haunted with fear. "You are of this family after all."

"But who is she?" Cecily asked. "What is she?"

"I have spent a lifetime trying to answer that question yet still do not know," the countess admitted. "All I have is what my mother told me. The wraith is a herald. She arrives when the death of a LeClercq is at hand. She wreaks mortal havoc on the lives of those around you. Killing those closest to you and driving you mad, until you either sacrifice your own life to appease her hunger and she drags you to hell along with the souls of everyone else who has died in the days leading up to your demise."

Cecily shook her head. "I . . . I don't understand. Is she a ghost? One of your ancestors?"

"You ask the wrong questions," the countess said, coming over next to Cecily. "She is the living embodiment of the LeClercq curse. She comes to us all. The question is when."

"Did she come for my grandparents?"

"I have long believed so," the countess said. "Though Marguerite refused to believe it."

"My mother?" Cecily asked, her voice small in the large room.

The countess turned to the window, distraught. "*Oui*," she said gently. "She sacrificed her life the same as my mother sacrificed hers for Marguerite and me. Like so many LeClercqs before."

"But how? If Marguerite wasn't even a LeClercq, why does it follow her family, too?"

"Marguerite thought she was immune to the curse," the countess explained. "That by virtue of being adopted, not of blood, it might pass her by. But when her daughter-in-law was killed and her son blamed, this view was shattered. She must have known that it was the doing of the wraith. Fortune or no, blood relative or not, she had been marked as a LeClercq and the curse did not care whether she had turned her back on her name or not."

So many things made sense now. The seemingly endless cycle of tragedy and death. Marguerite's monumental grief. Her mother's escape to America.

"Whatever horror our family is guilty of, whatever violation, offense, whatever transgression produced such a monstrous curse cannot be undone," the countess said. "In my many inquiries into its origin, I have encountered several instances of LeClercqs changing their names. Going overseas. Attempting to hide. A great-uncle of mine became a priest. A great-aunt of his became a nun. LeClercqs have led lives of opulence and hedonism but also of penitence and shrift. It does not matter. The wraith comes for everyone in our family without exception. And once you see her, you are next."

"She's going to kill me?" Cecily asked, incredulous.

"No, that is the insidiousness of the curse," the countess said. "She does not do it herself. You must make that sacrifice as your mother, Marguerite, and Louis all did. Only you. If you know her appearance means either your death or that of someone close to you, how long would you last? Louis held out and she took his bride. Your mother had no intimates, no attachments except you. When the wraith appeared, she knew she couldn't wait."

Cecily choked out a sob. It was too cruel. To know her mother sacrificed her life for hers felt like a crushing weight on her heart.

"She couldn't fight back? Try to get away?" Cecily asked.

"As I said, once you've seen her, your days are numbered and there is no escape," the countess said. "It was in watching the agony Louis and his wife's deaths put Marguerite through that made me realize there was only way one way to end the curse for good. There can never be another LeClercq. The line and the fortune stop with me. No one should ever be made to face this abomination of a choice again."

"But if somehow I'm the last LeClercq, what does—"

"You have already seen the wraith," the countess said coldly. "I wish there were something I could say to comfort you. Tell you the curse could be unraveled by ritual or incantation. Even by righting an ancient wrong. But you will believe me when I say all has been tried over the generations."

"So, that's it?" Cecily asked. "I'm going to die?"

The countess fell silent. Cecily shook her head. She had to get out of there. Back to a world that made sense. She got to her feet and ran from the room. She hurried down the stairs to the front door.

"Cecily?" René asked as she passed the parlor.

But Cecily kept going. She felt like throwing up. No, she felt like leaving everyone and everything behind, fleeing to the woods, and never, ever interacting with another person as long as she lived.

Her vision blurred as she pushed through the front door, ran past the parked cars, and into the overgrown garden. It wasn't until her legs went out from under her that she realized she was hyperventilating.

"Hey, you OK?" It was Bash hurrying over with a bottle of water. "Seems my job right now is to chase after you with liquids."

He sat down next to her and passed the water. She drank the entire thing, gasping between swallows. Her head throbbed.

"Are you sure you should be out of bed?" Bash asked.

"Is that your *Scrubs* medical training kicking in?"

Bash laughed. "Common sense."

Cecily nodded. "I had to get out of there."

"Did she scare you? The countess, I mean."

"Something like that," Cecily admitted.

"I understand. She is enigmatic. Fearing so much but surprisingly forceful. A strong, conflicted will. The gardener before me said she was always unusual. Clever and curious. Despite growing up surrounded by pain and trouble, she still loved to travel and be of the world when she was younger. The older she got, though, the fewer people she sees."

"You've heard of the curse?"

"Of course," Bash said. "But there's what they talk about in Félice and what I've learned of it here in the garden."

"What do you mean?"

"I can show you," he said. "If you think you are up for it."

Curious, Cecily got to her feet and followed the young man through the garden to the rear of the chateau. The estate's towering chestnut trees had begun to shed leaves with the coming of the fall, creating a thick carpet of yellows and reds amid the grass.

"You keep your trees in great shape," she commented.

"Thank you," Bash said. "They were doing well on their own when I started. I look for ways to help them help themselves."

"Do you have any evergreen oaks here?"

"Wow, you know your trees," he said. "I'd thought they were extinct until I saw a few out in the woods but no, none on the grounds."

"You know the forest?"

"Trying to. I want to get hired on as a forester by this arts foundation the countess is leaving all this to. Part of that has been helping to catalog the neighboring woods as they plan a few walking and cycling paths."

"Sounds fun," she said, glad to talk about something that made sense.

"Never seen anything like this forest," he admitted. "It's like stepping out of a time machine. But, I suppose, so is working around something like this."

He pointed ahead. The thirteenth-century abbey Cecily had glimpsed from René's car lay half-hidden among the trees. It was large and expansive. Much bigger and blockier than the chateau, with walls of great stone rising three stories supported by heavy buttresses every few yards. There were several gorgeous-looking stained-glass windows along the first floor, but the windows on the second and third more resembled those of a castle or prison, hardly large enough to see through. A narrow, man-made canal shuttled water into the abbey on one side where Cecily saw a large yet still waterwheel.

"That was what counted for running water in the thirteenth century," Bash explained. "Goes right into the kitchen and out the other side."

"It's huge," Cecily said.

"And cold and drafty and falling apart," Bash said.

"You've been inside?"

"Once or twice. The countess keeps it locked but has me clear out the courtyard every so often. We don't need the key to get in there, though."

He led her around the side of the medieval building to where the tallest ladder Cecily had ever seen leaned against the outer wall.

"Up there?" she asked, still queasy.

"As I said, if you're up for it," Bash replied.

Cecily wasn't sure she was but wanted to know what was inside. She took a deep breath, stepped up onto the first rung as Bash steadied it from the side, then climbed. She stopped after a few yards to look down. The sight was dizzying.

"The trick is to not stop," Bash said. "Keep going until you get to the top."

She did as suggested, reaching the roof thirty seconds later. Though it was slanted, she managed to get her balance and hold the ladder for Bash. Once he was up, they both looked out over the estate, past the walls, and to the lush surrounding woods.

"Beautiful, isn't it?" Bash asked.

"It is," she agreed. "But what did it tell you about the curse?"

"No, that's down there," he said, leading her up over the top of the peaked roof to the other side where a second ladder waited.

It led into a large courtyard within the abbey's walls. About half the size of a football field, it was filled with statues and busts sculpted in everything from marble to bronze. But like everything in the garden, the sculptures had been overtaken by a vast thicket of thick-stemmed plants marked by thousands of tiny red flowers.

"Are those . . . crowns of thorn?" Cecily asked.

"They are," Bash confirmed. "They call them Christ thorns around here. Be careful. Every stem has hundreds of barbs."

They descended into the courtyard, Cecily staring at the statues as they went. The sculptures themselves were pedestrian. Artless renderings from life that would seem as at home over a tombstone as in a bank or accounting firm. The writing on the pedestals under each statue named a different LeClercq.

"This isn't a cemetery, is it?" Cecily asked.

"A memorial garden," Bash said. "They're arranged so haphazardly it feels like they are in storage. They didn't know where to store the old statues, so they shoved them in here."

Cecily grinned. She made her way close to a Comte Philip LeClercq who, unlike several others, was completely clean shaven with short hair and dull eyes. Under his name on the pedestal was chiseled *neuvième.*

"It means he was the ninth Count LeClercq," Bash explained. "The ninth count since the peerage was created in the twelfth century though these days the monarchy is long gone. Titles like 'countess' don't mean much these days."

Cecily laughed and gently pushed past the thick, thorn-covered bushes to the other statues. While most were men, there were a few women in the garden as well. Some were sculpted as great beauties. Others in hats with delicate plumes or dresses representing several historical periods. She searched the faces for one that resembled the wraith, wondering if this was why Bash had brought her here.

"What does this prove about the curse?" Cecily asked.

"Belief in it," Bash said. "Going back centuries. Look behind the pedestal."

This wasn't easy given the Christ thorns, but Cecily finally glimpsed the back of the pedestal for what her limited French told her was the twelfth Comte LeClercq, named Guy. There were four thin, yet distinct scratches partially obscured by the bushes at its base.

"How many marks?" Bash asked.

"Four," Cecily answered, surprised.

"Go to the next one," Bash said.

Cecily picked her way to a fourth Comtesse LeClercq. She thought the statue's face, in some distant way, resembled her own mother, then remembered Marguerite's adoption. These weren't blood relatives of hers.

"What do you see?" Bash asked.

Cecily leaned behind the pedestal. There were six deep scratches in the pedestal. "Six marks," she announced. "What do they mean?"

"You've heard how the curse is meant to work?" Bash asked. "The wraith appears to the LeClercq heir or heiress demanding their sacrifice and marking them the next to die?"

"Um, sure," Cecily said, Bash's matter-of-fact tone conflicting with the countess's surreal insistence that Cecily's time on the planet was coming to an end due to the same circumstances.

"But if they don't sacrifice their life, the wraith slaughters someone close to them," Bash continued. "The villagers say it can be anyone and has included workers here at the estate. Nuns in their abbey. Clerks in their offices. Anyone in their orbit could be added to their butcher's bill, making these LeClercqs responsible for their deaths."

"What does that have to do with the scratches?" Cecily asked.

"Back then, it wasn't as if you could say anything against the local aristocracy," Bash said. "Raising a voice against them was the same as speaking against the monarch. So, those in the area would sneak onto the estate, take up Christ thorns, and mark the pedestals of the statues. Four marks meant the count or countess took four people with them. Five represents five souls. Six for six. Seven for seven. And so on."

"All before they took their own lives?" Cecily asked.

"If you believe the local legend, yes," Bash said.

Cecily checked several other pedestals. She saw four on one, three on another, eight on the next. She came upon one of a countess who, judging by her dress, was from a more recent century. Her pedestal was unmarked.

"This one's bare," she said.

"Then none died by her hand," Bash said. "Draw your own conclusions."

Cecily didn't know what to think of this. How could anyone's belief in something so unknowable be so strong that they'd take their own life? But also, how could anyone not do so if it meant saving the lives of those closest to them?

The countess was right. It was a grotesque dilemma.

The old woman's words returned to her. What odious horror must some ancestor of hers committed to exact this kind of curse?

"Look over here," Bash said.

He stood alongside a statue practically devoured by plants. Christ thorns wound around its body like several lengths of chain to hold it in place, red flowers bursting to life across its chest and head like blood oozing from countless lacerations.

The sculpture underneath looked as average as all the other LeClercqs. Narrow face. Large eyes. Thin lips and thinning hair. Sharp nose. On the pedestal was chiseled Comte Sabastien LeClercq with no number.

The first Count LeClercq.

"The locals acknowledge the pedestal markings are imperfect and the work of the superstitious," Bash said. "Some have cuts from years when plague swept the land. Others during wartime. There's no telling how many unrelated deaths were blamed on the LeClercqs. But there were no wars or plagues during this time."

Cecily pushed the Christ thorns aside to get a better look at the statue's base. She saw the first few marks, six or seven, at most. She shot a curious look back to Bash. He pulled on work gloves and held all the branches back at once.

"Behind there," he said.

Cecily gasped. Dozens of scratches had been carved on one side of the pedestal and continued around the back. Her fingertips traced over them as they stretched beyond where she could reach. There were hundreds upon hundreds of them, too many to count.

She turned to Bash. The look on his face was grave and inscrutable.

8

"Eglantine and I tried to find you," René said on the drive back to Paris. "I could not say if the old lady put the fear of God into you or, maybe, you had one of your I-need-to-drink-in-the-splendors-of-nature episodes. Imagine our relief when you suddenly appeared alongside the handsome gardener."

His words were light, but Cecily could hear the concern in his voice.

"I heard from Thérèse," he continued. "It was not so easy booking you on a last-minute flight back to your rundown *taudis* in America's most notorious slave port, but she is a miracle worker. I asked Eglantine if she would assist you with Marguerite's estate. She says if she cannot help, she will find someone who can."

He handed her Eglantine's business card. Cecily stared at it for a moment, then shook her head. "But what about the curse?" she asked.

"What about it?"

The urgency of the countess's warnings had worn off a little while she was with Bash, but the terror she'd felt in the woods had not.

"If my mother wasn't safe from it in America, how can I be?" Cecily asked. "The countess told me what happened to her own mother. What actually happened with my grandfather, Louis, and his wife."

René listened quietly for a moment, then exited the highway, pulling to a stop alongside a farm field.

"What're you—"

"Cecily," René said quietly but firmly. "Listen to me. When there is great tragedy in life, it is simpler to believe it the result of a magical curse. It is a way of denying the unfairness of life. What has happened to you, what happened to your mother, what happened to Marguerite and to poor Constance is unfair. Too much pain for anyone to bear. But there is no witch or wraith or ghost. No curse. Only the vagaries of life."

"I know what I saw," Cecily said. "I even took a photo of it. I just lost my phone."

René took her phone from his pocket. "This phone?"

She snatched it away. The battery was almost dead. She went to the last photo taken expecting to see the face of the wraith. But the image was too dark. All she could see were the tree and the knot.

"I saw it on the plane before," Cecily protested. "Then again in the woods. It's the same monster I saw as a child. The same the countess saw."

"*Un moment*," René said. "Did the countess say she'd seen it? Truly face-to-face? Or did she describe it from what her mother told her many years ago?"

Cecily couldn't remember. "I don't know."

"It was not the countess who was there when her mother died; it was Marguerite. She saw her in the tree. She saw what the police, the medical staff, the local newspapers—everyone—reported as a suicide by hanging. There is a coroner's report in the police archive in Félice. There was an inquest that confirmed the coroner's findings. But the countess has decided it was a wraith's vengeance."

"What about the townspeople?" Cecily asked. "Bash showed me the thorn marks on the pedestals."

"Oh, the *thorns*?" René asked sarcastically. "Have you tried to scratch marble with a thorn? Did you even take a good look at the scratches? Enough to wonder why some barely look older than others? Local kids have been daring each other to sneak over the walls of the LeClercq estate since the war. Those scratches have been made by everything from penknives to screwdrivers."

Cecily fell silent.

"As for you, you have seen the wraith three times, you say," René continued. "First, when your mother died. Second, on your first plane ride ever when you were so terrified you needed pills to fall asleep. Third, moments after you saw your great-grandmother with her throat torn out. I would almost worry more should you not have had a grand mal nervous reaction in each of those instances."

"But Louis," Cecily said. "The countess said—"

"Louis was a drunk who never forgave his mother for turning her back on a great fortune condemning him to a middle-class existence," René said. "Did the countess tell you he'd just lost his job? That the police had several witnesses who saw him attack his wife? There are many more boring, violent, terrible men in this world than wraiths, but if a reporter can tie a crime to a curse, they can sell more papers. If only Louis had lived to see how quickly he became a LeClercq in the public eye after his death."

"That's part of what I didn't understand," Cecily said. "He wasn't a blood relative."

"Exactly! There is no curse except what you choose to believe," René exclaimed. "How many marriages do you think there have been to the LeClercq family over the years? How many children? Grandchildren? Cousins? Nieces and nephews? *Thousands*. Has the curse chased them? No."

"But it followed my mother," Cecily said.

"Your mother, Sandrine, was abandoned by her wonderful but deeply flawed grandmother," René said, taking Cecily's hand. "She lost her husband to cancer. Her mother to domestic violence. Did she ever talk to anyone—even once—about that trauma? A counselor? A therapist? A coworker?"

"No, she stayed away from people," Cecily admitted. "Wouldn't go near them. It was pathological. She was terrified."

"Then I wonder if that is what Marguerite wanted you to learn by coming to France," René said.

"What?"

"You asked if she believed in the curse," he said. "For much of her life that answer was no. But as she grew sick, Auberon and I watched her turn into a different person. One driven to learn all she could about a curse she had dismissed decades earlier. She told us her death would summon the wraith and no one would be safe. Old as she was, she would disappear for days visiting archives. Chasing leads. Trying to explain an elusive curse that could no more be unraveled than smoke. There was nothing behind it. Nothing she could uncover in the last months of her life anymore than the countess could over a lifetime."

René stared out the windshield for a moment then shook his head. "I hate that my friend, my beloved friend, had to die alone and afraid in the woods," he said, voice barely above a whisper. "It wasn't the knife that killed her but her belief in this ludicrous curse that had finally entangled her at the end of her life. She should be here. She should be here to meet her great-granddaughter. Just as your mother should be here. And her mother before that."

Angry tears filled his eyes. Cecily put her arms around him. He returned the embrace.

"I miss my friend," he said, wiping his eyes.

The pair sat in the car for a long time, the only movement the grasses outside the window playing in the afternoon breeze.

It was midafternoon by the time they reached Marguerite's house in the Marais. Thérèse had called twice, updating René with Cecily's flight information. Takeoff was at midnight, but she admonished Cecily to be through security early as they closed the customs checkpoints at eleven.

"I will," Cecily had said, readier by the minute to be back in the South Carolina wetlands. Back where things made sense.

Given all that had happened, she couldn't imagine that René still wanted to go to Pauline's, the restaurant where Marguerite had made the reservation. When he told her he and Auberon would pick her up at six, she tried to beg off.

"We will drop you at the airport after," René said. "I cannot let you leave Paris with nothing but tragic memories. Let Marguerite's generosity be how you remember her."

"But I don't even have anything to wear," Cecily said.

"Go upstairs and look in the closet," René said, shooing Cecily out of his car. "Thérèse dropped off some dresses to try."

Cecily nodded and headed inside. She had little to pack but wanted to shower and nap before dinner. She tromped up to the third floor and was amazed to see that the dresses Thérèse left for her were all made from Marguerite's designs.

The photos she'd seen did them little justice. Her great-grand-mother's understanding not only of the geometry of plants but also of their gradients of color was incredible. One dress was red with thin golden vines striping it like almost invisible piping. Another was blue with flower petals in pinks and whites cascading down the front. A third was indigo with a pattern of leaves near the hem rising in a circle as if blown aloft by a passing car.

The last one was like the dress she'd seen Marguerite, Constance, and Sandrine wearing. All white with a dramatic palm leaf across the front. She could count on one hand the number of occasions she'd worn a dress, not one of them by choice. She looked forward to wearing this, though. She put it on. It fit perfectly.

She went to the rooftop garden and retrieved Marguerite's antique necklace from the sapling. She placed it around her throat and made a mental note to tell René that someone would have to take care of the oak. She undressed, showered, took a quick nap, then put the dress back on again and carried her pack downstairs, determined to push aside the day's events long enough to enjoy the evening.

She had just reached the kitchen when there was a knock on the front door. Cecily opened it to find René on the doorstep clad in a burgundy silk suit with three scarves and matching leather shoes that came to sharp points. Alongside him, Auberon wore a charcoal-colored suit made plaid with a checkerboard pattern in a dark red that almost matched René's outfit. His shoes were a deep blue. Both outfits were complemented by plant-themed lapel pins with sprigs of recent cuttings jutting up from them like jeweled boutonnieres.

"You two look wonderful," Cecily said.

"As do you," Auberon said, then stepped aside. "Your chariot, Mademoiselle."

The car at the curb behind him wasn't René's purple Prius but a bright-yellow Peugeot with the top down. It was as if someone challenged René to find a more garish vehicle than his own and he'd succeeded.

"What is that?" Cecily said.

"*Alors*, it is called a convertible," René explained, as if to a child. "They were invented in the 1920s but became fashionable years later. It allows someone to drive in the open air."

"We borrowed it from a friend," Auberon added. "We thought it might benefit someone whose preferences do not include confined spaces."

Cecily smiled. "Thank you," she said, then inspected their lapel pins. "Marguerite's work?" she asked.

"But of course," René replied, eyeing Cecily's dress. "How nice for her to leave us such pretty things to remember her by. Shall we?"

Auberon opened the back door for Cecily, and they all climbed into the Peugeot. René settled in behind the wheel, picked a playlist from his phone, and turned up the stereo as they roared away from the curb. Thundering electro-dance music blared from the car's speakers.

"Turn it down!" Auberon yelled.

René, of course, turned it up.

They sped through the Paris streets, music blasting as the City of Lights flew past. Cecily had never been in a convertible before and was surprised at what should've been obvious. There was so much more to see! Before, she'd seen Paris out the window of René's car at street level. Now, she could see it all. The scale and beauty of the city revealed itself anew even as the ever-present, late-summer rain clouds darkened the sky.

Curious about their destination, she typed Pauline's into her phone and searched for local restaurants. Nothing came back except a tiny lunch café half a dozen blocks away that was closed at night. The restaurants they did pass were packed with people in crowded shopping districts. She was relieved to fly by these.

When they turned onto a quiet residential neighborhood flanked by four-story row houses on either side of the street with no shops and very few streetlights, she wondered where on earth they might be taking her.

René pulled the car up to the curb and parked.

"Are we at Pauline's?" Cecily asked.

"*Oui?*" René said as if it was self-evident.

She followed the men down the dark sidewalk. There weren't even lights on in the neighboring houses.

"It is dead because these are mostly law offices, doctor's offices, a few accountants, a consulate or two, open by day alone," René explained. "These are the people who dash out of their office at six, maybe meet their mistress or paramour for a liaison at six thirty and are on the RER train home to their partners and children in the suburbs by eight. Leaving Paris to the Parisians."

They stopped in front of one of the anonymous houses. There were no numbers or signs. Cecily had no idea how they'd distinguished it from the others. René held open a tiny iron gate to let Cecily and Auberon in first, then jogged up the steps to the front door where he pressed an unmarked call button.

"*Allô?*" an elderly woman's voice asked from the speaker.

"*Bonsoir. C'est René, Auberon, et Cecily LeClercq,*" René said quietly.

There was no response. Cecily glanced at her escorts. Both grinned. Thirty seconds later, the door opened and a woman easily into her eighties or nineties appeared in the doorway. René and Auberon fell over themselves to greet her in rapid-fire French filled with flattering tones. The woman nodded idly then noticed Cecily.

She asked a question of René, who nodded as he put his hand around her shoulder. "*Oui*, Marguerite," he said. "*L'arrière petite fille.*"

The look of indifference left the old woman's face. She took Cecily's hand, kissed both her cheeks, then stared straight into her eyes, speaking softly in French. A pair of tears trailed down her cheeks. Cecily didn't need to understand the language to know she was saying how much Marguerite meant to her.

"Merci," Cecily whispered when she was finished.

René, teary-eyed himself, nodded to the elderly woman. "Cecily, this is Pauline and here is her restaurant."

The trio followed Pauline down a short hallway and into a small apartment. They passed through a cluttered living room before coming to a midsize dining room with three small tables set with dishes, glasses, and cutlery. Four people were packed tightly around one of the tables as a couple sat at the other. Pauline led Cecily and her friends to the last table, where they settled into mismatched chairs. Pauline then disappeared through a swinging door into the kitchen.

Cecily felt skittish around the other people but thought she could withstand it for a quick meal. It wasn't overwhelming. At least, not yet. What made it easier, she realized, was the company of René and Auberon.

An elderly man stepped through the swinging door holding a chalkboard as tall as he was. Written on it in French were the names of several dishes.

"Jacques, Pauline's husband, with the menu," Auberon confided.

The man read out the whole list, pointing at each as he explained their qualities in unadorned French. While his words might have been plain, the smells from the kitchen promised anything but.

"I hope you can remember all that," Cecily said when Jacques returned to the kitchen. "Maybe you can order for me?"

"*Alors*, you don't order at Pauline's," René said. "Those were tonight's courses."

"Which ones do we get?"

"All," René said. "Hope you're hungry."

Before Cecily could respond, a woman in her sixties ("Their daughter, Helen," Auberon whispered) exited the kitchen carrying a heavy wire wine caddy. She wordlessly visited each table and filled the glasses with liquid.

"The bottles don't have labels," Cecily observed.

"Pauline and Jacques get their wines from the best independent vintners in France," René explained. "The growers give them a discount. The labels are off so they can still charge the restaurants around the corner ten times as much."

Auberon raised his glass. "To Marguerite, a much-beloved friend," he said.

"*Un ami bien-aimé*," René agreed, clinking glasses with Cecily and Auberon.

What followed was the most opulent meal Cecily had ever experienced.

There were appetizers of melon and pâté followed by a

lobster soup carried in fresh from the stove by Pauline, who ladled it directly into bowls in front of each diner. No sooner had Cecily finished the soup then her bowl was taken away to be replaced with more wine and a course of ravioli.

"This is incredible," Cecily said.

"We have only begun," René replied.

Half a roast chicken arrived next prepared in a rich sauce surrounded by tomatoes and mushrooms. Pauline lowered the birds onto everyone's plates while Helen ladled the sauce. More wine appeared. Cecily began to run out of fresh silverware, making her believe the meal might be nearing its close. She was about to ask René when Pauline emerged from the kitchen to replace the plates and enough forks, knives, and spoons to eat a dozen more courses.

"This place is nuts," Cecily said.

"When you come to Pauline's," René said, lifting his wine-glass, "you get traditional French cooking made by people who care far more about flavor and an intimate setting than table turnover and social media."

"With a kitchen like this, you do not have to buy a bushel of two hundred radishes every day," Auberon added. "You buy the twelve best and use just them."

"Were they famous chefs at some other restaurant before?" Cecily asked.

"Not at all," René said. "Jacques was an army cook making meals for the very many. In retirement, he wishes to cook for the very few."

A beef dish was brought out, followed by one of quail. Then beans and butter. Then vegetables that tasted as if they'd been pulled from the ground earlier that day. When Cecily again thought the meal might be nearing its conclusion, entrée-size portions of pork, duck, and crepes showed up with even more wine.

"The crepes have to be dessert, *non*?" Cecily asked when she'd finished hers.

No sooner were the words out of her mouth when apple cake arrived paired with port.

"You were saying?" René asked, grinning.

By this point, Cecily felt faint. She managed to down the cake and wine but winced when the kitchen door swung open yet again. This time, Pauline, Jacques, and Helen arrived together with nothing in their hands. The guests all applauded. The cooks smiled and cleared the last plates. The diners at the two other tables slowly rose and left. When Cecily moved to follow, Auberon put his hand on her wrist.

"No more!" she said. "They won't be able to fit me on the airplane!"

Auberon smiled but said nothing. Pauline and Jacques came out of the kitchen with an old and almost empty bottle of wine and fresh glasses. Pauline spoke quickly to Cecily. René translated.

"This is a bottle of fine port from the year Marguerite was born," René said. "They kept one here for her to have a drink with them on her birthday every year. They drank from this bottle the last three years. Now, we finish it together."

Pauline filled glasses and everyone raised them in toast. "*À la tienne.*"

Moments later, Cecily and her friends were back on the street. A drunken René hung off Auberon as he thanked Pauline for a wonderful night.

"Merci beaucoup," Cecily added.

"*Puissiez-vous vivre une vie longue et saine*," Pauline replied, kissing her cheeks.

"She wishes you a long and healthy life," René translated as they wandered back to the car.

Auberon struggled to keep his husband upright, so Cecily got on the other side of René and the three of them made better progress. They were almost to the car when a distantly familiar sound reached Cecily's ears. It was a piece of music. A song. She couldn't quite place it, but she knew it by heart.

"What is it?" Auberon asked.

Cecily nodded to an open upper window of a nearby building. "That song. I know it."

It hit her. It was the French disco pop singer her mother used to love dancing to.

"You do not," René said, scoffing. "You cannot know this. His music never made it to America."

Ignoring him, Cecily sang along in phonetically learned French. Auberon laughed and joined in.

"You know this?" Cecily asked.

"*Oui*," Auberon said. "It's Cloclo!"

"No, it is too mundane!" René protested as Auberon whisked him across an imaginary dance floor. Finally, he sang along as well. "How do you know this?"

"My mother had his tapes," Cecily explained. "We danced to him in the kitchen."

René smiled. One song ended and another began. The three of them sang along to the next track, then the one after that. Cecily checked her phone. They'd been at Pauline's for over three hours. It was time to get to the airport.

"We have an audience!" Auberon exclaimed, pointing down the street. "*Veuillez chanter!*"

Cecily glanced at the newcomer to see if they were singing along. She couldn't see the person's face, but even in the dim light, she could make out the watcher's white dress, long black hair reaching all the way to the sidewalk, and fingers tapering down into spikes.

It was the wraith. She'd found her again.

Once you see her, your days are numbered. There is no escape.

9

Cecily spun René around. "We have to go."

"*Pourquoi?*"

"It's her," Cecily said, pointing down the sidewalk. "It's the wraith."

René seemed to sober up. "*Chérie*," he said. "Did we not speak about this?"

"You can see her this time, right?" Cecily asked.

René rolled his eyes and waved his arms. "Hey! Who goes there? Friend or foe?"

The wraith didn't move. René shrugged. "See? It is three against one. She does not stand a chance."

Pedestrians moved along the block near the wraith. One by one, as they drew alongside her, they slowed and turned to look at Cecily as well. It was exactly like the passengers on the jet as if in drawing near, they were swept into the wraith's thrall.

Cecily stepped away from René and Auberon. The wraith and her followers didn't seem to notice. They were still staring at Cecily's friends. She remembered the Christ thorns in the abbey's courtyard and a horrible thought came to mind.

"You have to get out of here," she told Auberon. "Get in the car and go."

"What are you talking about?" he asked. "We are taking you to the airport."

"Now!" Cecily barked. "Get somewhere safe!"

Before Auberon could answer, she took off running. Directly toward the wraith.

"Cecily!" René yelled.

She ignored him. The mob now fully inhabited by the wraith saw her coming. They crouched like predatory animals readying themselves to attack. Cecily had no idea what she was doing but picked the nearest one, saw that his eyes had gone black and red as he clenched his fists, and ran straight toward him. She bowled into him with such force that he went flying.

She glanced at the others and sneered. "What're you gonna do about it?"

They opened their mouths as one, howling out an angry, inhuman roar that sounded like the rush of a hurricane rumbling up from the bowels of the earth. Every nerve in Cecily's body flashed in terror at the otherworldly cacophony.

She ran.

She had no destination in mind. She was running for her life. She fled past empty row houses, blocks, parked cars, and abandoned intersections. Her pursuers were a few yards behind her. All of them had been perfectly normal moments before. They'd been on their way home. To a friend's house. To meet up with people.

Now they were possessed and directed by an unholy creature.

What was so disturbing about their pursuit was their silence. They moved on her like wolves. The only sound was the rush of wind pushing past them as they darted ahead. They didn't speak. Their footfalls barely echoed across the asphalt.

Cecily's lungs burned and her legs grew numb. She was in

good shape but not good enough. She wouldn't be able to go many more blocks in this residential maze before she'd collapse.

Music swelled up ahead.

Thank God.

It was bright at the end of the street. Cecily put on a last burst of speed and reached an intersection flanked by two busy restaurants. She ran toward the maître d' of the one closest.

"I need help!" she cried as he eyed her with alarm. "People are chasing me! Can you call the police?"

She glanced behind her. In the shadows across the street, the wraith stood watching her. Her eyes burned with tempestuous fury. A hatred. A desire for vengeance.

When Cecily looked back at the maître d', the young man and all the customers in his restaurant stared back at her. Their eyes slowly darkened, turning black in the dim light. She turned to run, but her path was blocked by her pursuers. They'd boxed her in.

Every street in Paris has borne witness to some bloody horror, René had said.

This one would soon bear witness to hers.

She glanced to the restaurant's outdoor seats. There were steak knives, an empty chair, even a heat lamp. All could be employed as weapons. But these were innocent people momentarily inhabited by the wraith. It wasn't in her to injure or maim them for actions they weren't responsible for.

She turned to the nearest of the possessed, a young woman in a server's uniform.

"Come on then!" she barked.

All the people on the block bared their teeth at her at once. A terrifying spectacle. They were going to tear her apart.

The sound of a revving engine drowned out the music still

playing from one of the restaurant's speakers. A bright-yellow convertible edged its way around Cecily's would-be killers and pulled to the curb.

"Get in!" Auberon shouted from behind the wheel.

Cecily threw herself in the back seat. Before she'd even closed the door, Auberon was off again. They flew down the main road as the restaurant patrons howled in anger.

"Are you all right?" he asked, panicked.

"It's the curse," Cecily said. "We have to get away from here."

"And go where?"

"Far away from people," Cecily said. "As far away as possible."

He nodded, unsure. Cecily looked to René for help. Besotted with wine, he stared blearily out the passenger side window as if nothing were happening.

Cecily tried to shake the image of all those eyes turning on her at once, but it was too horrifying. She thought about her mother. Had she ever seen something like that? Was that why she avoided people?

"Where are we going?" René asked. "Shouldn't we be on our way to the airport?"

Cecily glanced at the sidewalk. As they passed pedestrians and delivery drivers, maintenance workers and a police officer, all turned from their conversations or work to stare at the passing convertible, their eyes darkening into oily pools. A few gave chase, but the car quickly outdistanced them.

Cecily didn't think the wraith would give up so easily.

The airport would be crawling with hundreds if not thousands of people. The prospect was alarming. It was the last place they could go.

"Drive to Félice," she said. "Go to the woods."

"The woods?" Auberon asked.

"We'll be safe there."

Auberon took the next left and wove his way through the city. He opened a map on his phone. The highway up to Félice was a solid red line of traffic. Cecily, looking over his shoulder, shook her head.

"Is there another way?" she asked, frightened of getting stuck in a car surrounded by other people.

Auberon checked for alternate routes. One wound straight through the city, green the whole way. "This adds a few minutes, but there is no traffic," he said, pointing to a hill in the distance topped by the large white cathedral, Sacré-Cœur. "Through Montmartre."

They drove swiftly through the empty streets. René's head lolled right and left, then focused on what lay ahead. "Wait, where are we going?" he asked. "Not Montmartre. What self-respecting Parisian goes there at night?"

He angled his head back to look at Cecily. "Are you feeling better?"

"Sure," she lied.

"Good," René said, slumping down. "Maybe if we're lucky, we can stop in and see their choir of nuns. They're quite beautiful. Their singing, I mean. Not necessarily the nuns themselves."

Auberon sighed at his husband's latest offensive remark. Cecily stared out the window, waiting for any of the people they passed to turn their horrific visages their way. None did. She didn't breathe easier.

They neared the cathedral. Seemingly endless stairs descended away from a wide plaza in front of it. Cecily figured the view from there would be magnificent.

"It occurs to me, 'Montmartre' means Mountain of the Martyr," René said. "It is where they beheaded Saint Denis, the patron saint of Paris. He then picked up his severed head, preached about repentance, and wandered off to what is now the suburbs to die. There is that good restaurant near there."

Auberon rolled his eyes and patted his husband on the knee. "You are incorr—"

The wraith appeared in the street directly ahead of them. Cecily screamed. Auberon spun the wheel. The Peugeot clipped the bumper of a parked maintenance truck and went airborne. Cecily grabbed onto the seat in front of her as the car slammed onto its passenger side and slid several yards down the empty street. Sparks flew up as the asphalt tore at the car doors. The windshield shattered and fell away.

When it stopped moving, Cecily carefully extracted herself and checked on her friends. Auberon was unconscious, a nasty wound drizzling blood from his forehead. He groaned, confirming that he was alive at least. Cecily reached for her phone but couldn't find it.

She had to get help.

"René? Are you all right?" she asked, though he didn't look as if he'd received a scratch.

"Who can tell?" he said groggily.

"Stay with Auberon. I'll be right back."

"Where are you going?"

"To get help," she said, eyeing the darkness for any sign of the wraith.

She hurried down the sidewalk, looking for an open business or anyone with a cell phone. But as René had intimated, the neighborhood was deserted this late at night, with only a few lights on in distant apartments.

Frustrated, Cecily turned around until she was looking up at Sacré-Cœur itself. There were several lights on inside. She ascended the long stairs up to its front plaza, fearing the whole way the lights would turn out to be decorative and the building locked up. When she finally arrived and found the front doors open, she was relieved.

She passed through a narrow vestibule and a second set of doors before stepping into the cathedral's colossal nave with its high, vaulted ceilings, dozens of rows of polished oak pews, and racks of flickering candles against a side wall near a font of holy water.

"Is anyone here?" she cried, looking from the confessionals to the altar.

She imagined a priest emerging from the sacristy, eyes turning black, a murderous expression on his face. No one appeared.

She moved down through the pews. There had to be a phone in the rectory or somewhere nearby. But as she thought about calling the police or paramedics, she envisioned the first responders arriving at the crash site merely to feast on Auberon and René.

Even if they didn't attack, she imagined that they would somehow know this was all her fault. That this violence was inflicted on her friends simply because she lacked the courage to sacrifice herself to save them.

She shook this off. If René was right about the thorn marks on the statue pedestals, that they were made by kids, what else might he be right about with regard to the curse? The countess admitted that she'd spent an entire lifetime trying to understand it. Trying to figure out what had started it and how to stop it. In the end, she knew nothing with certainty.

She heard one of the outer doors creak open. The light flickered in the vestibule, visible from under the door. Someone was coming. She gauged the distance between herself and the altar, but it was too far. She had nowhere to hide.

The door swung open. It was René holding a cell phone.

"Found your phone. *Again*," he said, waving it. "An ambulance is on the way. Auberon is out of the car but woozy. You need to come back out. I think you may need to go to the hospital as well. We are worried about your condition."

"You can't be here, René," Cecily said. "She's not going to stop! I have to get away."

René eyed her harshly. "I do not know how I can put this more succinctly and precisely," he said. "There is no curse. There is no . . ."

He trailed off as if hunting for the right word.

"No what?" Cecily asked, taking a step toward him.

René's mouth was open, his eyes fixed on Cecily. The rest of his body started to contort in pain, hands flexing and unflexing. Neck twisting around. Legs shaking as he was lifted two feet off the ground.

It was the wraith. Her eyes burned into Cecily as they had in the woods and on the plane. She wore but a single emotion. Furious anger. She lifted René higher, as if offering him up to the angels sculpted into the ceiling above.

"No!" Cecily shouted, realizing what the wraith meant to do.

René stared helplessly at Cecily one last time, mouth moving like a landed fish. Then the wraith extended a finger across his neck and tore his throat out.

10

THE NEAREST HOSPITAL, Bretonneau, was ten minutes away. The ambulance arrived at Sacré-Cœur in less than five. It had been called by a priest who'd heard Cecily's screams and came running. Cecily tried to staunch the flow of blood cascading from René's neck with her own hands.

"Do something!" she yelled at the priest, her friend's blood staining the cathedral's marble floor a cardinal red.

The paramedics applied a field dressing to the wound as Cecily held René's hand. They warned her that he could go into cardiac arrest. René opened his eyes and tried to speak but couldn't.

His gaze found Cecily's but soon lost it again. He looked helpless, a small child who couldn't understand what was happening to him. By the time they reached the hospital and the paramedics pried Cecily's hand from his, there was no pulse.

She followed as they rushed him into the emergency room. A nurse blocked her from going further, nodding to the waiting area. "*Vous êtes de la famille?*" the nurse asked.

Cecily shook her head. She took out her phone but wasn't sure how to get in touch with anyone else. She didn't know where Auberon was. Didn't even know if René had any family members in the area. Where did Auberon say he was from? Lorraine? She couldn't remember his last name.

She filled her thoughts with these questions, forcing them to push away the repeating image of the wraith cutting René's throat. She couldn't escape it. It was there when she closed her eyes, when she looked around the waiting room, even out the doors to the parking lot. There was no way to flee the memory or the feelings of guilt, shame, and sorrow.

She had done this. She had caused it to happen. All René did was befriend her and try to help her through the past couple of days. And now this.

"Cecily?"

Thérèse, virtually unrecognizable to Cecily with no jewelry on at all, stood in front of her looking confused. Cecily embraced the startled woman.

"Where is Auberon?" Thérèse asked, worriedly. "Is he all right? The *docteur* said she tried to reach René, but there was no answer."

Cecily couldn't find the words. She stared at Thérèse, eyes growing glassy with tears. She felt so helpless. Thérèse finally seemed to notice the bloodstains on Cecily's dress.

"No," Thérèse whispered. "No."

She sank into a chair. A woman hurried over from the triage desk and put her arms around Thérèse. It took Cecily a moment to realize she'd come in with her. Cecily put her hand on top of Thérèse's for a moment, felt the room swirling around her, and stepped away.

She emerged out into the gray Paris early-morning twilight. There was a taxi stand nearby, but the idea of being confined inside a car with a stranger terrified her right now. She checked her map and began walking home.

At some point in the night, it had rained. She'd abandoned the heels she'd taken from Marguerite's closet. The water was cool under her bare feet. It rose to her ankles when she stepped off the curb to cross the road to avoid people or to speed up as she passed a busy café.

She wanted to be around no one. She didn't trust anyone but also feared what she might inflict on others. If she could only get back to Charleston, but then she thought about Ina and Hideo. Aunt Olivia and her grandmother. How much violence would she unleash on them if she returned? No one would be safe.

She had nowhere to go. Better to stay in Paris where she was a stranger.

When she got to Marguerite's house, she took off the ruined dress, collapsed onto the bed, and waited for the tears to come. None did.

Cecily awoke a couple of hours later. She checked her phone, hoping for word on René, but found nothing but a voice mail from the assistant medical examiner up in Val d'Oise, Gens, saying they had to delay the release of Marguerite's body.

"It is the police," he said apologetically. "Everything takes more time out here, but they claim there is a jurisdictional issue. Call me back at your convenience."

Cecily tossed the phone aside and headed downstairs. She wasn't hungry but tore a few chunks of bread from a loaf and popped them into her mouth. She was looking for coffee when a woman's face appeared through the frosted glass of the window in the front door.

Cecily screamed. The woman, who wore the yellow uniform of a delivery service, jumped backward.

"*Pardon. Êtes-vous Marguerite LeClercq?*" she said through the glass. She held up a thick envelope.

"I am . . . *je suis* Marguerite's *arrière petite fille,* Cecily?" Cecily said in broken French. "I can sign for it."

But the messenger pulled the envelope back. "*Personnel et confidential,*" she said. "Must have signature from Marguerite LeClercq."

"She . . . Marguerite passed away. *C'est mort.*"

The messenger shook her head. "*Désolé.* It will return to sender."

Cecily sighed and nodded, figuring it couldn't be too important. She was about to close the door when the messenger checked her scanner.

"*Un moment,*" the messenger said, scrolling through a note. "Cécile LeClercq?"

She held out the scanner. On a tiny screen, Cecily saw the French spelling of her name.

"*Oui.*"

"*Désolé,*" the messenger said again, handing a stylus to Cecily. "Your name was added."

"What? When? I mean, *quand?*"

The messenger showed her the screen. It had been changed two days earlier in the late evening. Hours before Marguerite's death.

"Who changed it?" Cecily asked urgently.

"Only Marguerite LeClercq," the messenger said.

She tore open the packet and found three smaller envelopes inside. Each had the logo of a genetic testing service where the return address would go. One was labeled *Marguerite LeClercq.* The next was labeled *Dominique Dutoit.* The last *Gaby Dutoit.* She didn't recognize either.

She opened Marguerite's envelope and found the results of a DNA test. She translated it with her phone app and found it simple and straightforward. Marguerite's ancestry was French and *only* French going back several centuries. In an accompanying letter, it stated that her relationship to Dominique and Gaby Dutoit was negligible, less than a 2 percent match.

Having never heard of these people, Cecily wasn't that surprised. What she didn't know was why Marguerite would want to find out if she was related to them.

Dominique Dutoit. Gaby Dutoit.

D. D. and G. D.

She hurried upstairs to retrieve the book on the LeClercq family. She unfolded the family tree in back. Sure enough, the initials Marguerite had penciled in, which Cecily had thought might be relations of Aline, were D. D. and G. D.

She looked up the names in her phone. There was no address for a Dominique Dutoit but one for Gaby in a small town called Chambly. It was fifteen kilometers west of Félice on the other side of the Oise River from the LeClercq Forest.

She opened Dominique and Gaby's tests. They confirmed that they were not related to Marguerite. But there was a fourth sample mentioned with these results. To this individual, listed by number with no name attached, the percentage jumped up to an over 95 percent match.

Cecily was stunned. She thought about what René had said about Marguerite's investigations during the last few months of her life. These had to be related. It was the addition of her name to the delivery service's website??? That seemed to confirm to her that Marguerite had left breadcrumbs behind for her to piece together. The necklace on the lost sapling. Now the genetic testing results.

So, who was this unidentified individual?

And just like that, a theory began to form in Cecily's mind.

She made a quick phone call, showered, and dressed, threw the envelopes in her backpack, and hurried out the door. It was the middle of the day, but the Metro station her phone had directed her to was packed. She went to the end of the platform, forced herself not to look at her fellow passengers, and was rewarded with an empty train car.

She took it up to Gare du Nord, the train station in the north of Paris with routes out to the suburbs. She hurried to the lower platform where the RER trains were, keeping close to the walls and avoiding all the people.

Unfortunately, the RER train passengers were evenly divided throughout the double-decker cars. Most, however, stayed on the bottom levels. She hurried down the platform until she found a car with an empty upper level and slipped inside as the door slid shut.

She settled onto a molded plastic chair, keeping an eye on the stairs as the train raced north from Paris. She felt like she was daring the wraith to attack. She wanted to feel strong. All she felt was scared.

She needed to conserve her phone's battery life, but it was impossible not to check if anyone had texted her about René or Auberon. Nothing. She texted Thérèse but got no answer. She called the hospital and asked, in broken French, if there was any update on Monsieur Chaumière. The response included a lot of negative words she assumed related to medical information not being given out over the phone. Before they hung up, the nurse mentioned a surgery. Cecily exhaled. At the very least—the *very* least—this meant René still clung to life. For how much longer, she didn't know.

An hour later, the RER train pulled up to the platform at Félice, the second to last stop before the line's terminus. Cecily was the sole passenger to disembark. Waiting on the platform was Bashir alongside a pair of bicycles.

"Hey there," he said, eyeing her with concern. "Are you all right?"

"I'll let you know in a sec," she said, looking around the platform.

They appeared to be alone, but she didn't even know if the wraith had to be present to have someone in her thrall. In truth, it felt like she knew less about the curse today than she had yesterday.

"What are you doing?" he asked.

She'd told him a little about what happened the night before on the phone. Now she told him the rest. His face darkened as his concern grew, the reality of the horror cutting deep.

"I am so sorry for your friends," Bash said. "Also, for you."

"I appreciate your delivery of the bicycle," Cecily said. "I can't ask you to accompany me given the danger I bring."

Bash rolled his eyes. "You think I would let you take this journey alone? You are trying to solve this curse, yes?"

"I don't see any other way to stop it," Cecily said.

"Aside from the sacrifice of your own life, you mean," Bash said.

"No," Cecily countered. "I can't believe that part. So many people have tried to end it that way, yet it goes right on killing people. I don't want to absolve myself. I want to stop it."

"Then I will help you," Bash said. "I do not want this to go on a minute longer either. Anything I can do to stop it, I will do."

"You're sure?"

"I am."

"Then thank you."

Bash nodded and rolled the bicycle to Cecily. She climbed on and followed Bash as he cycled back through Félice. She felt dizzy as they swung past the millennia-old church, the aged residences, and all the shops. There were people around. Too many people. It had the opposite effect of her dash through Gare du Nord. She kept it together there in a large, enclosed building surrounded by a hundred times as many folks. But there was something about the people on the sidewalks that filled her with fear.

Maybe it was how it mirrored the incident of the night before.

She wanted to close her eyes but was afraid she'd crash. Instead, she focused on the back tire of Bash's bicycle. She let the steady repetition half hypnotize her, almost ramming him once as they passed the grocery store along the highway on the opposite side of town.

As soon as they crossed over and were under the tree canopy, Cecily relaxed. Despite what had happened to her there, a feeling of safety returned. She belonged here. Not Paris.

Rather than stay on the road, Bash led her onto a narrow trail she hadn't noticed earlier. In seconds, they were deep within the forest. Cecily saw a lightness in Bash as well. He might not have needed the woods like she did, but he was more comfortable there, too.

"Did you grow up near trees?" she asked.

"Not at all," Bash replied over his shoulder. "I was in a packed apartment in Bobigny with all my siblings *and* my grandparents. Getting out of there even to explore a nearby park was a treat. Oh, look. A friend."

He pointed through the trees. Cecily's heart leaped, fearing who it might be. It was a wild boar. It eyed them curiously, then dropped its head to the ground again, sniffing for food.

As they kept going, Cecily imagined they must be in a particularly distant part of the forest. She'd seen a few telephone poles and wires as she and René left the LeClercq estate the day before. Out here, though, there were no signs of civilization.

Then she spotted a fence post. The woods broke apart to reveal a large horse paddock. A single chestnut mare glanced up at the two cyclists as they passed. The path through the forest widened. The tops of houses appeared off to their right.

"Wait," Cecily said as they neared a small neighborhood of gray houses, some still under construction. "I thought we were in the deep woods, LeClercq land as far as the eye could see?"

"We were," Bash said. "Took a detour back into civilization as the trees get thicker close to the Oise and it's harder to push through."

They turned off the trail and onto the small street, passing the uniformly ordinary two- and three-bedroom houses. Their only unique feature was a narrow, shallow canal that ran in front of them interrupted by the occasional sidewalk leading to a front door. A pair of large swans paddled along in it as if it was a river.

"I'm so used to seeing centuries-old buildings," Cecily observed. "These look like they were built last week."

"There is a lot of new demand," Bash said. "They added an express train line up to Gouvieux and Chantilly. The cars used to be empty. Now there are thousands of commuters going into Paris from these neighborhoods every day."

These are the people who dash out of their office at six, maybe meet their mistress or paramour for a liaison at six thirty and are on the RER train home to their partners and children in the suburbs by eight.

Cecily saddened at the memory of René's tossed-off observation. Last night had been such great fun, a much-needed respite after the past couple of days. She'd never enjoyed the company of others like that before.

They cycled through a roundabout, passed through a neighborhood of larger family homes with long driveways and broad front yards. Children played basketball and rode bicycles. If it weren't for all the European-made cars in the driveways and, well, a clay surface tennis court alongside one of the homes, Cecily could imagine they were in an American suburb.

"What was the address again?" Bash asked.

Cecily checked her phone and told him. He took a right turn up ahead. They crossed the river and entered a slightly more mature neighborhood. There were more trees here, a number of orderly young birches, and shops housed in older stucco buildings all in faded shades of pink, orange, and yellow.

They finally reached a small stone cottage with a slanted tile roof and green shutters over the windows. A white mulberry tree, maybe the first Cecily had seen in France, stood in the front yard. The pair left their bicycles at the curb and approached the front door. Bash knocked.

"*Puis-je vous aider?*" a middle-aged woman asked when she opened the door to eye the pair with uncertainty.

Bash stepped forward. "Dominique Dutoit?"

"*Non,*" the woman said, followed by a string of words in French.

"She says that Dominique is her mother, but she's asleep right now," Bash translated for Cecily.

"Gaby Dutoit?" Cecily asked.

"*Oui?*" the woman replied, looking more perplexed by the moment.

"Can you ask her if she knew Marguerite LeClercq?" Cecily said.

Bash was about to translate when Gaby shook her head. "Marguerite LeClercq? How many more of her visits can we expect? The last upset my mother very much."

Cecily looked past Gaby to the interior of the house. A television was on. A small child peered around the corner from the living room. The foyer wall was a mosaic of family photographs. Cecily peered at them, curious.

"I am sorry Marguerite upset your mother," Cecily said, inching closer. "She was my great-grandmother. She wasn't well. But I received the results of the DNA tests. I thought you would like to know that you and your mother are not related to Marguerite."

She took the envelopes out of her backpack. Gaby eyed them as if she might strike them from her hand.

"That is what we told her!" Gaby exclaimed. "We agreed to the tests, but they were unnecessary. Please. Leave us in peace."

Cecily took one step closer and spied an old photograph of a man in a military uniform alongside his young bride. "Can I see that?" she asked.

Gaby glanced back, seemed to consider denying her request, then carefully took the picture down and handed it to Cecily. She and Bash stared at it for a long moment before Cecily handed it back. "Merci," she said, eyeing the bride's pale eyes and familiar, restive expression. "We will not bother you again."

Gaby nodded primly, headed back inside, and shut the door behind her.

"That picture," Bash said as they retrieved their bicycles. "Was it . . . the countess? It resembled her."

"No, but I think it was her birth mother," Cecily said, airing the theory she'd begun forming in Marguerite's apartment.

"Who do you mean? Sandrine LeClercq?"

"No, Georges and Colette Manzanarès," Cecily said. "When Georges was killed early in World War Two, Colette, who had no family of her own, was left destitute and gave up her daughter to Sandrine to raise."

"The half sister," Bash said, remembering. "But that is your great-grandmother, Marguerite, no?"

Cecily waved the DNA tests before shoving them into her backpack. "Maybe not," she said. "I need to speak to the countess. I think I know why the curse has followed Marguerite's side of the family."

If she was right, it might mean that the countess had lived her entire life in fear for no reason. It was a horrible realization.

The pair got on their bikes, headed away from the Dutoit house, and crossed back over the Oise as the LeClercq Forest stretched out ahead of them. It was a deep green wall of trees that stood like a living refutation to the construction on the opposite bank.

"We can take the road north around the top of the forest and come down the highway on the other side," Bash explained. "It will be much faster than cutting through the woods."

Cecily nodded. As they followed the Oise, towns and new construction continued to appear on the western banks of the river while the silent forest ran along to the east. After several more miles, the Oise widened. A tributary split off in front of them. Bash slowed and pointed back to the woods.

"We are at the northern limit of the forest," he explained.

"This tributary, la Thève, runs all the way to the highway, boxing it in."

Cecily checked her phone's map, her position showing up as a blue dot. The forest really was tremendous, but she saw what Bash meant. The Oise and Thève to the west and north, the highway to the east, and the dirt farm road to the south served as borders. It was easy to understand, even in a time before the roads were in place, how a king could carve it out to hand over to a count.

"When the countess bequeathed this to the arts foundation, it was with the understanding that none of the forest could be sold or developed," Bash said, heading along the Thève. "It must be kept together as a single parcel in perpetuity."

"That's good to hear," Cecily said. "There aren't a lot of old-growth forests like this anymore."

"True, but it made the legal side of it very difficult," Bash admitted. "The first map of France was not even made until the early sixteenth century. There were no land deeds. No real records. They had to dig through medieval archives to even prove the LeClercqs were the owners of the land in the first place so that the countess could give it away. Even then, Eglantine says they must estimate."

Cecily stared into the LeClercq Forest. Her thoughts returned to the evergreen oak sapling on Marguerite's rooftop garden. If the genetic test results led her to the Dutoits, what would the sapling lead her to? She had to find where it belonged. She had to return to the woods, to look for other evergreen oak tr—

"Cecily," Bash whispered, nodding to the forest.

"What is it?" she asked.

"I saw something," he said. "Movement."

Cecily went rigid. Light flickered among the shadows. A silhouette of a dark figure slipped from one tree to the next.

The wraith.

Cecily looked back to Bash, terrified by what she might see. Rather than the black-eyed stare of one of those possessed by the wraith, his face was filled with fear.

"Go!" Cecily yelled.

She started pedaling as the shadowy movement in the woods grew closer. She hadn't gone more than a few yards when two people in black tore out of the woods, faces obscured by dark masks, and launched themselves at Cecily. Though she was in motion, they lifted her from the bike saddle and slammed her to the ground on the side of the road.

She managed to look back at Bash as three more people, all in black, ran from the woods and took hold of Bash. He was thrown to the road and swarmed.

"Bash!" Cecily cried, her arms and legs pinned to the ground.

Her wrists were drawn back, but rather than yanked from their sockets, plastic bands were slipped over them and pulled tight as one of her attacker's knees drove into the space between her shoulder blades.

She finally managed to see what was printed across the back of one of the people who'd grabbed Bash.

Police.

11

CECILY WAS UNDER arrest. She didn't understand what the police were saying to her, but that much came through. Part of her realized that the movement in the woods wasn't the wraith. Another part feared arrest that much more.

Her mind went to the events of the night before. Was this about René? Had they figured out that his wounds weren't from the car accident at all as she'd stammered to one of the paramedics? Did they suspect her of being capable of such violence? Or did they merely know she lied about having seen nothing?

She was terrified of getting caught up in the legal system, not least of all because it would make things quite easy for the wraith when she did come for her. She might even be handcuffed. Served up to the other prisoners or guards all inhabited by the monster. She'd be at their mercy.

As they bundled her into the back of a police van, she glimpsed the faces of two of the officers, their masks now removed. They were the detectives who'd been present when she identified Marguerite's body. Now they were questioning Bash.

Bash met her gaze, then turned away.

Cecily's heart sank. What the hell was she going to do?

It was a long drive to the police station. Though the sun was shining outside, the back of the van was freezing cold.

With her hands bound behind her, Cecily couldn't even try to warm up. By the time they reached the precinct, she was shivering. The officers who led her in didn't seem to notice or care.

She expected someone at the station to speak to her in English. No one spoke to her at all. She wasn't fingerprinted or photographed or charged. Instead, she was led to a small, unbarred room, sat down in a chair, and had the ties cut off her wrists. She waited for an explanation, but her escorts quickly exited, leaving her alone.

She sank into the chair. There was a clock on the wall. It was now noon. She wondered if the police had picked up her phone and backpack. She wondered if it mattered. The clock went all the way from noon to one. No one opened the door. Cecily grew hungry.

If this was about René, she wondered if something had changed. If he'd gotten worse. If he'd died. She tortured herself with these possibilities until she finally put her head on the table in front of her. She was asleep in seconds.

"My God, Cecily!"

Her eyes flew open. The clock said it was two thirty. A uniformed police officer held open the door for a panicked-looking Eglantine. The young lawyer hurried in and threw her arms around Cecily's neck.

"We are getting you out of here right now," she said, seemingly as much to the officer as to the young American. "Come on."

"Where's Bashir?" Cecily asked as they exited the interrogation room. "Is he OK?"

"*Pourquoi?*" Eglantine asked. "You have spoken to no one?"

Cecily shook her head. Eglantine led her to the front desk where they retrieved her backpack, phone, and even her bicycle, which they wheeled out to Eglantine's car. Cecily kept looking to the lawyer for an explanation. Eglantine said nothing until they were in her car.

"Bashir is OK. He is not physically hurt," Eglantine said. "But he has been arrested."

"For what?" Cecily asked, alarmed. "He was with me all morning."

"It is for the murder of Marguerite LeClercq," Eglantine said quietly.

Cecily had to resist the urge to laugh. "What?" she asked. "That's absurd! Bash?"

"*Oui*," Eglantine confirmed gravely. "The police have suspected for a couple of days that this was not suicide, or so they say. They came to search the estate today. They think the blade used to kill her was one used in the garden."

"No, no, no," Cecily said. "That's not right. That's not what happened."

"They also found Marguerite's blood on his work boots in the shed," Eglantine said. "They suspected him because they found tire tracks in the mud from his truck."

This was too much for Cecily. Had Bash been possessed by the wraith the night of the killing? Could he be guilty of what they were accusing him even if he might not have been cognizant of the act? It was too horrible to consider. What judge or jury would believe a ghost made him kill someone?

"Also, it seems, he has confessed," Eglantine added with finality.

Confessed?

"To murder?" Cecily asked, incredulous.

"No, he confessed to being present during her killing," Eglantine said. "He described details only a witness would know. The police say this is common in cases like this. A murderer's guilt makes them disassociate. To claim to be a bystander and incriminate themselves with details as their subconscious wishes to take credit or blame. They believe he will soon tell all."

Cecily shook her head. This was madness.

"Where is he?" she asked. "Can I speak to him? I have to speak to him."

"I doubt that is possible," Eglantine said. "He is being questioned and then will more than likely be charged. The countess asked me to arrange for him a lawyer. The medical examiner called as soon as he heard."

Cecily wondered if the countess thought Bashir had been in the thrall of the wraith, too.

"May I see the countess?" Cecily asked.

"Unfortunately, when she heard the news about first Bashir and, sadly, Monsieur Chaumière, she had a nervous attack," Eglantine reported. "The nurse is with her again and is hoping she will sleep. I can call you when she is ready to receive visitors."

"Thank you," Cecily said.

"I am driving into Paris now," Eglantine said. "All this anguish is worrying on the countess and she wishes me to accelerate the final bequeathment of her estate. If you would like a ride to the Marais, I would be more than happy to take you."

"Can you drop me in Félice instead?" Cecily asked. "I'd like to stick around here in case I can see Bash. I have to know what he saw."

Eglantine nodded. They soon reached Félice.

"Are you certain you do not need a ride?" Eglantine asked as Cecily pulled the bicycle from the back.

Cecily assured her she was fine. As soon as Eglantine's car was out of sight, Cecily climbed on her bike and headed out of the village.

It was midafternoon but the dark clouds that had gathered overhead made it look later. Cecily's phone said sunset was a few hours away. Still. she hurried. She felt the first raindrops as she crossed the highway and neared the LeClercq Forest. She was under the tree canopy a few minutes later, which kept her dry.

She thought it'd be hard to backtrack to where she and René had come upon the giant evergreen oak the day before. She hadn't thought to pin it on her map as she'd done with various backwoods discoveries she'd made in the past, but she needn't have worried. The route René took came back to her as soon as she was in the forest. A lifetime spent hiking through the woods and memorizing the way they were laid out was paying off.

The rain was coming down hard now, some of it hitting Cecily, though she didn't mind. It was the darkness that made things difficult. She climbed off her bike and walked it through the trees until the undergrowth became impassable. Her shoes sank several inches into the mud as she trekked forward, threatening to pull her under.

But then she saw it.

The dark clearing appeared like a patch of night hidden in the woods during daytime. It drew her close like a black hole despite the terror she'd felt the last time she'd been here. She knew it was physically dangerous. The roots could give way and the multiton trunk would collapse into the sinkhole below, dragging everything around down with it. But she was willing to take this risk.

She had to know why Marguerite had come here. Had to know whether Bash had been here, too.

The tree seemed even larger than before. No water penetrated its upper branches, but some sluiced under it through the gaps Cecily had made in the ground cover toppling through the web of lateral roots. She chose the thickest of these roots, tested it with her foot, and slowly made her way to the trunk. Dirt and wet leaves shook loose, drifting down into the sinkhole below. The root bounced up and down like a wire, threatening to send her over the side as well, but she kept her balance.

By the time she reached the trunk, it was so dark that Cecily almost ran directly into it. She turned on her phone's flashlight, and momentarily feared she'd come face-to-face with the wraith. The light illuminated nothing but tree bark. There was no sign of the monster she'd last seen tearing out René's throat.

Except.

Except for the thin claw marks along the trunk made by the monster's fingers.

So, it hadn't been Cecily's imagination. René must not have seen her. She ran her fingers over the claw marks to be certain. They were deep and narrow, as if made by razor-sharp scalpels. She didn't want to think about what they could do to her own flesh.

She remembered something. She grabbed onto the large tree trunk and carefully stepped around to the side where she'd climbed out. She shined the light down into the pit, illuminating only mud and grass.

She thought she had felt brick under her fingers. Could she have been wrong?

She leaned over the gap between the roots and scraped at

the mud with her heel. It slowly wore away, revealing more earth. Frustrated, she pocketed her phone, grabbed onto the root, and lowered herself back into the hole. The ground was slick from rainwater. One wrong step and she'd drop like a stone.

She edged her toe down through the muck until it hit something solid. Blindly, she worked the mud away from it until she could make out that it wasn't a rock but something flat and smooth. Leaning onto the oak's stiff roots for support, she lowered herself a few more feet until she was directly in front of the flat stone. She turned her flashlight on again to get a better look.

Brick, she realized, was a misnomer. Bricks were made of dried clay. These were fieldstones stacked together and bound with masonry.

Was this the Castle LeClercq?

Her pulse raced. She descended a few more feet and exposed more of the stones. The wall wasn't flat but curved. It wasn't a castle, she realized, but more likely an old well.

Something skittered across her fingers. She shrieked and almost tumbled off the wall only to realize it was rainwater trickling down from above. She reached for one of the roots to steady herself. She wanted to see how far the well went down before climbing back up, but the water made it slippery.

When she took her next step, there was nothing there. She felt around with her toe, but the wall seemed to be in motion. It was sliding downward, the stones separating from the earth on the other side.

"Gah!" Cecily screamed as the wall gave way entirely.

Her hands slid from the roots and she was airborne, weightless. Her breath rushed from her lungs as she fell through the darkness. She'd never felt so vulnerable. She was terrified of the pain to come—if she somehow survived the fall.

She landed in water. No, not water. Something soft like liquid earth. A gentle, mushy rise of subterranean loam. Its consistency was somewhere between oatmeal and quicksand. She clawed her way out to a more stable surface, relieved to be uninjured but facing a new fear.

How would she get out of here?

The air smelled of damp earth and decay. She turned on her phone's light, but the cavernous space swallowed all but the faintest glow. She was in a cave, likely a onetime aquifer from which the well pulled water. She angled her phone around as hundreds of tiny, bioluminescent mushrooms on the wall and cave floor glowed a dull blue.

It was also very cold. Her clothes were soaked. Her breath hung in the air as she exhaled. If she were trapped down here, hypothermia would kill her long before starvation. She scanned the walls for anything that suggested a way out. A tunnel. Roots or branches she might use to climb back up into the well.

What she saw instead was a face. It stared at her through the gloom, its slate-colored skin drawn taut over its skull. Cecily stumbled back but had nowhere to go. Had the wraith waited until she'd descended into her own lair to kill? There'd be no escape this time.

But the face didn't move. If it noticed Cecily, it made no response. It appeared still like a statue. Cecily peered at it through the darkness. It wasn't the wraith. It didn't look like her at all. There was no long hair or eyes of black. Just the skin was the same.

Given the beatific expression on its face, she wondered if she really was looking at some buried statue or idol. She illuminated it with her camera light and gingerly touched it with the tips of her fingers. The skin gave way, cracking apart like centuries-old parchment.

It wasn't a statue, but partially decayed human remains. She cautiously chipped aside the caked earth, keeping the rest of the body lodged in the cave wall. The skin below the neck wasn't smooth like that on the skin on the face, but partially melted like scar tissue on a burn victim.

The person's expression wasn't beatific but hardened and resigned. It was as if whoever it was had been in tremendous pain when they died. The victim of some brutal murderer. More earth crumbled away, revealing the ridge of the corpse's spine and an exposed ribcage. It tilted forward and muddy water trickled from its eye slits, giving it the appearance of crying black tears.

"Jesus Christ," Cecily whispered.

The body pitched forward. Cecily hopped backward, but her foot was stuck in the mushy loam and she fell. The water level had risen as more rain had come down to fill the cave. The ground was looser. In pushing herself up, Cecily's hands played across several scattered objects just beneath the surface.

She shook the silt and loam aside and found herself sitting on a pile of bones. Lots of them. Skulls. Femurs. Ribs. Fingers. Vertebrae. Teeth. Several of which looked as if they'd been bashed apart or splintered by a sharp or blunt object.

She had encountered plenty of animal cadavers in the woods without getting squeamish. There was something vastly different about human remains, particularly ones that had been hidden away. This was no grave. These people had died in tremendous pain.

At first, Cecily wondered if these were victims of the

wraith, thrown down here as Marguerite or René might have been in a different time. But there was something about the body that had remained intact. The similarity of its skin to that of the wraith made her think it must be something else. Something tied to the curse itself.

Who are you? she thought, staring into the eyeless face as black rainwater bled through its eye slits. *Who did this to you?*

You did, a voice in Cecily's head whispered.

And somehow, she knew it was true. This wasn't the work of something supernatural. This was what the wraith meant to avenge. The deeds of the LeClercq family.

Cecily's family.

12

IT TOOK TWO hours for Cecily to get out of the well. She could only escape through the hole she'd come down and it was twelve feet off the cave floor. She'd scoured the area for stones or roots to boost herself up, but there was nothing high enough. She'd scraped out enough chunks of the wall, looking for something buried in it, that she almost started a cave-in.

As she was doing this, more and more rainwater poured in, the trickle becoming a torrent. Soon, the cave began to flood. She added drowning to her list of possible deaths, then realized this might be her way out.

She turned off her phone, positioned herself under the well, and waited for the fast-rising water level to lift her off the ground. Some water still drained away farther underground, but enough stayed to carry her skyward like a frigid, liquid elevator. It took a long time, but she was finally lifted up into the well itself, where she began to climb.

This was far easier said than done. The walls were slippery and kept collapsing. The roots this far down were thin and wouldn't take her weight. Still, she managed by pushing aside the fieldstone and jamming her feet directly into the wet earth behind it. She gained enough purchase to push herself up a few more yards until the roots grew thicker. She used them to scamper up the rest of the way.

When she reached the surface, the ground was all mud. She tried to claw her way out but kept sliding back down as if she was scaling ice, not earth. At the last second, she managed to grab onto the base of the trunk and hold tight. She edged her feet up to the roots until she hung under it like a gibbon and climbed the rest of the way out.

It would soon be night. She was freezing cold in the deep woods. Her cell phone had no bars of service. She looked for the wraith, fearing she'd escaped one death only to walk into a trap. At least the rain had stopped. She tromped through the woods, retrieved her bicycle, and made her way to the farm road.

The moment she had service, she scrolled through her recent incoming calls and dialed the first number.

"It's Cecily LeClercq," she said as calmly as possible when the line was answered. "I need your help."

Twenty minutes later, Assistant Medical Examiner Gens, along with three members of the National Police, were following her back through the trees. The officers eyed Cecily's appearance with both disdain and suspicion, one making a cutting remark in French to Gens.

"What'd he say?" Cecily asked.

"He thinks you are dragging us out here to divert suspicion from Bashir Maleh," Gens admitted. "I hope it is not that."

"You'll wish it was," Cecily assured him.

When they reached the tree, the officer who Gens recruited based solely on the fact that she was a member of a local climbing club, set her anchors, stepped into her harness, and attached her belay. She popped her helmet onto her head, flipped on its lamp, and then offered Gens, Cecily, and the others a jaunty salute before heading down.

When she returned five minutes later, her joviality had drained away. She was all business but very pale. She reeled off directions to the others, her voice shaking. Her gaze flitted over to Cecily but then hastily went elsewhere.

Gens spoke quickly to a couple of the other officers, then came to Cecily. "Um, I think you cannot be here, but they will want you close," he said. "Is there somewhere nearby you can go?"

"Yes," Cecily replied. "But what did she say? Who are those people down there?"

Gens shook his head. "She doesn't know. Judging by the condition of what she saw, we may not know for some time."

Cecily cycled over to the LeClercq estate, hoping to slip through the front gates but instead found them locked tight. She leaned her bicycle against the wall and searched for a horse chestnut tree tall enough for her to use to climb over. She had several to choose from.

Once she made it onto the grounds, she hurried to the house and knocked on the front door. It, too, was locked.

"Countess?" she called.

When no one answered, she headed around to the side. A door she thought led into the kitchen was locked as well. She was about to go around back when she saw a tiny light glowing in the abbey.

As imposing as it had been in the daylight, the abbey appeared downright ominous at night. Cecily couldn't believe she'd scaled the outside of the building on something as flimsy as Bash's ladder. That was what confounded her. If he'd been there when Marguerite was killed, why hadn't he said something? Was he afraid of getting caught? Afraid Cecily would suspect him of being involved? She knew he wasn't a murderer.

Maybe that explained why he was so adamant about helping her unravel the mystery around the curse, though.

She slipped into the abbey's foyer. Even in the semidarkness, the building was impressive, with vaulted ceilings rising some fifty feet in the air, giving the antechamber a cathedral-like feel. A staircase of wide, heavy oak beams went up to the second floor, each step so large that it looked cut from its own tree. The wall to her right was covered with intricately carved wood paneling two stories in height. She couldn't make out the design. Maybe a pastoral scene from the Bible. Perhaps a representation of the Garden of Eden.

"Countess?" Cecily asked the silence.

When there was still no answer, she ventured down a corridor to her left. She passed an ancient kitchen, the one that must've benefited from the waterwheel and man-made canal Bash had shown her. Opposite the kitchen was a large dining hall, the stained-glass windows of which she'd seen from outside. It wasn't hard to imagine long monastery tables running the length of the hall with enough room to feed hundreds, all warmed by the largest fireplace she'd ever seen.

Taking up half the wall on one end of the room, it was so tall and wide, Cecily could have parked her camper truck in it with room to spare.

She spied something in the foyer she hadn't noticed before. There was a door cut into the paneling. A light breeze blew through its narrow frame. She pushed it gently and it opened.

On the other side was the abbey's chapel. Like the foyer, it was stone with high flying buttresses and a vaulted ceiling.

At the rear was an altar. Closer to Cecily were several rows of rotting oak pews. Dominating the space was a great evergreen oak tree bursting up through the marble floors to almost scrape the ceiling.

Cecily could hardly believe her eyes. Though not as tall as the one in the woods, its trunk was almost as wide around. Its upper branches coiled around the ceiling and, in a couple of spots, had broken through. Illuminated by moonlight, Cecily could see where rainwater had sluiced all the way down the trunk to its roots below.

It was the one from Marguerite's drawing. The great oak tree surrounded by walls.

She walked through the pews to the base of the tree, where she ran her fingers over the bark. Rainwater from a broken ceiling would hardly have been enough to grow such a massive specimen. She imagined the trees surrounding the chapel sending nutrients underground to this oak, keeping it alive in their own contained ecosystem.

"The nuns thought it was a miracle."

Cecily turned. The countess sat on one of the pews, obscured in shadow.

"It is," she agreed.

"After it broke through the floor, they watered it themselves and opened the windows to allow in fresh air and sunshine," the countess went on. "If you reach around the back, you'll find several notches hacked into it by Jacobin axes during the Terror. They tried to cut it down but gave up when it proved too difficult."

Marguerite moved to sit next to the countess. "How are you feeling?"

"How do you think I feel?" the countess snapped. "I have

dedicated my life to ending this curse. Yet the wraith has returned bringing its violence with it. I am prepared to die—"

The countess revealed a thin knife in her hand.

"—but so much feels left undone. Your appearance here suggests the curse will live on."

Cecily took the countess's hand in hers and gently removed the blade.

"The curse isn't coming for you," Cecily said quietly. "You are not the Countess LeClercq. On paper, you are. But by blood, no."

"What do you mean?" the countess asked, as if having not heard properly.

"Do you know the name Dominique Dutoit?" Cecily asked.

"I do," the countess said. "The Dutoits are related to Marguerite's birth parents, Georges and Colette Manzanarès, *non*?"

"Yes," Cecily agreed. "But I think Georges and Colette were your birth parents. Not hers."

Cecily took the genetic tests from her backpack and handed them to the countess.

"What are these?" the countess asked, sifting through the letters.

"Marguerite asked the Dutoit family to submit to genetic testing to trace their shared ancestry," Cecily said. "Only there was none. The lab discovered that she was not related to them at all. But that another individual, whose name isn't listed, is. Could this be you?"

The countess hesitated. "Perhaps," she said. "I know Marguerite communicated with Eglantine about a medical issue. It is this?"

"I think so," Cecily said. "We can ask her when we see her next."

The countess rose from the pew, walked to the tree, and put her hand on the trunk. Cecily could only imagine what the countess was feeling. She'd spent a lifetime buckling under the weight of a terrifying birthright only to be told she might have endured all the worry for nothing.

"Why would Mother do this?" the countess asked, her voice soft and without malice.

"I have a terrible feeling you were meant to be a sacrifice," Cecily said.

"A sacrifice?"

"Something you said gave me the idea," Cecily acknowledged. "I wonder if she made the switch hoping she could trick the curse in some way. Like changing a name or fleeing the country. Adopt a child. Tell the world it was the true heiress. Save her biological offspring."

The countess stared up into the tree. Cecily waited for the countess to become furious at her late mother. Instead, she simply shook her head in sorrow.

"That poor woman," the countess whispered. "How desperate must she have been to do such a thing? How scared?"

Cecily wondered if she could be so charitable if she'd just learned her adoptive mother meant for her to die.

"And poor Marguerite, too," the countess added. "I should have thought of that. There was one clue."

"What's that?"

The countess pointed at the necklace, Marguerite's necklace, still hanging around Cecily's neck. "That is the one thing Sandrine left to Marguerite. It was given to her by her own mother and has been passed down through the years."

Cecily touched the tiny vial on the silver chain. "Why? Isn't it for perfume?"

"Cyanide," the countess countered.

Cecily recoiled. *Poison?*

"Which, if Marguerite left it for you to find, may suggest she believed the same as you," the countess surmised. "That following her death, you are the true countess LeClercq. Not me."

She scoffed. "My God, the things I would've done differently in my life if I'd known," the countess said. "Seen the world, maybe. Fallen in love. Raised a family. Danced in Piccadilly Square. Anything but hide away here, dispensing of someone else's ill-gotten fortune."

They sat in the growing darkness a while longer. Cecily thought the news of her find out in the woods could wait until Eglantine returned. But when she and the countess finally exited to return to the chateau, they were caught in a flashlight beam coming from the front gate.

"Countess LeClercq? Cecily LeClercq?" a voice called out. "*Êtes-vous ici?*"

"*Je suis là,*" the countess replied. "*Que veux-tu?*"

Cecily spied a police car behind the two men. She thought she knew the answer to the countess's question.

The officers spoke quickly to the countess in French. The old woman glanced to Cecily several times in alarm.

"I was going to tell you," Cecily said. "But the information about your adoption took priority."

"You will still have to tell me," the countess said. "What they say does not make sense. Right now, they want us to go into the woods with them."

The pair followed the officers to their car. They were whisked swiftly through the dark forest until they arrived at the now-familiar dirt road. The grass had been flattened by the parade of emergency response vehicles that were waiting with flashing lights among the trees.

It looked like an invasion.

"*Mon dieu*," the countess whispered as they slid past yet another coroner's van.

It was worse once they were out in the cold night. Several officers in white protective coveralls passed up and down the muddy trail carrying heavy plastic equipment crates. Everyone wore the same expression of grim forbearance as if still coming to terms with the magnitude of the task at hand.

"What is this unholy enterprise?" the countess asked, frightened.

Cecily squeezed the countess's hand.

The area around the tree was no longer dark. Work lights plugged into noisy generators illuminated the scene. The dirt and leaves had been pulled from the clearing, exposing the oak's roots. It resembled the explosion of some distant star, blackened chunks of the superstructure blown in every direction and then frozen for all time. The tree itself looked diminished, naked without the groundcover beneath its canopy but no less a feat of natural engineering that it remained upright.

Helmeted climbers rappelled into the pit beneath the tree with empty backboards as others, shrouded in white and carrying bodies, were gently lifted out. Because of all the surrounding oaks, the excavated corpses were lined up haphazardly around the woods, placed wherever space could be found.

Gens spotted them and came over.

"How many have you found?" Cecily asked.

"Twenty-two so far," Gens said wearily. "They think there could be twice that below. There are many partial bodies and the bones have been mixed together over time."

Twenty-two. It made Cecily think of the hundreds of Christ thorn markings on the first Count LeClercq's pedestal back at the abbey. Could this be evidence of his work?

"From how long ago?" the countess asked.

"We do not know," Gens admitted. "There are differing levels of decay, but they believe this is a mass grave from a single event, not a place where bodies were dumped over time."

The countess absorbed this as best she could. "What can we do to help?" she asked.

"It is, like so many matters of bureaucracy, mostly a formality, but as the property owner, we need to ask if you can identify any of the victims," Gens says. "Is that all right?"

Cecily paled. Other than the one with the preserved face, the bodies she'd seen were little more than broken bones.

"*Oui*," the countess replied, her voice distant as if she were already trying to remove herself from the scene.

Gens led the pair to the first row of covered bodies. A forensics tech lowered the first sheet to reveal a surprisingly well-preserved young man, short in stature, his mouth and eyes closed. His taut skin was slate in color, the same as the wraith.

Cecily mentally scrolled through the faces on the sculptures in the abbey's courtyard. Could this be a LeClercq?

The countess stared at the body in amazement before shaking her head. "I do not know this man," she said, prompting the tech to replace the sheet. "But why does he look like that?"

"There seems to have been a layer of peat down there," Gens explained. "It creates a highly acidic, oxygen-free environment that prevents normal decomposition. It preserves the body, the bones, and even the hair. Bodies conserved in this fashion are discovered from time to time. They are called peat men or bog bodies."

The tech lowered the sheets from a few more bodies. Some were like the young man, well preserved and looking more asleep than dead. Others were badly decayed, or their features were contorted in agony as if they were experiencing great violence in their last moments.

The countess dutifully reported that she didn't recognize any of them. Gens recorded her responses. They stopped before getting to the end of the row.

"These are too decomposed for there to be any identifying characteristics," he explained. "Thank you for your assistance, Countess. I will have you driven back to the chateau."

He signaled to a nearby officer. Cecily put a comforting arm around the older woman.

"Let's get out of here," she whispered.

The countess nodded gratefully.

A cry went up from beneath the tree. A couple of forensic techs hurried to the side of the pit and grabbed onto a rope.

"What's going on?" the countess asked, alarmed.

Cecily wasn't sure. The rope went taut. One of the techs turned a crank to draw it up.

"I think they found another body," Cecily said.

A few seconds later, another backboard carrying a body reached the surface. Judging from the shape beneath the sheet, this one was more intact. As the techs swung it to the side, the sheet flipped back, momentarily revealing the corpse's face.

Cecily went cold. A tech replaced the covering, but Cecily was already in motion. She pushed past the officers and techs until she was alongside the backboard.

"I need to see it," she said, dizzy as she said the words. "Please."

The tech shook his head. "*Non*. Step back. S'il vous plaît."

"You don't understand," Cecily said. "I recognize her."

The tech eyed her with alarm. Gens hurried to Cecily's side. The tech glanced to Gens, who nodded. The tech eased the backboard to the ground and pulled the tarp back. Cecily gasped.

It was the wraith.

13

THE BODY BELONGED to a young woman. Her eyes appeared to be missing but her teeth were visible behind pursed lips, jagged and broken. Her long black hair, matted with mud and loam, ran down past her feet. The skin was flayed from her fingers and toes as if she'd tried to climb her way out of the well, the bones now protruding and whittled into points.

Cecily couldn't breathe. She expected the wraith to rise off the backboard, expected the faces of all the surrounding officers and techs to turn toward her, hungry and ready to tear her apart.

But the body on the backboard didn't move. It was too small to be the wraith. Too real.

Cecily looked her over for any indication of injury, but it appeared she'd died how Cecily feared she herself might. Entombed alone in a cold, dark cave surrounded by the dead.

She wondered if the woman had known any of these other victims. Were they her family? Her friends? Neighbors? Lovers? If true, how monstrous to be surrounded by their bodies as you lay dying. Enough, Cecily imagined, to unleash centuries of generational vengeance against the family who was responsible. The family whose lands hid these deaths for so long.

She surprised herself by taking the woman's hand.

I will find out what happened to you. And I will put you to rest, she promised the body.

The lifeless husk, betraying no more sign of who she might've been in life than Marguerite's body had, made no response.

Eglantine was waiting at the front gates when they returned. She hurried to the countess's side to help her in, shooting a worried glance to Cecily. "The police called and said they found a crime scene? Bodies—more than one?"

The countess weakened at Eglantine's words, almost sinking to her knees. Cecily shook her head. "I'll explain in a minute."

The pair helped the countess get upstairs to bed. She said little as she took off her shoes and put on her nightdress, as if still seeing the corpses and not the young women in front of her.

"Eglantine?" the countess asked. "Will you allow me a moment with Mademoiselle LeClercq?"

"Of course," Eglantine said and stepped out of the room.

Cecily helped the countess get into bed, the old woman looking more aged and tired by the minute. "When we were little girls, Marguerite and I wondered what horror our forebears must have committed to bring on our curse," she said. "Our imaginings were always fanciful, like fairy tales. Stolen pirate treasure, offending a witch. I fear that the truth, something so banal as mass murder, never occurred to us."

"Do you know anything about what might have been in that part of the woods?" Cecily asked. "People don't usually dig wells in the middle of the forest."

"I know nothing about that well," the countess admitted. "But for our mother to have gone there, to have died there, and the same now with Marguerite, I wonder if they knew what lay beneath the surface."

Cecily nodded, unsure. "Get some rest, Countess," she said, stroking her hand.

"No, you are the true countess," the old woman said. "I am a resident of this house until death. You seem to be the inheritor of all else."

Cecily absorbed this, realizing that it was true and knowing what she had to do about it.

She found Eglantine in the kitchen, making the two of them cups of tea. The lawyer looked frazzled. "I called the nursing agency. They are sending someone," she said. "Is she all right, Madame, the countess?"

"I can't imagine she is," Cecily admitted. "Given all she's gone through the past few days."

"I should have been here," Eglantine said. "She is not young. This is all too much for her."

"Is there any word about Bash?" Cecily asked.

"Indeed," Eglantine said. "They believe he will be out in the morning."

"Really? That's incredible. But why?"

"It was your friend, the medical examiner, Gens," Eglantine explained. "Though he believes Bash when he claims he was a witness, he says the wounds to Marguerite were inconsistent with someone of Bash's size. He listed many reasons why Bash must be freed."

"When did he say this? Before he knew of the bodies under the tree?" Cecily asked.

"He called from the site," Eglantine said. "I think it convinced him that Marguerite did go there intending to take her own life. That she meant to atone."

Maybe the countess was right. Marguerite did know what

WRAITH

was there. This, despite Cecily having a hard time believing she could descend into the well on her own.

"René mentioned you might be able to help me with Marguerite's estate," Cecily said. "I know you are in the final stages of dissolving the countess's fortune. I was wondering if you might do the same for what few things Marguerite owns. Her house, her possessions."

"Why?" Eglantine asked. "You do not fear the curse, too, do you?"

Cecily wanted to tell her all she had learned but hesitated. One less person to think her crazy.

"No, no," Cecily replied. "I just need to go home. I want to get back to my life and away from all this. The arts foundation the countess is donating her estate to sounds like something Marguerite would wish to support as well. Is it possible?"

"Simplicity itself," Eglantine said. "If you are certain?"

"I am," Cecily confirmed. "How quickly can it be done?"

"I can start tonight," Eglantine assured her. "I can even have preliminary documents to you by tomorrow. It is so urgent?"

"It is," Cecily said.

"Then it shall be done."

"Thank you," Cecily said, relieved. "Merci."

Cecily's sleep brought nightmares. She was the wraith attempting to claw her way out of the earth. Up through the soil. Up through the stone. To rise back up through the well to the surface. Only for each time to be denied. For the universe to assert its cruelty by confirming this would forever be her grave, though she wasn't dead.

The only living thing to hear her cries was an evergreen

oak. It sent its roots down as fast as any tree could manage to lift her out only to be a century too late.

She awoke, sunshine washing over her face through the rain-slicked glass ceiling of Marguerite's rooftop bedroom. It was warm and welcome. She sat up. The out of place evergreen oak sapling was where she left it, right outside the bedroom door. Its leaves were lush and green from the constant rain and brilliant sun. It was healthy now but wouldn't be for much longer.

"Where do you belong?" she asked it, questioning her sanity when she paused to let it answer.

There were voice mails on her phone from Thérèse. She closed her eyes, fearing the worst, then found several texts from her as well.

René is awake.

Cecily experienced a lightness like none she'd felt before. After the unrelenting darkness of the past few days, it arrived like a miracle. She wrote back to ask when he might be out of the hospital. Thérèse replied shortly thereafter.

Not soon.

A moment later, she added: He wishes to see you.

Cecily didn't even think this was a possibility. She got ready to head out, texting Eglantine the good news to pass along to the countess. On her way downstairs, she stopped halfway and hurried back up to the rooftop garden to take cuttings of as many flowers as she could find.

The usually placid neighborhood filled with pedestrians. Cecily flinched in surprise and realized it was a Saturday. Her old fears of being surrounded by people amplified by her recent encounter with all those the wraith possessed. She thought she could bull through it. Get to the street and make her way to the hospital. But it wasn't happening. Her mind became overwhelmed. She had to get back inside the house.

Even this proved impossible. Her hand fumbled with the knob and she dropped the keys and flowers. She'd been so overjoyed moments before. To lose it like this reminded her of how vulnerable she really was. She leaned against the wall, closed her eyes, and slid to the ground. She imagined herself back in the wetlands of the Waccamaw River, tucked in the hollow swamp laurel oak where they'd found her after her mother's death.

She made herself remember the scent. The texture of the rotting wood of the trunk beneath her fingers. The cool air whistling through cracks in the bark. Mostly, she tried to bring back the sense of calm. She forced out the sounds of those passing in the street and focused on birdsong, both real and imagined.

When she opened her eyes again, the pedestrians remained—some eyeing her quizzically—but the crushing nature of their presence had been dispelled. She got to her feet, collected the flowers, and walked toward the hospital, keeping as much distance between herself and others as possible.

The receiving nurse at the hospital shook her head when Cecily asked to see René, replying with a curt, "Family only," in English. Before Cecily could reply, Thérèse appeared at her side, barked, "*nièce*," and hustled Cecily down a nearby corridor.

"How is he?" Cecily asked once they were alone. "I thought he was going to die."

"So did the doctors, but no one fights like René. He would never go so easily," Thérèse said. "The accident has taken his, uh . . . *voix*. Voice? He will not ever speak again."

Never speak again? The idea that René might never again rant or rave in his mad, explosive manner felt particularly cruel.

"He lives, and this is the most important thing," Thérèse added. "Though, *oui*, Paris will be the quieter for it."

Cecily's stomach churned, but she knew she had to be strong. Auberon appeared at a door at the end of the hall. There were stitches across his forehead and his right arm was in a cast. He hugged Cecily, but she thought it cold. The embrace of a sleepwalker. "I am happy you are well," he said.

"And I you," she said, holding him tight.

"When you see him," Auberon said, "do not react with surprise. He is not himself."

Cecily nodded, unsure of what he meant. Auberon opened the door to the hospital room. Cecily was perturbed to see René sharing a room with a much older man, shrunken and bald, but it was the only bed in the room.

"Visitor for you, *mon cher*," Auberon said quietly, touching the man's hand.

The old man was René. His head was shaved. A curving zipper of sutures marked where he'd had surgery above his right ear. His neck was obscured under a mass of bandages, so many that Cecily couldn't tell the extent of the damage. Tubes and wires ran up his arms and over his chest. His mouth, barely open, revealed at least three missing teeth. From when his head struck the cathedral's marble floor, Cecily imagined.

"There was swelling of the brain," Auberon said bitterly, indicating René's head. "They removed a piece of skull to relieve it. That was the scariest moment."

René roused. His groggy, unfocused gaze landed on Cecily. He raised a shaky hand. She quickly took it. His eyes seemed to sigh. She knelt beside him.

"Good God, you look bad," she whispered tenderly. "They warned me not to stare, but they didn't warn me-warn me if you know what I mean? But how could anyone prepare for a sight like this? Anyway, I brought you flowers as, my God, there must be something pretty to draw the eye in this depressing room."

Thérèse gasped. Auberon made a choking sound. René stared at Cecily in horror for a moment but then the light returned to his eyes, recognizing her pitch perfect echo of his own affected boorishness. His chest quaked with laughter as he smiled. He tightened his grip on Cecily's hand. It was weak, but she could feel the warmth under his skin.

After a moment, René signaled for a nearby tablet. Auberon handed it to him as Thérèse emptied a plastic water pitcher to place Cecily's flowers in. René scribbled something on the tablet, not typing but writing on a blank screen in loping script.

"He asks to be alone with you," Auberon told Cecily after reading it.

She nodded. Auberon kissed his husband gently on the cheek and then exited with Thérèse. As soon as they were gone, Cecily leaned her forehead against René's arm.

"I am so, so sorry," she whispered.

He stroked her hair gently with his other hand. When she raised her head, she saw tears in René's eyes. With a mournful look on his face, he wrote something out on the tablet and turned it to show Cecily.

You cut flowers from Marguerite's garden! What manner of plant killer are you? What a waste!

Cecily laughed, as did René. He pointed to a chest of drawers, indicating for Cecily to walk over to it.

"You . . . you want me to pull them over on you?" Cecily asked. "To put you out of your misery?"

René shook his head. He wasn't being funny now. He

pointed to the top drawer. Cecily went over and pulled it to her, finding a large sketchbook wrapped in a plastic grocery bag. She took it out and opened it, recognizing the sure hand of her great-grandmother's work.

"What is this?" she asked.

The hospice in Chantilly sent us Marguerite's possessions, René wrote on his tablet. *Including her last drawings.*

Cecily turned the pages. There were plants, leaves, and trees but also illustrations of doctor's offices, waiting rooms, medical equipment, and even a recovery room not unlike the one Cecily sat in now. There were several drawings of this to follow, all from different angles. Some looking out the window, another looking down at Marguerite's own feet as she lay in bed. A third showed her closet.

The next showed the wraith.

Cecily almost dropped the sketchbook. René, watching over her shoulder, had a fearful look in his eyes. In the drawing, the wraith was hanging upside down as if clinging to the ceiling. Cecily turned the page. The next image showed the wraith towering over her from the foot of Marguerite's bed.

The one after that was a close-up of the monster's face with her mane of black hair filling the entire page. It was terrifying for Cecily to imagine Marguerite at the mercy of this creature.

René pointed from the sketchbook to his neck. Cecily nodded. *Who is she?* he wrote on the tablet.

"A wraith," Cecily admitted. "An avenging ghost somehow tied to the LeClercq curse. She killed my grandmother. Drove my mother to take her own life. She's who I saw under the tree that day. Now she's after me."

You? René asked.

"The countess says that if she appears to you, your days are numbered," Cecily explained.

Remission or not, Marguerite knew she was going to die? René added.

Cecily considered this. It made sense. It explained why Marguerite would add Cecily's name to the signature list for the Dutoit's genetic tests. What didn't make sense was that she'd gone to the tree without her necklace. She'd kept it around her neck her entire life whether she admitted to herself she believed in the wraith or not. Yet, when it finally appeared, she left it behind in her house.

Why?

Cecily turned to the last page of the sketchbook, hoping there would be an answer. The final drawing was of a copse of evergreen oaks. There was a mammoth evergreen oak in the center, filling the page as much as the face of the wraith had, its branches roping away from its trunk the way the wraith's hair had her face. Behind it were several more evergreen oaks, some younger but given their spacing, of the same family.

Toward the bottom, four saplings rose from the earth including one that looked identical to the one on Marguerite's terrace. Cecily stared at it, wondering if her great-grandmother knew it would be her final sketch.

Then she spied what looked like letters hidden among the grass surrounding the saplings. It was a single word scribbled in a shaky hand, Marguerite's final testament.

Beauverie.

14

"BEAUVERIE? WHAT DOES that mean?" Cecily asked.

René shrugged. *It is no name known to us. No city. No thing. Spelled Bouverie, it is a flower.*

Cecily took out her phone and looked it up. There was nothing. The last name of a long-dead French painter, but that was it. What could it mean? Hidden in the grass like that, it felt like another buried clue for her to find like the necklace and the ancestry tests.

The question was, from whom was Marguerite hiding it?

Cecily stared at the word for so long that she didn't notice a nurse entering to announce that visiting time was over. She gripped René's hand again and then kissed his forehead.

"If you plan on dying here, try getting a *little* better first," she said. "Otherwise, you will make such a hideous-looking corpse."

René smiled, wrote *idiot* on his tablet, then faded to sleep. Auberon stepped back into the room. Thérèse came to walk Cecily out of the hospital.

"Do you know this word, *Beauverie*?" Cecily asked.

Thérèse shook her head. "No? Why?"

"Never heard Marguerite mention it? Maybe in reference to her childhood or the LeClercq Forest?"

"Not that I recall," Thérèse admitted. "She did not speak of it often. It was only recently that changed and her interest in her past and that of the countess was piqued. It became a puzzle to solve in her last months."

"Why?"

"Her cancer, I think," Thérèse said. "Before, if her sister called or wrote, she would not reply. More recently, well, she still did not reply but communicated briefly with her lawyer and then went back over previous letters and messages."

Cecily returned to Marguerite's house and began going through her files and photo boxes, looking for any reference to Beauverie. She checked the index of the LeClercq paperback but found nothing. A Google search returned plenty of entries, mostly suggesting she'd misspelled Bouverie, but nothing that related to Marguerite or the LeClercq Forest. She found many old receipts, clippings, and travel documents going back several years.

In each case, she discovered not a single reference to Beauverie.

It was maddening. She left the sketchbook in René's hospital room but had snapped a few photos of the last drawings, including the tree marked with the elusive name. She checked and rechecked the spelling. Though the hand that scratched out the word might have been unsteady, the letters themselves were clear.

Increasingly frustrated, she reached for her phone, hoping to speak with Eglantine or, better yet, the countess. It rang before she could dial.

"Bonjour!" Eglantine said as soon as Cecily answered. "Today, it seems, is the day of good news."

"You got my message about René?"

"I did," Eglantine replied. "And I must tell you that Bashir is out of jail and free. The ongoing absence of a murder weapon was too confounding to the courts. He surrendered his passport and is under house arrest, but anything is better than prison."

"Can I talk to him?" Cecily asked quickly.

"You can try his phone, but when I called, the number was cut off," she said. "He may want his privacy."

"I understand," Cecily said. "I had a question for you and the countess. Do you know what Beauverie is?"

"No, it sounds like a varietal of wine," Eglantine replied after a moment's hesitation. "Shall I ask the countess?"

"Please," Cecily said, then felt bad for not inquiring about the countess's condition. Given all she had learned the night before, would the countess be dismayed? Or elated?

Cecily heard a few words in French, including Beauverie. The countess's voice could be heard in the background. The only thing Cecily could make out was, "*Non, pourquoi?*"

"She has not heard of it but admits there is much she has forgotten," Eglantine said. "Is it important?"

"I don't think so," Cecily said quickly.

"All right," Eglantine replied. "As I said last night, I will likely have the first documents relating to what is, effectively, a simple renunciation of your inheritance for you by tonight but can wait until tomorrow morn—"

"No," Cecily interrupted. "The sooner, the better."

"*D'accord,*" Eglantine said. "That is what the countess desired as well. I will call you later."

That answered Cecily's question. The countess still meant to rid herself of the LeClercq fortune.

Cecily hung up and returned to Marguerite's drawing. She'd thought it was a place name but could Beauverie be the name of the wraith? A nickname for the tree? For the forest itself? She went back to her phone, looking at every map she could of the LeClercq Forest and surrounding area, but found nothing.

Though Bash told her there were no maps of the LeClercq lands dating back to the beginning as, well, there were no French maps back then at all, she figured there had to be some from the eighteenth or nineteenth centuries that might have a Beauverie on them. What if it had been a location—a restaurant, a person's house, anything—only to have gone away in the last century or so? Hadn't everyone talked about how much things changed during the Terror?

She paused. Was she over-reacting? Making too much of a hastily scrawled word that could be something wholly unrelated?

No, she decided. She had to assume any loose thread she came across had been placed in her path deliberately. She had to uncover the meaning of Beauverie.

She went online, finding nothing but images of old maps. Little she could blow up or pore over. She did notice that many of the maps were housed on the same servers, those of the Geography Department (specifically, *Cartographie et analyse des informations géographiques*) at the Paris-Sorbonne. The library's main page said they allowed nonstudents access to the maps but not for checkout.

Good enough.

Marguerite set off, calling Bash's phone as she exited. It didn't even ring but played a message in French that said the number was disconnected.

She closed her eyes. Right now, her focus was on getting to the library and discovering what she could about Beauverie. Everything else would have to wait.

The streets of the Marais were as filled with people now as they had been earlier. Cecily thought she'd be OK, but her sense of being overwhelmed began all over again. She got an idea, though, and hurried back inside. She went to the evergreen oak sapling in the rooftop garden, clipped off the four-leaved tip of a branch, and pinned it to the strap of her backpack. The fresh smell filled her nose. When she touched it, the texture set off comfortable sense memories as well.

It wasn't a perfect solution, but she thought it might work for a few hours.

She made her way through the heart of Paris, across the Seine, and back to the Sorbonne, avoiding people as best she could. The good thing about it being a Saturday was that once she reached the Sorbonne, the pedestrian traffic lessened.

The geographical library was in a large, gorgeously appointed room with generous oak tables, wide enough to unroll even the biggest charts on, and cabinets with long drawers for maps that were kept flat.

She approached the library clerk, fearing her French wouldn't be up to the task. The Indian student behind the desk, however, wore a name tag announcing the six languages she spoke, including English.

"No one looks for those maps," the librarian, whose name was Indrani, said as she led Cecily to the right section. "I am always pulling the same maps of the catacombs, of Versailles, of battlefields from Agincourt to Normandy, but seldom forests in the Ile-de-France."

They reached a section of shelves toward the back of the library where Indrani indicated four drawers. "What you are looking for is in here," she said. "Leave them out when you are finished instead of putting them away, and one of the clerks will reshelve them."

"Thank you," Cecily said, then got down to work.

She pulled out four maps that focused on the Val d'Oise and included villages she'd visited, like Chambly and Félice, with the Oise River and its tributaries cutting up through the center. The LeClercq Forest was demarcated, time and again, by a wide green patch but without showing any roads or trails cutting through it.

Judging by how far she'd traveled up the farm road each time to zigzag in toward the tree, she was able to estimate the spot where it and the well were located. She would be able to use this on maps that predated the current roads.

For the next three hours, she searched for Beauverie. She pored over topographic maps, climatic ones, road maps, physical maps, county charts, and reproductions of centuries-old atlas fragments. She went backward through time; some villages became larger and more regionally prominent as others grew smaller, indicating how much they'd expanded by the time the twenty-first century rolled around. In one case, a village southwest of Paris called Oradour-sur-Glane that existed for some time vanished and then reappeared a few miles away, only to return as two different villages on later maps.

Cecily looked this one up on her phone. The inhabitants of the original village, over six hundred people, were massacred by the Nazis during World War II, some burned alive in various buildings. After the war, the village was rebuilt nearby and the original was set to be bulldozed. The French president at the time, DeGaulle, halted the razing, making the remains of the village a historic site so that no one would ever forget what happened there.

She made a mental note to ask René about it. It wasn't only Paris where every street had witnessed some bloody horror.

But from urbanization to industrialization to the establishment of rail lines and then to highways, the LeClercq Forest never changed. On every map, it remained as green as the English Channel stayed blue. Across all these maps, there wasn't a single mention of Beauverie.

"Maps of the kind you are looking for not only do not exist but also they had no reason to make them," the librarian explained when Cecily went to ask about it. "The land belonged to the king, and the king, in establishing a peerage, put someone in charge of it, like your Count LeClercq. The land could as easily be taken away if a LeClercq fell out of favor. If there was a dispute among those farming the land, the count would resolve the issue, not a surveyor."

"When did that change?" Cecily asked.

"Over the last century or so," the librarian explained. "With the coming of roads, running water, telephone lines— all the things the regional department oversees—measuring distance to the last meter became a necessity. We have a lot of those maps online for municipal use, but I don't think they would have what you are looking for."

Cecily didn't think so either. She thanked the librarian and headed for the exit. It had been a wild-goose chase. The LeClercq Forest, as far back as maps existed, had always been the LeClercq Forest. There was no well. No Beauverie. No reason to think there had ever been anything there except for trees.

So, what had her great-grandmother been trying to say when she wrote it in her sketchpad?

She stepped out of the library, expecting the streets to be as empty as they'd been earlier. Instead, it was as if all of Paris had been waiting for her to emerge. Hundreds of pedestrians filled the sidewalks and streets. Traffic came to a standstill.

She thought they might all be heading to a sporting event or concert, but there were as many people walking in one direction as the other.

This time, a couple of oak leaves and a little self-hypnosis wouldn't cut it. Cecily considered hurrying back into the library but saw on the door that it would be closing in twenty minutes. This wasn't a solution. She looked up and down the block. More people joined the two-way procession. She had to get out of there while things were still moving.

She took a deep breath, lowered her eyes, and stepped into the sea of people. Almost immediately, she felt like she was drowning. She couldn't breathe. People jostled into her on one side and then the other. She gasped, trying to avoid looking into any of the faces for fear one would turn into the wraith.

She knew this was irrational. She felt weak for believing it. But it didn't matter. Every touch sent a paroxysm of fear and nausea through her body. This was a mistake. She had to get away. Had to—

Her body reacted before her mind did. A door opened to her left, and she stepped through it as two people stepped out. She gasped for air and collapsed into a chair once the door closed behind her, cutting off the noise of the street. She thought she'd stepped into a restaurant, then saw it was a comic book store. She'd inadvertently sat down at a table where three young women played a spellcasting game with cards.

"Sorry," she said.

The girls shrugged. Cecily now heard distant music from outside and spied multicolored lights strobing up from a rooftop down the block. The pedestrians all cheered.

"What's going on?" she asked the shopkeeper.

"*Nuit blanche*," he replied, tapping a poster on the window.

White night? The poster showed a silhouette of Paris at nighttime with the moon and stars above. The streets were filled with people as if it were a summer festival at midday. As she was trying to decipher the meaning, musicians in commedia dell'arte–style costumes and masks wove their way through the stopped cars, singing as they went. Rather than be annoyed, the drivers applauded and filmed the artists with their phones. Dancers followed, cutting straight through the crowd, and even leaping onto a couple of the vehicles.

Cecily's phone vibrated. Eglantine's number was on the caller ID.

"*Allô*," Eglantine said. "I am stuck in traffic but moving slowly to you. I forgot it was Nuit Blanche!"

"I stumbled into the center of it," Cecily said.

"Where are you?" Eglantine asked.

"Near the Sorbonne. I went to check out the map room. When I came out, there were hundreds of people here."

"*Alors*, yes," Eglantine chimed. "That will be the entire city soon."

"But what is it?"

"Nuit Blanche is when the whole city stays up until dawn, one night a year," Eglantine explained. "Restaurants, shops, and exhibition spaces are all open and occupied. Artists shut down boulevards for performances. Concerts are everywhere. Parents let their little ones stay up to see the attractions. It is fun. I have your documents. If we finish our business, maybe we can enjoy it together?"

Cecily couldn't imagine anything worse but didn't say as much. "Where are you now?"

"Driving to Marguerite's house, but it may be faster to park and walk, as there is much activity in the Marais."

"I'll head in your direction."

"See you soon," Eglantine said.

Cecily hung up. There were more people passing by the shop's front door now. It almost made Cecily throw up. A shop-worker entered from a stockroom carrying a box of comics. Cecily got an idea. She waited until the worker was halfway through the store and walked into the stockroom as if lost. The shopkeeper called after her in alarm, but she kept going, spied a door leading out, and exited.

Thankfully, the door led to an alley.

She jogged to the end. The road it emptied onto was sparsely populated. She didn't think it would be like this all the way to the Marais, but it was a start. She checked her map app, came up with a route of back alleys and narrow streets, and set off.

Once she'd relaxed a little, she looked around. Every window of the three-story apartment building to her right was filled with painted plastic baby-doll heads as recorded cabaret music flowed down from the rooftop. Half a block later, a string quartet performed on the steps of a church in fuzzy animal costumes as puppeteers carrying marionettes delivered wine and pastries to passersby. Cecily ducked away from them only to narrowly miss a group of gymnasts in multicolored leotards vaulting themselves across the street's benches and bollards as if trying not to touch the ground.

A block later, she passed a restaurant filled with patrons who barely reacted to the surreal activities happening around them.

The performers she passed on the way to Seine—jugglers, mimes, DJs, dancers, graffiti artists creating vast murals on the sides of buildings, clowns, magicians, singers, and even a tightrope walker balancing on a wire high above someone in a matador's costume pretending to bullfight a bored cat—could have an audience of zero, a couple of dozen, or even several hundred but gave it their all just the same. Cecily realized the evening's activities weren't simply about entertaining but also about giving artists the outlet to do whatever they wanted.

Some of the installations and performances were breathtaking. Fantastic. Profoundly moving. Some were silly, intentionally or otherwise. Some went over her head while others stretched for a meaning so obscure that Cecily shrugged and moved on. What mattered was that no one in Paris was absolved from taking part as either artist or participating member of the audience.

She was struck by something hard to quantify. She wished she could get swept up in this collective feeling. Enjoy being an anonymous member of the crowd. She wondered if these documents Eglantine was bringing could, with the stroke of a pen, really undo a curse that had caused so much damage. Unlikely. Maybe once the police identified the dead at the bottom of the well and given their bodies a proper burial?

Again, the gulf between herself and normalcy seemed insurmountable no matter what she did. If she dispelled the curse and somehow vanquished the wraith, could that unravel a lifetime of conditioning?

She wasn't optimistic but hoped the universe would prove her wrong.

She crossed the Seine and reached a wide boulevard where traffic was cut off for several blocks to allow pedestrians the run of the street. There weren't any musicians, clowns, or dancers on this one. She thought it might be in reserve to use for a concert or something later on but then every light within three blocks switched off, plunging the street into darkness. She held her breath. Everyone stopped in their tracks, unsure of what was happening.

Music arrived from high above. It began with quiet notes from a piano before adding a choir. Then the ground beneath everyone's feet glowed to life, illuminated by spotlights and high beams hidden in the trees and on the rooftops of the nearby buildings. The white light softened to a shade of crystal blue, undulating like the waters of the South Pacific. It spread the width of the boulevard and rose up the walls of the surrounding row houses like a filling bathtub.

Photo-realistic sand and coral emerged from the ground as fish, sea stars, and marine mammals burst to life as if from thin air. They were few in number at first but soon shrimp, plankton, and sardines were joined by dolphins, sharks, marlins, and whales swimming over every tree, kiosk, and lamppost down the three blocks. The reef grew larger and more complex, giving Cecily the feeling of looking at the seafloor from a glass-bottom boat. Anemone, stingrays, and even a large sea turtle materialized beneath her, the latter swimming up the side of the nearest building before seeming to disappear into the stars.

"*C'est magnifique!*" someone cried nearby.

Some gasped. Others laughed in amazement. All were taken in by the spectacle.

The current sped up. The sea creatures swam faster and faster as the music reached a crescendo. An image of a tub drain appeared in the center of the block. The water spun like a cyclone, sucking the animals down as the blue of the water returned to a bright, obliterating white before, all at once, the three blocks went dark.

A suitably ominous voice boomed out, "*Chaos climatique,*" from a nearby loudspeaker as the lights strobed a few times for impact.

Cecily scrunched her brow at the somewhat anticlimactic, on-the-nose punctuation of an otherwise effective piece. Maybe she simply liked animals more than people. She glanced to the other spectators to see if they felt similarly.

They stared back at her as one.

Gone were their expressions of wonder or amusement, replaced with the wraith's familiar fury. Their eyes were black, their veins pulsing with rage. Sweat beaded across their foreheads and down their hands. Their mouths were open as if they were salivating at the chance to devour her whole.

Cecily was surrounded.

15

THERE WAS NO René to pull her to safety. No Auberon to ride to the rescue. Cecily was completely alone. She knew how fast the mob inhabited by the wraith could run. They were practically superhuman. They didn't tire or get distracted. They tightened the circle around her with preternatural calm and focus. Her breathing came in short, stuttering bursts. She feared she'd hyperventilate. She turned around, hoping to see a break in their line, a single avenue of escape, but there was none. She was completely at their mercy and knew one thing above all else.

She was about to die.

Her thoughts were interrupted by the boisterous chatter of drunken English tourists stepping onto the wide boulevard half a block away. They were on the far side of the circle, probably too engrossed in their own conversation to hear her shout. She ran straight for them anyway.

She didn't have a plan but hoped the tourists wouldn't fall under the wraith's sway. The footsteps of her pursuers from the opposite side of the circle echoed close as the ring collapsed to form an arrow. The ones directly ahead of her formed a wall.

"Oy, what's going on?" one of the tourists bellowed.

Cecily broke left before reaching the mob. The arrow of

her pursuers did not. All but a couple of them slammed into the others, sending them flying. A few clawed at Cecily while those on their feet kept running after her. She'd broken the wall, though, so it wasn't hard to veer right and head straight for the tourists.

"Hey! Are you OK?" one of them asked.

"They beat up my friend!" Cecily yelled. "I have to get to the police!"

This worked better than she expected. The English tourists, mostly young men, straightened as if called to arms. They moved toward Cecily as if to help her out. She slowed down, her possessed attackers behind her did not, then she sped up again.

The wraith's minions slammed into the tourists. Entangled, the possessed mob flailed and punched at the group. The tourists punched back. Someone started yelling. More people flooded into the street as a full-on melee broke out.

Cecily kept running as sounds of violence echoed around her. People were being injured. Perhaps even badly. All because, as with René, she thought her precious skin was more important than theirs.

No. It wasn't that. Not at all. She shut her eyes, forcing these thoughts from her mind. If she didn't stop this, it would keep going and going on down through the generations. She had to stay alive to put an end to it.

Police sirens echoed in the distance. She hoped this would end the fight but also prayed it wouldn't make it worse.

She rounded a corner, hurried between buildings, and found herself in a church courtyard. People were talking inside the adjacent chapel, but the courtyard was empty. She caught her breath and checked her map. She wanted to get to Marguerite's house and lock the door behind her. Would she be safe from the wraith and her minions there? She didn't know but would worry about that if and when she arrived.

As she was putting her phone away, it vibrated with Eglantine's number on the caller ID.

"Almost to you!" Eglantine sang out on the line. "Where should we meet? It's so festive in the streets."

"I'm feeling sick," Cecily said quickly. "Can we meet tomorrow? I'm sorry for making you waste your time."

"Sick?" Eglantine asked. "Do you need anything?"

Electronic dance music erupted nearby. Cecily covered her phone, but it was too late.

"Wait, where are you?" Eglantine asked. "Do not lie to me! If you are already out partying, I can meet you."

"No, no, I'm—"

Cecily's voice was drowned out by more music, this time arriving as an echo. Cecily realized Eglantine was so close that the music came from her phone as well.

"Are you near the rue d'Argenteuil?" Eglantine asked. "We hear the same music."

Cecily paled. If the wraith were nearby, the last thing she wanted to do was lure Eglantine closer.

She hung up. When Eglantine rang back, Cecily ignored the call and hurried out of the courtyard. She needed to put as much distance as possible between herself and the lawyer. Which ruled out the Marais. That was the first place Eglantine would look. No, she needed somewhere away from people and away from Eglantine.

She hurried from the courtyard and through the church to discover that she was in a high-end shopping district. The stores were all open and taking part in Nuit Blanche, but their windows looked professionally done by expensive, trendy artists that centered the store's name or logo.

They were all surrounded by customers. Cecily ran the opposite way. Her lungs burned and her feet ached, but she kept going. No one noticed her or thought her odd. It was Nuit Blanche after all.

She ducked under an arch and, to her surprise, found herself outside the Louvre. It was dark and silent. The palace buildings were lit up, but no one was inside. Cecily thought the museum might be sitting the festivities out but then spied the movement of a couple of hundred dancers in front of the Louvre's trademark glass pyramid. There was a DJ booth but no speakers. The dancers all wore headphones, the music piped directly into their ears.

She'd seen silent raves before but never with this many participants. Given the backdrop of the museum and dark clouds overhead, the dancers' zombielike movements reminded her too much of those inhabited by the wraith. Across the roundabout from them, there was a long statue garden, but it was roped off with signs saying in three languages that it was closed for Nuit Blanche.

Perfect.

Cecily jogged over, hopped the ropes, and ran down the center of the garden to a large, round fountain. Even in the dark, she had unobstructed views in all directions. No one would be able to get within a dozen yards without her seeing them first.

There were a few trees as well as numerous statues nearby, but she felt safer on open ground. The statues reminded her of the courtyard garden at the LeClercq abbey. She'd had an idea about how to contact Bashir. She wasn't sure how long she'd be stuck in the garden but figured narrowing it down would pass the time.

She took out her phone to make a search only to inadvertently answer an incoming call.

"Cecily!" Eglantine cried. "I have been so worried when you did not answer. Are you safe? Injured? Given all the calamity recently, you can understand my concern."

Cecily went to hang up but was interrupted by fireworks launching up from the DJ stand near the Louvre and exploding overhead, their brilliant colors reflected on the pyramid's glass. She heard the explosions from Eglantine's phone as well. This time, it wasn't an echo.

"Wait, where are you?" Cecily asked.

More fireworks rose behind the DJ stand, followed by applause. Eglantine was near the Louvre, maybe even in the garden.

"Eglantine!" Cecily cried. "I . . . I can't explain, but you have to stay away from me. Please!"

Eglantine didn't reply. Cecily could still hear the fading sounds of the ravers cheering the fireworks but not a word from the lawyer. There was but silence. Cecily hung up and scanned the garden. There was no movement. She saw trees, stone benches, and statues atop their marble pedestals. No people. No Eglantine.

She stood up, trying to get a clear view of the Seine. She couldn't go back the way she came. Couldn't get to the Marais. But if she could find somewhere unpopulated. Maybe by the river—

She heard a footstep. She froze. When it was followed by silence, she wondered if she'd misheard. Maybe an echo of something far away. She glanced to the Louvre, wondering if any dancers had come her way. The wide path back was empty.

Then came a second footstep. The sandy gravel gently crunching beneath someone's heel. Cecily ducked, scanning the hedges and statues for anything as tall as a person. Nothing moved save a few tree branches gently swaying in the breeze.

Well, not nothing. Something flapped near the base of one of the statues. She thought it was a loose bag or piece of trash picked up on the wind. But it was too high for that. It appeared attached, like someone had put a skirt on a statue.

She exhaled. Nuit Blanche, she guessed.

She was about to turn away when she realized that the statue's face, itself unseeable in the dark, was angled directly at her. Its shape was familiar.

The wraith? It was here?

She grabbed her phone. She needed to warn Eglantine. Get her away from here as quickly as possible. She dialed her number.

And a small, distant light glowed to life in the statue's hand.

"Oh God," Cecily gasped.

The statue came to life, dropping the phone as it lowered itself from the pedestal. Its eyes never left Cecily. She stared back as if hypnotized. Then it bolted straight for her.

"No!" Cecily barked, wheeling around to dash away.

Her first instinct was to run toward the Louvre, but she knew the minute she got there, the face of every dancer would turn her way with murder in their eyes. The same held true with the district filled with high-end stores. That left the Seine.

She couldn't swim away. Even if she managed to get onto one of the glass-covered tourist boats, everyone on board could turn on her in the next instant. She hoped for the impossible. Some kind of small boat or rescue craft tied up along the river that she might steal.

It was no kind of plan. No better than nothing. But it was all she had.

Eglantine was gaining on her now. As with the mobs in the street, she didn't make a sound except for her rushing footfalls. It was like being pursued by a predatory cat. Cecily was almost out of the garden but didn't think that mattered to her would-be attacker. The wraith would have Eglantine strike her in the middle of a busy street if she had to.

She reached the steps leading down to the voie Georges-Pompidou, the four-lane boulevard that ran alongside the Seine. Its streetlights illuminated the look of mad, single-minded determination on Eglantine's face. As if there was nothing else in the world for her besides her pursuit of Cecily.

She dashed across the street, dodging cars as she looked over the edge of the concrete barrier to the river below. A ramp led down to a landing. There were no boats. Cecily sprinted down anyway, heading along the wide concrete quayside that ran just above the waterline.

She had no idea how far it went but doubted it went forever. She eyed the water, the quay, and even the wall for so much as a rescue ring or floatation device. There was nothing.

As she neared a bridge, she glanced back to see how many steps she had on Eglantine. Her pursuer was gone. The one thing coming toward her was a slow-moving barge chugging its way down the Seine. She had a wild impulse to try to jump to it, but it was several yards from the quay and, even moving slowly, was going too fast for her to swim to.

She turned back around. There was a bridge up ahead with a service door leading back under the voie Georges-Pompidou. Maybe it led to the sewers or the catacombs. Maybe it was a closet. Cecily hurried to it, turned the door's handle, and to her surprise, it opened right up. There wasn't a closet inside but a well-lit access tunnel.

Perfec—

She flew backward through the air. Her field of vision blurred. Eglantine gripped her arm and shoulder. She'd somehow gotten out in front of her.

Suddenly, they were airborne.

Cecily shrieked as the lights of Paris flashed overhead, then were replaced with the black water of the Seine. She had no idea how deep the river was or how fast its current. All she knew was that it was freezing cold, like diving into a lake high in the mountains.

She sank a few feet under before succeeding to right herself and swim back to the surface. She'd managed to gulp down another breath of air before Eglantine grabbed her from below and dragged her under. She couldn't see her. Could only feel her tight grip on her legs and torso. She kicked back at her as best she could, but it didn't matter. Eglantine, as possessed by the wraith, was as strong as four or five people.

Cecily blindly kicked at her assailant and managed to surface a second time, gulping in air. The barge was almost on top of her. She panicked, fearing she'd be run down, then saw the men on the deck had turned a light on the surface and slowed the boat. They or someone on the shore must've seen them go into the water. She waved. Someone shouted. The light swung her way.

But she was already gone. Pulled back under. She flailed her arms, but Eglantine was on top of her, pushing her down with all her might.

This gave Cecily an idea. She swung her legs around with as much force as she could muster. Her underwater somersault threw Eglantine off-balance, using her momentum against her to sail past Cecily. Cecily dropped down as fast as she could, planted her feet on the detritus-covered river bottom, and launched herself skyward. She broke the surface in a pool of white light. Strong hands grabbed her arms. She was lifted from the water and onto the barge.

"*Tu vas bien?*" the bargeman asked.

Cecily took a few steps back, checking his face. His eyes were blue. They stayed that way. She pointed to the water.

"There's someone else down there!" she cried.

He turned the searchlight back to the river as another man joined them on deck. People gathered along the quayside, on the bridge, and by the concrete barriers on both sides of the Seine to watch and point. The faces she could make out weren't of those possessed by the wraith. Rather, they eyed her as if she were crazy.

"*Une autre femme?*" the bargeman asked.

"*Oui! Une femme!*" Cecily insisted. "Look!"

Everyone did, but Eglantine didn't surface. Cecily ran to the other side of the barge. There was no one there either. She looked to the quayside, expecting to see a soaking wet young woman climbing from the river. As time moved on and none of the people around her turned monstrous faces her way, a horrible feeling came over Cecily.

Eglantine was dead.

16

THE BARGE PULLED to the quayside where paramedics waited. Cecily was covered in cuts and bruises, but they were concerned with hypothermia. They wrapped her in blankets and gave her hot packs. She hardly noticed as she sat on the back bumper of an ambulance, staring into the Seine.

She felt numb. First René, now Eglantine. All she'd wanted to do was help. Help the countess. Help her. It cost her life.

Cecily shook her head. Where was the body? Without a body, she could still imagine Eglantine had survived. Maybe she'd been carried downriver. Maybe, at this moment, she was clinging to the quay, trying to pull herself out of the water.

"I have to go," Cecily told the paramedics, handing back the blankets.

Before the paramedics could respond, Cecily hurried through the crush of onlookers. She jogged the first couple of blocks, following the Seine and peering down to both sides as she searched for Eglantine. The city around her was celebratory. Pedestrians, cyclists, and a handful of people zipping around on mopeds sang along to songs being played, shouted to people they knew, and slid from one busy bridge to another without a care as Nuit Blanche continued.

There were thousands of eyes watching the Seine. Not a one spotted a body in the water below.

The stars were reflected on the waves in the river, marking its undulations. Cecily stared at every swell and turn, wondering if it could hide a body. Was that Eglantine clinging to a bridge pylon? Or merely a shadow?

There was something familiar about this. Then she remembered staring into the storm-charged waves slamming onto Myrtle Beach for any sign of her mother.

She closed her eyes and kept going. She reached the Eiffel Tower and was surprised to see that it was as large in real life as in her mind's eye. There were dancers at its base with a huge, multicolored light show going on above, beams firing from every level of the great structure.

Thousands watched from the grounds around it, stretching all the way to the Seine, with even more people on the bridge where Cecily stood. The sheer number of people didn't bother Cecily. If they all turned to rend her apart, she wouldn't have the energy or will to fight them off.

She stared into the Seine for another minute before turning to head back to the Marais. She touched the necklace. It was such a devilish trick, this belief that sacrificing your life could save others. Her mother died thinking she was saving Cecily. Her namesake, Marguerite's mother, died the same way. Strong women. Powerful women. Brought low by a lie.

They couldn't appease the past any more than they could change it.

Once back at Marguerite's house, she tore off the necklace and threw it across the rooftop garden, as furious at the destruction wrought by an inscrutable curse as she was distraught over the loss of Eglantine. She cried tears of frustration and anguish, collapsing into bed without taking off her wet clothes.

When the phone rang a few hours later, her teeth were chattering like dice in a tin can. She pulled a blanket over herself and reached for her phone. It wasn't the one ringing. She spied a landline next to the bed, an ancient, rotary model easily half a century old.

"Hello?" she said, raising the receiver.

"Bonjour!" The voice was so sprightly and joyful that it took Cecily a moment to realize it was the countess.

The countess. She wouldn't know about Eglantine yet. Cecily didn't want to tell her such horrible news over the phone. She had to get up to Félice.

"Um, good morning, Countess," she said. "You sound . . . well."

"Should I not be?" the countess asked. "Today is the big day."

"Big day?"

"You and I have documents to sign," she said. "The end of the LeClercqs for once and for always."

Cecily darkened. She'd have to tell her. "Documents?" she asked, stalling for time.

"Yes, Eglantine dropped them downstairs an hour ago," the countess said. "An entire packet! We were to sign them and courier them back to the *fondation's* lawyer in London tomorrow as it is Sunday, but I've arranged for us to travel there today."

She wanted her to go to *London*?

"Their lawyer said he would take receipt in person and countersign them this very evening. We will both be homeless! Penniless! But free forever of the curse!"

"And dancing in Piccadilly Square," Cecily said, echoing the countess's earlier wish. She was still trying to process what the countess said. She'd seen Eglantine?

"Precisely!" the countess cried, giddy. "It is but a two-hour train ride on the Eurostar. How often in life will you be in a position to make that happen? We can stay overnight and return in the morning."

Cecily ignored this. "But Eglantine—she came to the chateau?"

"*Oui*," the countess said. "I was sleeping still, but she left a note of instruction and the documents downstairs. Only she has a key. She and the nurse."

"But you didn't see her?"

"No, but who else would have the necessary papers?" she asked. "Mine and yours?"

Cecily wondered if she was dreaming. It had been Eglantine the night before. She knew this. She was the one who chased her from the Tuileries Gardens in front of the Louvre. She was the one who threw her in the Seine.

Or could it have been a stranger? Someone else possessed by the wraith?

No, she knew what she saw. Still, she reached for her phone and called back the last number dialed. When it went to voice mail, the voice instructing her in French to leave a message was Eglantine's.

"Cecily? Are you there?" the countess asked.

"Of course," Cecily said.

"Are you having second thoughts about your inheritance?" she asked. "Or third or fourth?"

"No, I'm ready to be rid of it all," she said. "What about you?"

"Second thoughts? Absolutely not," the countess said. "It is a fortune earned from suffering. I am only glad to be giving it away of my own free will as opposed to under threat. So, hurry along. I have little. Enough to fill a suitcase or two. When I leave the chateau, I will not come back."

"Where will you go?"

"Friends in Reims have long offered for me to stay with them, but I have refused, fearing the wraith's vengeance exacted on their lives," the countess said. "If that is no fear any longer, then I will happily retire to the cottage they've arranged."

She wanted to say no. That she had no interest in going to London or anywhere else for that matter. Not after all that had happened. But there was a part of her, however distant, that heard the joy in the countess's voice. A joy that had probably proved elusive most of her life.

Given all the lives Cecily's presence in France alone had decimated, it felt like the opportunity to do this one good thing to help the countess now that she was freed from the curse was as much a gift from the universe as anything.

"I'll go," Cecily said.

"Of course, you will," the countess said. "Our train leaves soon. Do not forget your special passport."

The countess hung up. Cecily fell back on the bed. Had the events of the previous night been some kind of hallucination? There were finger-shaped bruises on her arm where Eglantine had grabbed her by the Seine. If the curse was trying to make her think she was crazy, it was doing a good job.

She texted Eglantine. When you get this can you call me? It's urgent.

After Cecily emerged from the shower five minutes later, Eglantine hadn't texted or called back. Could it have been an assistant of Eglantine's who brought the papers? Could she have dropped them by the night before? If this were the case, why would she have left Cecily's documents as well? She was bringing those with her to the Marais.

It didn't make sense. She checked various news sites, looking for anything about a body pulled from the Seine the night before. Nothing came up, though she did read a story about drunken violence following a presentation from Action Climatique. Six people had been arrested, but there were no serious injuries. Cecily was relieved. She searched for Eglantine's name but still found nothing.

No drownings. No deaths. No Eglantine.

She tried Eglantine again on her way to the Metro. Still no answer. Being early in the day on Sunday, it was easy to find empty cars. She hadn't even considered what it would be like on the way to London with the countess. Could she beg off? Doubtful, especially given the countess's condition. She hoped there'd be empty cars on the Eurostar.

She switched trains at Gare du Nord and journeyed north. She doubted the Eurostar made pickups in Félice, so she searched for a map. Sure enough, she and the countess would have to come all the way back to Paris first. This was a bit much. She checked the Sunday traffic between Félice and Gare du Nord, saw she could shave half an hour off their time if they hired a car, then nosed around the Val d'Oise online searching for a car service.

No matter where she looked, she came up empty. Taxis, Ubers, and Lyfts didn't seem to exist there. She checked for buses next, landing on a municipal site. Though it didn't look as if buses ran on Sundays, she hit a button marked *carte* to check a map.

The map that appeared wasn't a bus map but one from the regional water utility showing the various water pipelines in the area to warn construction crews away from drilling through them. She was about to click away when she saw the LeClercq Forest.

René had mentioned that water lines went through the forest, but she hadn't expected there to be so many. Several seemed to be storm sewers handling drainage and sending rainwater into the Oise. Others, she wasn't sure what they were for.

Her gaze fell on a small symbol in the forest. There were no pipes running past it. The symbol resembled an old-fashioned water pump, the kind primed by hand. The map's key listed it as an abandoned water well. Her eyes went wide. It was the first time she'd seen the spot marked on any map. She checked to see when the map was made, but there was no date. She searched the site for Beauverie, but there were no entries.

She knew there must be abandoned wells all over the region, likely discovered by the same kinds of seismic surveys they conducted along the Waccamaw back home when they were looking for a place to build a landfill. But as she zoomed across the map, it looked as if the well under the giant oak tree was the only one.

Then she spotted the symbol again a few kilometers to the east. She copied the second well's coordinates and pasted them into her map. Her jaw dropped. The second well not only was on the grounds of the LeClercq estate but underneath the abbey.

Below the second oak.

Cecily was stunned.

She sank back into her seat, wondering what this could mean. She scanned around the LeClercq Forest for other abandoned wells. Nothing came back. Only these two.

What were the odds that from both wells would spring evergreen oaks?

When the train arrived in Félice, Cecily ran all the way across town. When she reached the gas station, she slowed. One of the coroner's vans that she'd seen in the woods used by those excavating beneath the tree was getting a fill-up. She didn't want to be seen in case Gens or others had more questions for her. They could wait. When the tank was full, a forensics tech she vaguely recognized screwed on the cap, replaced the nozzle, and drove the van back down the farm road to the site of the mass grave.

Cecily shuddered to realize that they might still be extracting bodies.

She shook this off and hurried down the farm road herself, relieved to be back within the trees. She'd almost reached the LeClercq estate when she realized the countess might be waiting out front, everything locked up for their impromptu journey to London. She'd have to come up with an excuse to go back in.

But the gate was wide open. The countess was still in the chateau. Cecily left her backpack by a tree and hurried over to the abbey. The front doors were closed but not locked. She slipped inside, looked for signs that the countess might be there, then moved into the chapel. With daylight streaming through the colorful stained-glass windows, the tree was like something out of a medieval tapestry. Beautiful and soaring with a suggestion of magic.

She moved to the base of the trunk, but there was no way to get under it. The heavy marble was cracked from the oak's roots but not enough for anyone to slip below.

There must be another way.

She remembered what René said. That the LeClercqs hid

resistance fighters in tunnels beneath their property during World War II. Couldn't that mean below the abbey?

She searched the chapel for trapdoors and stairs but found nothing. She circled behind the altar, along the base of the buttresses, and beneath the pews. All was solid. Not so much as a loose stone.

The floor out in the foyer was solid as well. She next checked the kitchen. Nothing there either. The dining hall's marble floor was as solid as the kitchen and corridor. She made her way over to the fireplace and felt a draft. The chimney, however, was sealed. The cool air was coming from somewhere within the fireplace itself.

She ran her fingers over the walls until she found the source. There was a loose panel in the side of the fireplace. Given that there was probably always a fire blazing away in it, the fireplace was perfect for hiding a secret entrance.

Cecily pried it halfway open before seeing a latch. She sprung it and a square door swung open on sunken hinges. Cool, damp air flowed out carrying the scent of rich earth. She'd found the tunnels.

She was about to step through it when she discovered that the hatch opened into thin air. There was no floor or stairs. Anyone who charged right in would plummet below. Clever nuns. Cecily turned on her phone's flashlight and discovered a wooden ladder pressed against the earthen wall directly below the fireplace. It descended deep into the ground.

The ladder, though old, proved to be strong enough to hold Cecily's weight. She climbed down into a narrow subterranean tunnel. It had hard-packed earthen walls reinforced with wooden beams like a mine shaft but little else. There were no wires. No signs of plumbing. All primitive. She wondered if it was merely some kind of cellar, then saw that there were several small rooms off the main tunnel.

She held her breath as she reached the first room, fearing what might lurk inside. Her light revealed a small, square-shaped space with a makeshift wooden bedframe, a stool fashioned from a crate, and an old wooden table. *Margarine Salée* was stamped or burned onto the side of the crate, suggesting to Cecily that it wasn't that old, likely from the past century or whenever salted butter became a transportable commodity. She noticed a hole cut in the ceiling. She shined her light into it, revealing edges blackened by candle smoke.

The next few rooms were identical. It was like an underground monastery. When she reached the last room, the darkness swallowed her camera light. It was much larger. An altar sat at the front with a pair of crucifixes made from scrap metal resting on top. If she needed further confirmation that this was indeed where the LeClercqs hid members of the Resistance, a pair of heavy latched wooden trunks sat alongside the altar listing the munitions inside. When Cecily lifted the lid, she found dusty hand grenades and hundreds of rifle bullets.

Would probably be a good idea to mention this to Gens or someone before the arts foundation took over the building and accidentally blew themselves sky-high.

But where was the well?

She checked back through the rooms but saw no sign of it. She ran her fingers along the floor and walls, looked under the bed frames and the altar. There was nothing. When she shined her camera light up one of the holes, she saw it was ringed by candle smoke. Piercing the dirt wall of the makeshift chimney was the tiniest lateral root from the great oak. Judging from its size, she estimated about where she was in relation to the chapel overhead.

She returned to the corridor, eyes on the ceiling, and imagined the tree overhead. She took eight steps down the hall, stopped, and looked right. There wasn't a room there but a solid wall. Curiously, there was a room directly across the hall, and judging by the interval, there should've been a room here, too.

She dug her fingers into the earthen wall. It held tight. She grabbed a stool from a neighboring room and used its legs to carve out a small dent. She wound it around and around in a circle, widening and hollowing the hole until the leg poked through to empty space.

Her hunch paid off. The room had been walled up.

It took several minutes to widen the hole until it was big enough to slip through. She'd already seen the roots of the massive evergreen spilling down from the room's ceiling before she crawled through, the taproot descending straight through the room like a gnarled spike. What she didn't see until she crawled all the way in was the pile of broken masonry it was stabbed into, shattered over the years as the roots tore the room apart.

The mouth of the second well.

17

CECILY STARED INTO the earth. Who had walled up the room? Could it have been a member of the LeClercq family trying to cover up their own misdeeds? Or someone else, more recently, trying to keep the wraith from emerging? If the latter, was it one more LeClercq thinking they finally knew how to defeat the curse?

If Cecily had learned anything, such tactics were fruitless. Whether by switching daughters, fleeing to another country, or, she feared, signing her own name to a stack of documents. The point of the curse seemed to be that it couldn't be undone. Now, Cecily merely hoped it could be understood.

She shined her light into the well. Unlike the one in the woods, its walls were mostly intact. Being sheltered from the elements probably helped. It also felt like a clue. The abbey wouldn't have had a well in the middle of its chapel. The abbey must have been built on top of it when the first Count LeClercq had it constructed. While she had no reason to believe the three hundred marks on Sabastien LeClercq's pedestal were scratched there in error, this confirmed or at least suggested he had something to hide.

Had he put the bodies in the well in the woods? She wondered if it would ever be possible to know for sure. What was he trying to hide in this well? She had to know.

She took hold of the taproot. It was solid and strung, thick, hair-like roots extending around like the rungs of a ladder. Cecily didn't think they'd all hold her weight, but she figured she could find toeholds on the wall of the well if need be. Pocketing her phone, she began her descent.

It was like climbing down a ladder. She moved slowly, determined not to trust the thin roots. Some bent but none broke. This well was deeper than the one in the woods, but she still managed to descend the stalactite-like taproot in half the time. The air grew cooler and damp as she neared the bottom. She stopped, unsure of how much farther she had to go. Her phone light revealed that she was six inches off the floor of the onetime aquifer.

She stepped off not onto the expected mush and loam but hard rock. The cave was mostly dry. She swept her light over the floor, expecting to see more bodies or bones, but it was empty. There were no corpses here.

So, why was it walled off?

She walked the length of the cave, its walls smoothed by years of swelling groundwater. There were no faces embedded in the rock. No hands. No skulls. Nothing.

Maybe her theory didn't make sense.

Her light picked up something shiny in the middle of the cave. She thought it might be a stone. A piece of quartz. As she neared it, it glinted like gold. It was a ring but one unlike any she'd seen before. It had a metal band, possibly gold, though it had become tarnished and discolored over time. On top, rather than a stone, there was an entire building, perhaps a castle, gilded in miniature. The castle would easily rise an inch off the finger of whoever wore it. Not a very practical ring.

She held it up, turning it around under the light. There were symbols or letters carved into the base, though Cecily didn't recognize the language. She took photos of the ring from all sides, thinking she might send them to Thérèse, and then put it back down.

She looked up to see where it came from.

It took all her willpower not to scream.

The ceiling, lit by her phone's light but also by thousands of tiny, iridescent mushrooms, was covered in bodies. The skeletons and half-decomposed corpses she'd expected to find strewn across the ground were embedded in earth. Broken skulls smiled down at her. Vertebrae snaked through ribcages and around fractured femurs. Fingers drooped down like moss hanging from a willow tree.

Including the hand from which the ring likely fell. She looked it over but found nothing else to identify the victims by. There were no articles of clothing here. No preserved skin. No peat mummies. Only bone. She did another walkaround of the cave, this time scanning the ceiling. There were far more bodies here than the twenty-two or so the police had extracted from under the evergreen oak in the woods. She lost count of the skulls after the first hundred.

If she'd thought the twenty-two people in the woods might have been the work of one person, she knew now how mistaken she was. This was the result of a massacre. Hundreds of people killed. Their bodies hidden away. It was as horrifying as it was numbing that something like this could be swept aside.

"Cecily?"

It was the countess. She couldn't come down here. Couldn't get near these bodies. Given the deleterious effects of the horrors of the last few days on the countess's health, Cecily feared learning the abbey was over another, much larger mass grave might kill her.

"Be right up!" Cecily cried out, trying to sound as calm and rational as humanly possible.

She took several photos of the skeletons embedded in the ceiling, then hurried to the taproot. She reached the top in seconds flat, thankful that the countess wasn't standing in the room when she got there. She ducked into the corridor in time to see the countess, carrying an electric lantern, descending the ladder.

"You found the catacombs!" the countess said.

"Um, I did," Cecily said, her hands shaking. "You knew about all this?"

"Of course," the countess replied. "Who do you think brought messages and food to the resistance fighters hiding out here once upon a time? *C'est moi!* Why are you here?"

"René told me about it," she said quickly. "I didn't believe it. Had to see it for myself."

"Voilà, now you have," the countess said, then peered past her. "What is that? What is at the wall there?"

Cecily stepped in front of the countess. "Nothing at all."

The countess stared back at her for a moment, a silent exchange passing between their eyes. Cecily feared she'd have to make up all sorts of lies now to keep the countess away. To her surprise, the countess softened and turned away.

"Come," she said. "It is time to leave this place to others."

A car was waiting at the front gate. "It was arranged by the arts foundation," the countess explained. "As you can imagine, they are anxious to get their hands on the estate."

Cecily nodded and headed to retrieve her backpack. While walking, she opened a browser on her phone and went to a remote burner email site, one in which accounts were deleted after sixty minutes. She'd used it to report plant poachers before. Now, she sent the photos of skeletons to Gens with a screenshot of the water department's map indicating the location. She then texted the ring photos and a brief explanation of where she'd found it to Thérèse.

The countess's luggage, all the possessions of a lifetime, fit into two small bags the driver loaded into the car with ease. Cecily expected the countess to linger. To stare back at the chateau or the abbey or the grounds as if to frame her last moments in the place in her memory.

But the countess did no such thing. She turned away from her home of almost a century, climbed into the car, and didn't look back.

"Shall we go?" she called to Cecily.

"Of course," Cecily replied, joining her in the back seat.

The driver wheeled the car around the overgrown rotunda in front of the chateau and headed for the gate. Cecily glanced at the countess. The older woman had closed her eyes. Cecily took her hand. The countess gripped hers in return. Her eyes stayed shut as they bounced past the gate—the driver hopping out to close them—down the dirt path, onto the farm road, and finally to the highway.

When even the LeClercq Forest was no longer visible in the rearview, the countess opened her eyes. "Enough of that," she whispered as if to no one in particular. "May I have my bag? The blue one?"

Cecily handed it over. The countess pulled from it a yellow padded return envelope with a courier company's logo on the side and passed it to Cecily. "Make sure you initial every page," she said. "Then sign the last sheet and add the date."

Cecily pulled the papers from the envelope. There were eight sheets. And this was only because there were French and English-language versions. She read through them. It was as simple as Eglantine suggested. Cecily renounced all claims on Marguerite's estate but also the LeClercq estate. The estate of Marguerite Varennes née LeClercq would be passed, in its entirety, to the trust dispersing the remainder of the LeClercq estate itself.

It seemed straightforward. Cecily signed and initialed each page and replaced them in the envelope.

"I do not know what I expected," the countess said when the signatures were done. "A thunderclap, perhaps? The roar of a thousand angry souls rising from the beyond? But not nothing."

Cecily bit her tongue. Why should there be a reward for renouncing a fortune likely built on mass murder? Instead, she nodded and handed the envelope to the countess.

"Now we can travel in peace," the countess said.

They arrived at Gare du Nord in the midafternoon. The foundation's lawyer called to tell them a driver would pick them up from St Pancras station and take them directly to the law firm's Oxford Street offices.

"I am sending your tickets to this number via text," the lawyer said, loud enough that Cecily could hear. "I look forward to seeing you soon."

"*Parfait*," the countess said.

They headed inside, Cecily staring straight ahead as they rode the escalators to the international platform on the second floor. She blocked out as many of the other passengers as possible, though the sounds of the loudspeaker and the numerous other people made that hard to do.

The sleek, white Eurostar train—the most futuristic mode of transportation Cecily had ever seen—was already boarding for the trip to London. A long line of people extended away from a small customs podium. Even more were already packed into the cars.

Cecily took a deep breath and went to join the line. This wouldn't be an easy trip.

"Where are you going?" the countess asked, moving toward an empty car two back from the engine. "*Première classe, ma chérie.*"

Cecily's entire body relaxed in an instant. She doubted they would have the car to themselves but was thankful there wouldn't be as many other passengers. Her phone vibrated.

"Eglantine?" she asked.

"Pardon," said Gregoire Gens. "It is your favorite assistant medical examiner."

Cecily turned from the countess to keep her from hearing her conversation. "Of course. How are you?"

"Exhausted. We have now recovered twenty-nine bodies from the well in the LeClercq Forest. The identification process will begin soon, but we have reason to think they are centuries old."

Remembering it was the first Count LeClercq who built the abbey over the well, Cecily wanted to say they should consider the early twelfth century but bit her tongue. This would have to wait. "Oh," she said instead.

"I was curious if you knew about any secondary sites," Gens continued. "I have received a number of photos now from, it seems, the LeClercq estate itself. I am reaching out to you but fear I should also contact Bashir Maleh. He had access to the estate as well."

Cecily hadn't considered the implications for Bash. "I can explain," she said quickly but was drowned out by the train station's loudspeaker.

"Where are you?" Gens asked, concerned.

"I'm with the countess," Cecily said. "We're dropping off legal papers. There is no reason to involve Bashir."

"We have a team on the way to the LeClercq estate right now," Gens said, growing frustrated. "If there is another grave, I must insist that—"

Cecily hung up. She didn't think it was the smartest thing to do. Her phone rang again right away. This time, she turned it off. She joined the countess as a young attendant checked their documentation and ushered them onto the train.

The first-class train car had about a dozen seats, half forward facing, half back. They were large and looked comfortable, with removable wood-topped tables between them. The countess picked a seat by the window and Cecily settled in across from her. Cecily's old claustrophobia kicked up. She felt her heart rate rising. The minutes ticked by as she watched the door, waiting for the other first-class passengers to join them.

But eventually the doors closed, an announcement came over the train's loudspeaker, first in French, then in English, telling the passengers to stow their luggage on the shelves nearest the door, and the train began to move. She glanced around to the empty seats, confirming what she already knew. They really did have the car to themselves.

A map appeared on a screen overhead. It laid out their trip, showing how the train first went straight north almost to Belgium before angling west at Lille before stopping at Calais, a French town on the English Channel. The train then went beneath the channel and rose with stops in Ashford and

Ebbsfleet before reaching London. The entire trip was meant to take two hours and twenty-eight minutes.

"I remember when it was an all-day journey or more," the countess said, following Cecily's gaze as the train gained speed on its way out of Paris. "There was a boat train from Paris to Calais, then a ferry. One could take a plane, but they were expensive and did not run as often. There was also the fun of waiting for the ferry at Calais. Marguerite and I would play on the beach watched over by Mother. On a clear day, you could even see the famous white cliffs of Dover on the other side."

The Eurostar was so much faster than the RER trains Cecily took to and from Félice. It was only minutes before they'd left Paris behind and were driving on toward the distant suburbs. She stared out at the fields and rural roads passing by, though most everything was a blur.

The high-speed train reached Lille in under an hour. Cecily had dozed off for part of the journey, as did the countess, but now watched apprehensively to see if any first-class passengers would join. None did. They were soon off again, angling west toward the English Channel, according to the overhead map.

It felt so strange to her that they were going to London. Sure, she'd moved around a lot as a child, but it was up and down the same highway mostly. One anonymous apartment traded after another eventually traded for a ramshackle mobile home. Now she'd been to Paris and was going to London. When she could peek out from behind the monstrous and surreal circumstances, she wondered if a future existed for her in which she lived without fear.

An RER train also leaving Lille pulled alongside the Eurostar on an adjoining track before the latter had picked up much speed. The passengers all stared at their phones, slept, or read magazines. Given that it was a late Sunday afternoon, there weren't many people on board without the daily commuters.

She noticed someone looking back at her, the face flickering in and out of sight as the Eurostar pulled ahead. For a moment, she thought it was an optical illusion. But no, there she was, looking straight through both trains' windows, meeting Cecily's gaze.

Eglantine.

She was there and then gone. Cecily gasped. It wasn't possible. She shook it off, figuring the young lawyer was simply on her mind. The Eurostar pulled past the next car. Cecily looked to see if Eglantine might be staring back from this one, too.

This time, everyone in the RER car was staring back. Cecily flinched away so quickly that her head struck the overhead rack. She blinked, convinced she was still seeing things. But no, the passengers' gazes were fixed on her.

The sight blinked away as the Eurostar pulled ahead. Cecily turned to the countess, hoping the old woman would look over and confirm that it was a delusion, but she was fast asleep.

Cecily looked back again and almost screamed. The passengers in the next RER car were scratching and pawing at the windows and doors as if trying to smash their way out of a moving train in order to board the Eurostar and attack Cecily. Their faces were contorted by the wraith's fury and hunger. Cecily backed all the way to the opposite side of the car.

She closed her eyes. The Eurostar outdistanced the RER train and arced away to the west. When she opened her eyes again, the train was gone. Thank God.

"Did something happen?" the countess asked, waking.

"It's nothing," Cecily said, forcing a smile.

As the Eurostar rattled on down the track, a new and

distant sound was added to the cacophony. Like a loose screw or a damaged latch. Cecily wondered if she'd struck the overhead rack so hard, she'd detached it from its bracket.

She detected movement at the back of the car. Half a dozen of their fellow Eurostar passengers stood on the other side of the sliding glass door between train cars. Their eyes were so bloodshot they looked black. Their jaws worked up and down. One of the passenger's fingers tapped at the sliding door handle, trying to activate it to step into the first-class car.

Like the passengers on the RER train, they were feral and ready to rip flesh from bone. Except, they weren't looking at Cecily.

They were looking at the countess.

18

"**WHAT DO THEY** want?" the countess asked, more confused than scared. "Are they trying to get in?"

Cecily recognized this bewilderment. The countess, for all her fears, had never encountered the wraith or her possessed mobs before. Not even once. Rather than panic, she was merely disoriented.

"We have to keep them out," Cecily said, forcing herself to sound focused as she looked for anything to block the door.

"Keep them out?" the countess asked. "If they mean us harm, should we not call the attendant?"

"Anyone we let in will become like them," Cecily said. "We have to keep ourselves safe. We can't rely on anyone else."

The countess's eyes went wide. "How do we do that?"

Cecily wasn't sure. The doors leading in and out of the first-class car didn't appear to be locked, but the passengers inhabited by the wraith didn't seem able to work the mechanism. At the top of the door, there was a lock to keep the doors sealed to prevent people from moving into first-class from the other cars, but it required a key.

Damn.

She searched for something to jam in the keyhole, but the

train was so new and so clean, it wasn't as if a screwdriver or chunk of metal would helpfully materialize.

"Cecily!" the countess cried. "There!"

Cecily wheeled around. Two porters and an attendant stood at the door leading to the engine. Their eyes had gone black as well. Rather than scratching on the door, one of the porters was slamming his weight into it, trying to crack the glass.

"We are pinned in!" the countess said, terrified. "What can we do? I thought I was safe from this. Is giving up the fortune not enough?"

Cecily didn't want to answer this. She knew the wraith was there because of her not the countess. The countess's breathing came in fits and starts. Cecily was afraid she would hyperventilate. She glanced at the electronic map. They had thirty-five kilometers to go before they reached Calais. But if those driving the train were possessed by the wraith, did that even matter? She prayed it didn't.

"We only have to last a few more minutes," Cecily said. "When the train gets to Calais, we'll be the first off."

"Then what?" the countess asked.

"We'll get as far away from people as possible," Cecily said.

Hoping to avoid more questions she couldn't answer, Cecily hurried to the luggage racks. She picked up the countess's bags. They were too light to do much. She shoved them against the door anyway. There was a large first aid backpack that she added to the pile before topping it with her own backpack, the lightest of them all.

There was a click. One of the other passengers had managed to undo the latch. Cecily slammed it closed again, but the wraith-possessed passengers attacked the mechanism with renewed vigor. They'd be through long before the train reached Calais.

"Are these removable?" the countess asked.

She pointed to the wooden-topped tables set up between the seats. Cecily ducked under one and found it held in its stand by two metal pins. She yanked them out, hefted the heavy table, and half walked, half dragged it to the door. It cracked the safety glass as she wedged it in place.

"They won't get past that," she told the countess, hurrying to drop a second table by the forward door.

The porters threw their weight against the door. The heavy table didn't budge. Cecily wondered what Eurostar would think of the destruction she left behind. She settled back in next to the countess, taking the old woman's hand. The banging from either side of the car was unnerving, but she had to keep calm.

"Now what?" the countess asked nervously.

"We wait until Calais," Cecily said, retrieving their bags. "The minute the train comes to a stop, we get off and—"

Her thoughts were interrupted by a strange clicking noise. She looked to both doors. Nothing had changed. The tables were still in place.

"Where's that coming from?" she asked.

"There," the countess whispered, her voice haunted.

It came from the car's small bathroom. The door handle shuddered as if jostled by little more than a breeze on the other side. It stilled, then danced up and down again.

Then the door opened.

Cecily launched herself at it. The attendant who'd checked them in stood on the other side, eyes as dark as blood, mouth wide open. Cecily kicked the door back into place, but the attendant's foot kept it from shutting all the way. Cecily threw herself against it only for the attendant to kick the door with such force that she went flying.

Cecily righted herself quickly and raised her arms, anticipating the next attack. The attendant flew at the countess instead.

"No!" Cecily roared.

The attendant shoved Cecily aside and grabbed the countess by the throat, lifting her off the ground. Dazed, Cecily punched the attendant in the back of the head, then slammed an elbow into her nose when she turned. There wasn't much strength behind it, but it caused the attendant's nose to explode with blood. She dropped the countess, who fell back into her chair, gasping for air. The attendant grabbed Cecily by the neck, ready to slam her into the window when the train suddenly decelerated.

Catching the attendant off-balance, Cecily to elbowed her in the ribs and sent her sprawling into to the aisle. Cecily took the countess by the elbow and helped her to the exit doors.

"We have to be quick," she said, the platform coming into view.

"*Oui,*" the old woman said, her voice hoarse and pained.

The train slowed to a stop. Dozens of passengers waited on the other side of the door to board. Cecily scanned their faces for signs of the wraith's presence. When she saw none, she hit the emergency exit button. An angry buzzer sounded, and the door slid open. She took the countess's arm, pushed through the crowd, and hurried down the platform.

The passengers, confused, stepped forward, as if thinking all the doors would open. When they finally did, the possessed mob rushed out directly into the crush of waiting people. Cecily scanned the area for a luggage trolley, then spied a porter standing by with a wheelchair. She led the countess to it and sat her down.

"Merci!" she said to the confused porter before whisking her down the platform's ramp.

She'd expected a small rural station. Calais, instead, rivaled Gare du Nord in terms of arriving and departing passengers as well as the number of waiting trains. She hoped this would work to her advantage as she quickly pushed the countess toward the glass exit doors near the front of the building.

"No," the countess rasped, pointing to a side exit near a food court. "Through there."

"Are you sure?" Cecily asked.

The countess nodded weakly.

The side exit opened into a long-term parking lot with plenty of cars but no people. Cecily glanced over to the front of the station and saw hundreds more passengers coming and going.

"Good call," she said. "Now where?"

"Bicycle path," the countess said, indicating a sidewalk that disappeared into tall grass. "Avoids the city. It will take us away from here."

Sirens erupted nearby. Figuring it was a good time to get out of there, Cecily took the countess's suggestion, pushing her through the parking lot and onto the trail. The tall grass quickly obscured them from anyone except a passerby on the path itself. After a ten-minute walk, they'd still seen no one.

The sharp tang of saltwater reached Cecily's nose on a cooling breeze.

"Are we near the channel?" the countess asked, raising her head.

Cecily wasn't sure but noticed the grass on either side of the trail rose from sand. "I think so. Maybe a little farther."

The sun was beginning to set ahead of them. The sky turned from blue to peach-streaked amber. The concrete path gave way to gravel, which soon disappeared into sand. A long, wide beach extended to the water beyond.

"*C'est belle*," the countess whispered, nodding to the view.

The sand extended uninterrupted for miles, appearing pink in the setting sun. Unlike the beaches in South Carolina, there were no rows and rows of hotels or tourists on blankets. A few people dotted the sand. A couple walking their dog. A seated young man working on a laptop. A family packing up after what was likely a long day.

There were a few wooden cabanas no larger than changing rooms.

"Can you see the Cliffs of Dover?" the countess said, breathing in deeply, invigorated by the sea air. "It seems clear, but my eyes fail me."

Cecily scanned the horizon but saw nothing but water so blue it was almost lavender. "I think I can," she lied. "Just barely."

"How do they look?"

"Like a lace border between sky and water," Cecily said, easing the wheelchair across the sand.

"Beautifully said," the countess replied, as if seeing the cliffs in her mind's eye now. "Marguerite and I sat here as little girls, imagining the terror our forebears must have felt seeing fleets of English ships filled with knights and warhorses approaching."

Cecily knew the countess's words were meant to elicit romantic images from the age of chivalry. Instead, it made her think of the dead bodies she'd found in the wells.

"Stop here," the countess said, the wheelchair getting mired in the sand. "I can walk now."

With Cecily's help, the countess kicked off her shoes, lifted herself from the chair, and walked to the water's edge. Cecily felt the old woman's pulse. It was scarily erratic. She was about to suggest calling an ambulance when she noticed the people dotting the beach had stopped their activities. They all stared at Cecily and the countess.

Cecily tensed. The countess grabbed her arm.

"Countess," Cecily whispered. "They're—"

"The water's edge," the countess said, raising a silencing hand. "Please."

Cecily held out her arm. The countess took it. Together, they moved forward. The other beachgoers were coming toward them now, slowed by the sand but closing all the same. They'd be upon them in less than a minute.

The countess stumbled. Cecily held her upright. "We can sit," Cecily said.

"No," the countess insisted, her breathing ragged. "Keep going."

At the bottom edge of the sun-touched horizon, they reached the waterline. The countess sank to the ground, extending her feet into the coolness of the channel.

"I am so sorry for visiting this pain upon you," the countess said. "This curse. You have endured so much already. Your mother's death. Your grandparents."

"It wasn't your doing," Cecily said. "It was the LeClercqs."

"*Oui*, yes, but I tried so hard to stop it," the countess said, her chest rapidly rising and falling as she fought for breath. "I did not want it to harm anyone else."

"Countess," Cecily whispered. "Until you, the LeClercqs

did nothing to confront their past or face their crimes and the pain they inflicted on others. You stopped all that. You took responsibility even if you didn't know what for and changed the lives of so many people through your generosity."

"No, no," the countess said, the water playing over her heels and allowing them to sink into the sand. "You are the Countess LeClercq, not I. I am but Aline Manzanarès, daughter of Georges and Colette."

"It's a beautiful name," Cecily said, feeling the pounding feet of the beachgoers drawing near, the sand vibrating around her.

"It is," the countess agreed. "This, I want you to know. If the curse has taught me anything, it is that you cannot change the past no matter what you do. You can only change yourself. Only you can bring peace to yourself."

Cecily nodded, protectively wrapping her arms around the countess, around Aline Manzanarès. She would fight to her last breath to keep the monsters from touching her.

The quaking stopped. Cecily waited for the first strike. None came. The beachgoers were walking away. Some looked confused as to what brought them to the water.

The sunset was reflected in the countess's half-closed eyes. The water lapped at her feet. Cecily held the old woman tight, praying for a next heartbeat that never came, as tears flowed freely from her eyes.

19

THE LIES CAME easy when the police arrived. Countess Aline LeClercq had been under a great deal of stress following the tragic death of her estranged half sister, Marguerite, a few days earlier. This, coupled with the discovery of a centuries-old mass grave on her property—

"Are you serious?" the Calais police detective interrupted, alarmed.

"This is the number of the medical examiner overseeing the excavation," Cecily replied.

—led her to travel to London, hoping to get away. She'd felt sick at Calais and disembarked. They'd walked out to the beach, she'd complained of a lack of breath, then passed peacefully of a heart attack while watching the sunset.

"Were you aware of a fight on the train platform?" the detective asked. "Was the countess injured there?"

"What fight?" Cecily asked, looking so hollowed out by the countess's death that no one mentioned the security footage that showed her fleeing the platform.

Eurostar put Cecily up for the night in a Calais hotel room. Perhaps, Cecily wondered, in hopes she wouldn't blame the incident aboard their train for the countess's heart attack. She spent the night staring out the window toward the English Channel. She couldn't sleep.

She hadn't really known the countess. She'd met her just a few days earlier. By all accounts, she'd lived an exemplary life. Dedicated most of it to charitable pursuits. She wasn't a LeClercq. Hadn't actually been pursued by the curse. Which left one alternative.

She was dead because of Cecily.

It was the only thing that made sense. On Cecily's butcher bill of violence wrought by the wraith beginning with René, the countess died because of her close association with the person whose death was imminent. The LeClercq heir or heiress.

Cecily wondered if the old woman died knowing this. The fortune was gone, wasn't it? The land? The money? The bodies had been uncovered. What more might Cecily have done to save the countess? What did the curse want from her? The answer might be nothing. Nothing at all except her suffering.

She thought about it throughout the night. It was on her mind when she was reunited with her backpack, the countess's two bags, and the countess herself in a steel casket provided by the railway. She managed to text and leave more messages for Eglantine about what happened, but it was Thérèse and Auberon who met her at Gare du Nord.

"*Ah là là,*" Auberon said quietly, embracing Cecily as she got off the train. "What you have endured."

"I couldn't save her," Cecily whispered into his shoulder.

"I know," Auberon replied. "Given all that has happened, I do not know if anyone could. Even so, it sounds as if she was allowed a peaceful death. She has you to thank for that."

Cecily nodded but didn't cry. She was so numb she could hardly function. Two morticians from a funeral home were waiting to take possession of the countess's body. Her funeral had been long arranged. There was little for Cecily to do other than sign three documents attached to a clipboard and accept a receipt.

Cecily watched the coffin as it was wheeled away, as little able to connect the person she knew to the body inside than that of Marguerite's in the medical examiner's office to the woman from all the photographs and inherited memories. She spotted a drop box for the courier service whose logo was on the packet of documents she and the countess signed. She sealed the envelope, dropped it inside, and followed Auberon and Thérèse out of the train station.

"What will you do now?" Auberon asked.

"Go home," Cecily said.

"You will not stay for the funeral?"

She shook her head. She couldn't imagine doing so. He nodded and gave her a quick hug before hopping in a cab to return to René's side at the hospital. Thérèse waited until he'd left before turning to Cecily.

"It must feel so minor right now, but I must ask you where you discovered this ring you sent me," she said.

It took Cecily a moment to even remember what ring she was talking about. Figuring she had little to lose, she told Thérèse everything. Thérèse flinched a couple of times as if her body couldn't handle the awful truth. When Cecily finished, Thérèse laid her hand on Cecily's wrist.

"I showed your photographs to someone who I think can help you with the identification," Thérèse said carefully. "I would like you to come with me."

"A jeweler?" Cecily asked. "A historian?"

"A friend," Thérèse said.

Cecily agreed and followed Thérèse to a taxi. To her surprise, it took them to the Marais. They passed under the horse chestnut trees growing near Marguerite's house, the sidewalks mostly empty of people on a Monday morning. Cecily wondered if they'd stop at the house first but then the cab took a left, drove them down a narrow side street, and pulled to the curb in front of a wide, square, red brick building at the end of the anonymous block. It had a few windows but nothing by way of decor or signs. It reminded Cecily of Pauline's. Was it fashionable in Paris for buildings to be unmarked?

When she realized there wasn't even a street-facing door, she thought it must be.

Thérèse led her around the side of the building and down a long, narrow alley. The sidewalk was replaced by wide, rectangular flagstones as old as Paris itself. They were shaded by tall linden trees, their wide leaves glowing bright yellow in the sun. Cecily imagined what the area might've looked like before it was paved. Was Paris once as thickly wooded as the Val d'Oise?

They came to an ancient wooden door inlaid with intricate, delicately carved designs that stood in contrast to the building's otherwise unremarkable exterior. There was a thin metal cylinder screwed into the doorframe with lettering similar to what Cecily saw on the ancient ring. Thérèse pressed a button on an intercom below it, then nodded to a recessed security camera on the wall behind them. The door buzzed and unlocked.

The inside of the building stood in stark contrast to its exterior. The red brick walls were covered over by decorative wood paneling Cecily took for French elm. It extended over the ceiling and floors, giving the two-story entryway a certain warmth. Stairs with modern, angular wooden banisters rose to the second floor past wood-carved sculptures of people in various forms of traditional dress.

If it wasn't for the security guard standing in a booth of bulletproof glass surrounded by closed-circuit TV monitors next to the front door, an honest-to-God machine gun discreetly by his side with a second guard halfway up the stairs, the building might have looked like the entrance to a small private club or church.

A young woman in a gray skirt and dark sweater emerged from an office behind the stairs and approached the pair with a smile. "Bienvenue, Thérèse," she said, then turned to Cecily and asked in English, "You are the Countess LeClercq?"

"Oh, no, I'm—"

Cecily blanched. The young woman was right. She *was* the Countess LeClercq, no matter if the fortune or any authority the title once held was long gone. The legacy and its burden and obligations remained.

"I am," Cecily said.

"You are welcome in our community here," the woman said.

"Thank you. I'm not sure where here is, though."

"Temple Emanuel Sholom of Paris," the woman said. "I am Esther Gondelman, an assistant to Rabbi Batalion. She awaits us upstairs with her father."

Cecily shot a curious look to Thérèse, who smiled encouragingly. They followed Esther up the steps to the second floor, light coming in from several stained-glass windows that appeared dark from the street. They passed many offices and a pair of empty classrooms before reaching a small library. Esther ushered Cecily and Thérèse inside, then closed the door behind them.

Rabbi Delphine Batalion was a middle-aged woman with dark hair and wire-rimmed glasses that lent her a scholarly appearance. She wore a black dress accentuated with a single silver chain. Her father, whom she introduced as Rabbi Zadkine, looked about twice her age. He wore a dark suit and blue tie.

"It is very nice to meet you," Rabbi Batalion said in English. "Thank you for coming."

"Thank you for seeing us," Thérèse said.

"Please be seated," the rabbi said, indicated two empty chairs around a small coffee table.

As she took her seat, Cecily noticed a large pot of yellow flowers by the window. They were unusual, with wide green bases and puffy pods of tiny flowers, their petals wrapped in on themselves, ascending the stem.

"Yellow gentians?" Cecily asked.

Rabbi Batalion nodded. "*Oui*. They are from Oradour-sur-Glane."

The name rang a distant bell. "The village destroyed by the Nazis?"

"You know the story?" the rabbi asked.

"I read a brief reference to it once," Cecily admitted, recalling the village that seemed to disappear only to return on a later map in the library. "Was it a Jewish community?"

"Not at all," the rabbi said. "It was a small village with a population almost doubled by refugees, including seven Jews, a descendant of whom brought me those flowers. Despite several trials after the war, no one seems to understand why the SS men killed everyone in the town. It was war, they say. People die. They were going to rebuild. President De Gaulle said no. So many other sites of great tragedy are hastily erased. Covered over by the perpetrators. Meant to be forgotten as quickly as possible. Do you know what I mean?"

Cecily remembered the day she learned a parking lot in Charleston had paved over the remains of a slave jail.

"I do."

"There is a lot of our history in France that we know, but even more that, as Oradour-sur-Glane almost was, got erased," the rabbi continued. "Going back to the seventh century, Jews have been expelled from this country by French kings. In the tenth and eleventh centuries, Jews were often given the choice to convert to Christianity or be killed or exiled, their lands and possessions confiscated. In 1096, the entire Jewish community in Rouen was locked in a church and burned alive. Do we know their names? Where they came from? The size of the community? No. It is only because the killers were proud of their deeds that we know of it at all."

"That's horrible," Cecily said.

"Yes, but while some of it was religious prejudice, it was also an easy and even acceptable way to steal or annex property," the rabbi said. "No one complained if land was taken from a Jew."

Cecily felt Thérèse's eyes on her. She knew why she'd been brought here. "Do you think the LeClercqs were capable of something like that?"

"Why not?" Rabbi Batalion said. "We have found time and again that what we might wish to see as motivated by an aberrant evil, an exception, is in almost all situations much more banal. More commonplace. It is not a question of whether the LeClercqs were capable of this. Of course, they were. Humans have committed atrocities against other humans since the beginning. What is one more massacre?"

Rabbi Batalion looked at her father. He leaned forward with a color printout of Cecily's photograph. "The ring you showed our sister is likely from the eleventh or twelfth century. It was a style used in weddings. The building represents either the couple's future home or the Temple of Solomon in Jerusalem. The writing, in Hebrew, wishes the couple luck and happiness. It is rare to find these in France. Those who killed the Jews usually melted their jewelry down. What it does not tell us is who it belonged to."

"But was there a community of Jews near Félice? In the LeClercq Forest close to the Oise River?"

"We know of no Jewish communities in that area," Rabbi Zadkine said. "I have spoken to several scholars and historians, but there is no record of who they might have been. Unless something is uncovered during the exhumation, it may stay that way."

"Do you know the name Beauverie? Could that be the name of the town?"

"Not likely," the rabbi replied. "That is not a Hebrew word."

Cecily's heart sank.

"It is probably something very ordinary that happened," the rabbi continued. "The king established a peerage, granting the first Count LeClercq the land. This was at the height of anti-Semitic fervor in the region. Desiring the land of Jews in the area, he possibly ordered them to leave but more than likely massacred them knowing they would be quickly forgotten."

"Not by the wraith," Cecily said.

"Pardon?" Rabbi Zadkine asked.

"There are those in my family who believe the evil has lived on in the form of a curse that has been carried down through the centuries."

Rabbi Zadkine fell into an incredulous silence. His daughter leaned forward. "We know of this LeClercq curse," she said evenly. "What we did not know, Thérèse explained to us. It reminded us of a dybbuk."

Cecily looked between the rabbis. Both seemed reluctant to talk about this.

"What's a dybbuk?" Cecily asked.

"If you look it up in a book, you'll see that it's a ghost or demon tied to Jewish mythology," Rabbi Batalion explained. "It's written that a dybbuk is created by the dislocated spirit of someone who dies under horrific or unnatural circumstances. They then torment or even possess the living, wandering the earth until whatever wronged or tormented them in life is put right."

Cecily couldn't believe what she was hearing. A dybbuk? She'd never heard the term. But the rabbi's description fit the wraith precisely.

"That's incredible," Cecily said. "A dybbuk is—"

"There is no such thing," the older rabbi said. "It is mysticism. Folklore. It has no basis in reality, nor do any serious Jewish scholars believe it has much basis in doctrine or scripture."

"But I've seen her," Cecily said. "I've seen this wraith. This *dybbuk*. She's attacked my friends. Possessed dozens of people. She slashed our friend René's throat! I watched her do it! Marguerite saw her kill her own mother as I saw her kill mine."

The room went very still. Rabbi Batalion raised her hands. "I am so very sorry for all the tragedies that have befallen your family," she said. "But when people come to us with instances of demonic possession or communication with spirits, it has been proven time and again to be an issue of mental illness or suggestion. We do not believe in curses here. At least, not ones visited on the living by the dead."

"So, you think I'm crazy? More than that, you think my whole family is crazy?" Cecily shot back. "People have died."

"That is not what I am saying," Rabbi Batalion replied evenly. "While it is my experience that too many look to the supernatural to explain the unthinkable, that doesn't mean it is not the case with your family. It is simply this curse, this wraith, while it has the trappings of Jewish folklore, has nothing to do with us. Nothing to do with the victims of your ancestors. It is more likely something that comes from within rather than without."

"What do you mean?"

The elder rabbi leaned forward. "Since you have been here, has it been only you who has seen the wraith?"

"No," Cecily said. "René saw her—"

Thérèse interjected. "René says he did not see who attacked him. In fact, he has almost no memory."

Cecily remembered being in his hospital room when he saw Marguerite's drawings in the sketchbook. What had he written? *Who is she?* Was he asking because he recognized his attacker? Or understood Marguerite was drawing something diabolical?

"On the road," Cecily said. "Auberon saw her."

"He did not," Thérèse said again. "He reacted to your shout. He believes he was drunk, as was René. He does not blame you—"

"*Blame* me?"

"—for what happened," Thérèse said. "He understands you were under tremendous pressure these past few days."

Cecily couldn't believe what she was hearing. She ran back through each time she'd seen the wraith. On the airplane. Underneath the tree. On the street in front of Pauline's. The mobs of people inhabited by her as they chased Auberon's car. On Nuit Blanche. On the train.

The countess had seen the possessed people. René and

Auberon must have, even if they didn't realize what they'd been looking at.

But none had seen the wraith.

She remembered telling the police about the woman who followed her across the storm-swept parking lot to the beach where her mother died, only for them to tell her there was no one but them on the several different angles of security footage.

It wasn't possible. Was it?

"This makes no sense," Cecily protested. "I can't possess people. I can't—"

Rabbi Batalion touched Cecily's knee. "There are things we cannot understand about this life," she said. "There have been those in your family who have felt the weight of your ancestor's heinous sin. That shame and guilt and horror have burned through them in a collective unconscious passed down from one generation to another."

Cecily thought about the countess's mother telling her and Marguerite about the curse as her own mother had done. How Louis must've learned about it. How her own mother learned of it.

"This in turn becomes its own curse," the rabbi continued. "One you burden yourselves with and one that, in some way we cannot understand, leaped from your subconscious into the physical world, made manifest by your anguish over the unthinkable. Some see ghosts where others see nothing. Simply because it came from within their own mind doesn't make it any less real, any less capable of affecting the mortal plain. Shame, for those who can feel it, is an enormously powerful emotion."

Cecily sank into her chair, attempting to fathom the implications of what the rabbi was saying to her. "I never met my great-grandmother, yet how she drew the wraith is exactly as I see her. How is that possible if it's only in our minds?"

"Your mother never told you what she looked like?" the rabbi asked.

"No."

"Never told you a scary bedtime story? Never made a Halloween decoration? Never spoke about ghosts and goblins?"

Cecily was less sure about this.

"Folklore as an oral tradition is passed down in many different ways," the elder rabbi added. "When you see this wraith, is she always the same? Maybe five or six traits that never change but nothing more?"

Slate-gray skin. Jagged teeth. Fingers that taper into points. Long matted hair. Eyes of black. A white dress.

"Maybe," Cecily said, unsure.

"Then is it a memory of something you have seen?" the rabbi asked. "Or are you remembering words spoken to you that your internal visualization is bound to?"

Meaning the wraith was a manifestation of words passed down to her from her mother. Not something external. Cecily looked around the faces in the room. No one believed her version of events. She was even beginning not to believe it herself.

So, what did she believe?

"Thank you," Cecily said, feeling hollowed out. "For speaking with me about this."

"Cecily," Thérèse said gently.

"No, it's OK," Cecily said. "I just . . . need to get away for a moment. To think about this."

The two rabbis rose. "Thank you for, we hope, reuniting

us with lost members of our community," Rabbi Batalion said. "It is so rare that we can—"

But Cecily was already out of the room.

20

CECILY RAN ALL the way back to Marguerite's house. Thérèse called her phone, but she didn't answer. When she rang a second time, Cecily turned off the phone. Had her mother considered this? Had Marguerite? Did any LeClercq suspect they were the authors of not just their own destruction but that of others?

And if true, was that the actual lesson of the wraith? That there was nothing to be fought or made right at all? That they themselves were the destructive force unleashed on the world and only through their extermination would all this madness end?

And why not? They had been allowed to prosper for centuries specifically by denying that chance to others. What of the descendants of those they had killed? What might they have created? Loved? Built? And even if the answer is absolutely nothing, how do you live with the knowledge that it was your family who judged them to thereby be unworthy of life?

Could you ever be punished enough?

That was the curse. If you believed in it, the answer was no.

Cecily entered Marguerite's house, grateful her key still worked. The arts foundation would receive its documents soon and Cecily would be turned out of this home. But until then, she was glad for the shelter.

She stared through the dark kitchen toward the stairs. The density of the plants hanging down past the windows let the sun in only as jagged blades of orange between long shadows.

"Are you here?" she demanded of the darkness.

She envisioned the wraith emerging from a pantry. Appearing at the top of the stairs. Dragging her fingers along the glass. Along the ceiling.

Cecily hurried upstairs, checking each room and each closet. She *wanted* to see the wraith. Wanted to prove the rabbis wrong if just for the temporary comfort of knowing something made sense.

"Where are you?" she demanded.

She closed her eyes, hoping to conjure the monster. Needing to conjure the monster. Did she want it to consume her? She went up to Marguerite's bedroom and spied the necklace in the far corner of the terrace where she'd thrown it. She touched it with her fingertips, wondering again why her great-grandmother might've left it behind.

She was struck by a memory. Bashir. He wasn't a LeClercq. He'd seen the wraith murder Marguerite. At least that's what he told the police. She had to find him. She walked the necklace to the second-floor bathroom and poured out its contents. She dropped the chain and empty vial into the toilet, hit the lever, and watched it disappear.

She tried Eglantine, knowing she wouldn't get her. To her surprise, she heard a new outgoing message for Eglantine's inbox. It was in French but was merry and chipper. It sounded as if she were saying she would be away for a couple of days.

That might explain why she wasn't returning calls or texts.

Could she not know about the countess by now? Given the tabloid treatment of Marguerite's death, she doubted it would be long before the countess was treated similarly.

"Eglantine, it's Cecily," she said after the voice mail prompted her to leave a message. "I need you to call me as soon as possible. It's urgent. Please."

As she hung up, the image of Eglantine sinking into the dark waters of the Seine leaped into her mind's eye. She shut this out as best she could, made a quick online search for a shop location, then hurried out the door.

"Um, bonjour," Cecily said when she got to the counter of the shop in Clichy-sous-Bois. "*Je m'appelle Cecily LeClercq. Bashir Maleh est-il ici?*"

The woman behind the counter, young and wearing a bright-purple hijab, eyed Cecily with suspicion. "LeClercq?"

"*Oui. Il est . . . mon ami,*" Cecily said, reciting the French she'd looked up on the surprisingly long journey to the neighborhood.

Despite its size, neither the Metro nor the RER trains had a stop there. She'd had to walk much of the way.

The woman disappeared into the back of the pharmacy. Cecily glanced around the small shop. Though it was about the size of two aisles of an American drugstore, the shelves running up both sides of the store were filled with just as many products. There were endless boxes of medications, medical equipment from canes to glucose meters, and household items from wet wipes to toothpaste. The main difference was there were usually one brand of each rather than ten.

"May I help you?" a woman, the spitting image of Bashir, in a lab coat and hijab, asked in English as she emerged from the back. Her voice was guarded as if already preparing to defend her brother.

"I need to see your brother, Samia," Cecily said. "It's urgent."

"'Samia'? Do we know each other, Mademoiselle LeClercq?" the pharmacist asked.

"I'm sorry," Cecily said. "I know my family has brought Bashir a lot of trouble recently, but I was hoping to talk to him. For my sake but also for his."

"You are the woman he was arrested with," the pharmacist said.

"I didn't mean to make trouble," Cecily said.

"What does it matter what you meant or did not mean to do if the result is the same?" Samia asked. "What is your business with him?"

"I wanted to tell him that the countess passed away last night," Cecily said. "I don't know if he knows that. I wanted to assure him it was peaceful. Not . . . fraught."

Samia Maleh's demeanor shifted. She eyed Cecily as if looking for signs of deception, then turned. "Follow me."

She led Cecily through a stockroom to a staircase at the back of the building. They headed up into a residential apartment where an older man sat at a laptop entering numbers into an accounting program. He eyed Cecily quizzically. Samia said a couple of quick words to him, then led Cecily down a hall to a closed door.

"Bashir?" she said, knocking.

The door opened a moment later to reveal a bleary-eyed, half-dressed Bashir. "Cecily?" he said with surprise. "How did you find me?"

Samia said something quickly in Arabic and nodded

toward their father. "Right," said Bashir, grabbing a shirt and jacket before following them back downstairs.

The pharmacist returned to her work as Bash and Cecily sat on the boxes in the stockroom.

"I heard about the countess," Bash said.

"Already?" Cecily asked.

"It's online," Bash replied, holding up his phone. "They didn't list a cause of death. It said the last Countess LeClercq passed away in Calais. You were with her?"

"I was," Cecily admitted.

"I'm so sorry," Bash said. "That must've been awful. Was it your wraith?"

Cecily explained what happened. Bash shook his head in disbelief. "I'm glad she was with you, though, and not alone."

"Like you were with Marguerite?" Cecily ventured.

Bash turned away for a moment, a haunted look on his face. "I'm not meant to talk to anyone about the case," he said. "But I need you to know I did not kill her, all right?"

"I know you didn't. You couldn't. But someone did. Did you see who?"

"It was very dark," he said. "There was someone behind her. She was lifted off her feet and her throat slashed. It was horrible. It was like with your friend René."

"I'm sorry you had to see this. Why were you there in the first place?"

"I'd been on my way home for the night when I saw a cyclist," Bash explained. "I was afraid she was lost. I followed her to the trail but then she left her bike behind and I worried it was more serious. Maybe she was dehydrated or disoriented. When I got to the tree, she was already off the ground."

"My God."

"I ran to her side. I tried to stop the bleeding, but the wound was too deep. I held her hand as she stared up into the tree. She tried to speak but couldn't. She was dead within seconds, I'm afraid. I stayed with her. Tried to move her, but she was too heavy. I hurried to town and called the police but anonymously. I didn't want trouble for my family or for me."

"What happened to the wraith?"

"Vanished," Bash said. "Disappeared into the woods. I saw the curved blade of a dagger flash in the moonlight. A footprint, too, maybe."

"What did it look like?" Cecily asked, remembering the wraith's toes tapering into points as if the flesh had been flayed from the bone.

"A heavy boot," Bash said. "Like a wellie. Isn't that what the English call them?"

Cecily scrunched her brow. "Are you sure?"

"Not at all," Bash admitted. "All I told the police was that her killer must have known she would be there. It was too remote. How else could they have known to be right there in the middle of the night like that?"

Bash was right. It didn't make a difference if it was the wraith. She would've appeared no matter where she was, especially if the rabbi had been right and it emerged from within Marguerite herself. But if it was someone else . . .

"I'm sorry I didn't call you when I was released," Bash said, lowering his voice. "The arrest really panicked my family. If it had not been for Eglantine and the countess's lawyers, I would probably still be locked up. They want me to stay with relatives back in Biskra for a while."

"What about becoming a forester for the arts foundation?" Cecily asked.

"That might have to wait," Bash said. "That reminds me. You remember asking about evergreen oaks? I looked them up online. Apparently, they found several of them in the Val d'Oise a few years back. It made the news because developers had to get permission to knock them down."

"On LeClercq land?" Cecily asked.

"No, just on the north side of the Thève," he said, scrolling through his phone. "Near where we were arrested, in fact. Here's an article on it."

He passed his phone to Cecily. She translated it into English and read it. It was short and exactly what Bash said. Developers clearing land to build a new neighborhood came across rare evergreen oaks. There were a couple that were culled but others were removed and transplanted. This sent a shiver through Cecily. This was a community of mutually dependent trees that dated back centuries. Orphaned, they'd probably last a decade.

There was a map next to the article. Cecily clicked on it and zoomed out. It was two kilometers from where the Oise met the Thève. Could Marguerite's sapling have come from there? She checked the date. It was five years earlier. The tree was too young.

But maybe it was from close by.

"I'm going to head up there," Cecily said. "To look around."

"I'll go with you," Bash offered.

Cecily shook her head. "I appreciate it. But not this time."

She headed out, having the same problem getting out of Clichy-sous-Bois as she had getting there in the first place. By the time she reached an RER train, it was afternoon.

Dark clouds suggesting rain hung over Félice. Cecily wished she'd brought a bicycle. She got an idea, and after tromping to the LeClercq Forest, slipped over to the estate. Though she'd been there less than twenty-four hours before, it looked changed. Much more overgrown, as if it had been the countess's presence alone that had held back the plants and trees for so long. Now they were ready to take over completely.

Cecily hurried to the work shed where the bicycles were kept, slipped one out, and cycled away into the gloomy afternoon.

There was a funereal stillness to the woods. Again, she felt that she was projecting. The forest couldn't mark the passing of the countess any more than the chateau itself. Yet there was no birdsong. No breeze. Little sun.

She used her phone to find the fastest route to the Oise. It used Bash's shortcut of the other day, sending her through the woods only to appear in the tiny neighborhood of small, gray brick houses before reaching the river itself. She broke north and followed the Oise for several miles, the LeClercq Forest to her right. She waited for the rain to come, but it never did. As if the clouds overhead were there solely to block out the sun.

As she neared the meeting of the Oise and Thève, the sound of construction equipment echoed over from the far side of the river. There were new and half-built houses rising from land that must have once been as thick with trees as the LeClercq Forest on the opposite side.

She crossed the next bridge and rode into the neighborhood, looking for residual signs of the evergreen oaks. They were all gone. The roads curved in great, almost beautiful patterns like curlicues. The houses lining them were grand, modern estates with a thin veneer of individualizing touches to make them look less like pieces of a planned community for the suburban rich.

If the LeClercqs came into money today, this might be where they lived.

There were a handful trees here and there, some quite large, but none older than a couple of decades and certainly no evergreen oaks. She circled around and went through the neighborhood a second time but didn't even see any stumps.

Marguerite's sapling couldn't have come from here.

She exited the neighborhood only to see the next several miles along the Thève had been cleared as well. Property lines had been marked and even a few foundations poured. More houses were soon to come. Cecily cycled on, looking for the end of the development only to finally reach it a couple of kilometers later where the plowed-under land ended abruptly at the edge of a forest.

A sign on the cleared land indicated that it would soon be the site of a geothermal power plant designed to be part of France's carbon-neutral future. She scoffed. There was a certain irony that thousands of trees had to be cleared in order for humans to reduce their carbon usage.

L'hommes, she thought in echo of her mother's most common sentiment.

The woods were dense. Impenetrable. Cecily cycled a short way up the road to see if there was another way in. Only a few yards away, she spied a second sign planted in front of the old forest. Her heart sank. This, too, was to be cut down?

Photographs on the sign promised modern homes, beautiful swimming pools, and large, multi-acre tracts. It was the name of it that stopped Cecily in her tracks.

It was to be called Beauverie.

21

CECILY DROPPED THE bike and stepped through the high grass to the sign. She couldn't believe what she was reading. But there it was in a luxurious blue script.

Beauverie.

She'd spent so long scouring the past for the name that she never considered it was something that didn't exist yet. There was no question now. Marguerite had been here. Had perhaps taken the sapling from here. Had wanted Cecily to come here. But why?

She glanced back over the Thève to the LeClercq Forest. It was barely a hundred yards away.

A wild theory formed in her head. It seemed impossible. She took out her phone and returned to the water utilities map she'd stumbled across while looking for a car service. The one that showed the abandoned wells.

She scrolled around the map until she found about where she was standing on the north shore of the Thève. She zoomed in on the woods that would soon become Beauverie. There it was. About two kilometers from where she now stood was a third well.

She stared at the image of the old-fashioned water pump. It might be a coincidence. There were probably hundreds of old wells across France. But between its location, the name

Beauverie, and the possibility of another stand of evergreen oaks hidden somewhere within, she knew she had to find it.

She clicked the utilities map to make it overlay her own map. Now, she appeared as a blue dot on the chart and could plan a route. She retrieved her bike, cycled down the road until she was directly south of the well, then entered the woods.

Though she was scared, she was also giddy. If her great-grandmother had really been on the trail of something, this was where it had led. The very last thing she'd written for anyone to find was a name given to these woods. She didn't know what she'd see there, but she prayed it held answers to her remaining questions.

This forest was as beautiful as the LeClercq Forest to the south and likely as old. There were small differences. The density of trees, for one thing. There was a section much younger than its surrounding trunks with all the telltale signs of a small forest fire, likely from a lightning strike. The trees had come back over the ensuing years, but they weren't as integrated with the surrounding specimens.

Still, everything else was in place. There was high grass and undergrowth. Signs of decay and of late-summer growth. There were suggestions of animal life, including an area of roots recently dug into by boar, as well as birdsong coming from the upper branches. Every indication of a well-operating, old-growth forest.

What it didn't have were oaks.

A kilometer in and she still hadn't seen any. There were no particularly large trunks or dark clearings. No acorns on the ground. No dead oak leaves in the underbrush. She kept picking her way forward, drawing closer and closer to the well symbol on the map. It couldn't be much farther.

When she was a few dozen yards away, she spied a clearing. There was no sign of an evergreen oak tree, but it was better than nothing. Reinvigorated, she hurried the last few feet to what she assumed would be some sort of meadow in the middle of the woods.

It was a large pond.

Cecily checked the map a second time. The blue dot was a few yards from the well. For the map to be right, the well had to be underwater. She sighed. That's what she got for trusting technology. The overlaid map and the well could be off by only a few dozen yards and she'd never find it. She'd counted on seeing some great evergreen oak that would lead her straight to it as happened in the LeClercq Forest and the abbey.

No such luck this time. She exhaled, unsure of her next move, then noticed the tree she was leaning against was a young oak.

In fact, there were several oaks around the pond. Maybe two dozen in all. Some were quite old. The more she stared, the more she realized what was missing. An elder. A mother oak. The tree that likely lived in the center of where there was now a pond.

The pond's waters were dark and dense with algae. She couldn't tell how deep it was but didn't think it could go down too far. She took off her shoes and socks, stepped into the frigid water, and almost sank right in. It was much deeper than it appeared.

She'd have to try another approach.

She circled the pond, wondering if the well might be at its center. Could the water be the result of an overflowing aquifer? No. That wasn't how ponds worked. Still, there was something unusual about the pond. It was symmetrical, almost a perfect circle. If she didn't know better, she'd think it was man made.

Her second time around, she chanced to look back into the woods and saw a fallen tree trunk. It was not very wide around. It might have succumbed to beetles or some other invasive species a few years earlier. The trunk had broken into segments when it fell, and white mushrooms grew from its decaying insides.

Not far away there was a patch of recently turned ground. Something with a complex root system had been planted there as early as a few months back. Cecily ran her fingers through the earth. Something small had been pulled from the earth here, leaving loose earth behind. With evergreen oaks in such short supply, she thought it too much of a coincidence. It was the birthplace of the sapling from Marguerite's apartment.

She was in the right place. Where her great-grandmother wanted her to be. The well had to be there somewhere.

She searched the woods beyond the pond for a third time, but it was hopeless. There was nothing to indicate a well or any other man-made structure unless it was buried beneath the dirt. She returned to the pond, thinking there was no way that Marguerite had swum around in it hunting for a well when she noticed that the lateral roots of one oak extended for several feet over the water. It didn't look right. For them to grow that way, there would've had to be soil there at some point.

Or not. Cecily crept over and eyed the roots closely. They hadn't been in dirt. She ran her fingers along their base. They were almost smooth. She spied a pair of rocks beneath the surface of the pond. No, not rocks. *Stone*. Could it be the well? She touched these as well. They were polished smooth but by hand rather than water. They were too large to have been part of a well. More like the giant fieldstones around the base of the abbey.

There were more along the shore. She pushed aside the grass and dirt at the water's edge and found an entire wall of stone sinking into the pond, including a pair as big as refrigerators. Water flowed between them in what Cecily thought might be a crevasse or break made by the oak's roots.

Only when she shined her camera's light into it did she see that it was a narrow corridor with walls of stone.

Her mouth went dry. Was this . . . a castle? Could she be standing on the ruins of the Castle LeClercq? She looked across the pond, back into the forest to where the LeClercq land was meant to end over a mile to the south. But if this was the remains of their actual castle, it certainly cemented any claim that this was part of their original property.

How could an error like this be made? She thought back to what Bash had said about maps and surveys. If they didn't even come about for several centuries after the castle was built, the boundaries of the land could've been forgotten or recorded wrong.

Except, the forest had never been touched. Not for a thousand years. Not until the arrival of this new neighborhood, Beauverie.

Somebody knew.

She peered back down the stone corridor. The water rose almost to the ceiling, but there was a narrow air pocket up top. She had to see inside. Had to know for sure if this was a castle or simply the remains of an old stone grain shed or something.

She removed her shoes and socks a second time and slipped into the pond. The frigid water was a shock. She almost laughed. France had proven far more dangerous than she'd ever heard. Wraiths, subterranean tunnels, and the ever-present threat of hypothermia were hardly in the brochure.

Her feet touched bottom. She'd expected dirt or sand, but it was smoother than that. It felt slick. Artificial. More fieldstones, maybe.

The gap between the large stones was so narrow that she had to squeeze through sideways, the force of the earth and time having pushed the walls together. She held her phone aloft to light the way, but there were still plenty of roots and branches beneath the surface to claw and tear at her clothing and skin. She tilted her head back to gulp in air, though the tight fit compressed her lungs.

She feared the corridor would lead nowhere. A flooded chamber at best. A wall. Instead, she reached the end and found a pile of rubble. Her light revealed that a section of stones from the ceiling had collapsed, damming off the water. She boosted herself over the barricade to see if there was anything on the other side.

There was a stone staircase descending into the earth.

Jesus Christ.

She pulled herself all the way out of the water, wet clothes clinging to her and made worse by the cool air of the subterranean passageway. The stairs on the other side, thankfully dry, were so steep that she had to lean against the wall to keep from falling forward. She passed several gaps in the stone walls, figuring more earth and roots had cracked through. But these gaps were framed. They were windows. She was in a tower.

She couldn't believe it. She'd thought the fieldstones were part of a foundation. But this suggested the castle had sunk into the earth. No wonder it disappeared! Had the castle been erected over a sinkhole? Its builders hadn't exactly had access to 3D seismic waveform tech, so it was certainly possible.

After a few more harrowing moments on the stairs, she reached the bottom and stepped into such a large chamber she first thought it was a cave. Her camera's tunnel-like beam was swallowed up by the darkness. The chamber was cool and the air damp. Condensation rose from the stone walls and slicked the floor. Piles of rubble indicated where sections of the ceiling had collapsed.

She crept across the uneven ground and peered into various chambers and corridors. A few had crumbled, the rooms filled with earth and stone. Others were eerily intact, with furniture and tools scattered around. It was as if they'd been left seconds earlier, their owners soon to return.

What she didn't find was a well.

She kept looking, circling back until she found a trapdoor made of solid oak in the floor of a side chamber. She lifted it. Light glowed up from below. She dropped her legs over the side and lowered herself in.

This chamber was shorter than the ones above. Cecily dropped to the floor and looked around. The room was small, like a prison cell. It had walls of stone but an earthen floor. Cecily stepped through its door to find several identical chambers off a main corridor. She was in a dungeon.

But one that's back wall had collapsed to reveal a vast cavern beyond, dimly lit from above. She stepped through the break into the cave. The ground was cold and wet, water dripping down from above.

Was she under the pond? That might make sense. The light drifting down shimmered a pale blue as if passing first through water. She was just wondering if the remains of the well were up there when she spied them in the center of the cave. They had fallen into a subterranean lake, a pile of broken stones and masonry. On top of it, lying on its side, was the largest evergreen oak tree Cecily had ever seen.

It had fallen from above, its branches, taproot, and trunk shattering apart upon impact. It was like some great sea creature beached on the land, unnatural, with its entire form out of the ground. It had been over 150 feet tall.

It was dead. There was no question of that. For how long? Cecily moved closer to the underground lake. It couldn't have been more than three or four feet deep. Most of the tree's leaves had fallen off but a few remained, including on the tip of a branch bathed in light. Here, a handful of rich green leaves strained up toward the sun. Not so dead after all.

It didn't make sense. How could the tree and the remains of the well be down here without there being some great hole in the ground up there? When her foot had touched the bottom of the pond, hadn't it felt . . . unnatural?

"The lake bottom is temporary," said a familiar voice from the darkness behind her. "Fiberglass and concrete. Does not have to last forever. Only long enough to finalize the sale."

Cecily aimed the light back in the direction from which she came. The person's presence wasn't a surprise. More like confirmation of what she'd suspected.

"Eglantine," Cecily said as the young lawyer stepped from the sunken castle into the great cave.

"Countess LeClercq," Eglantine replied.

"What happens when they build houses up there?" Cecily asked, pushing the apprehension from her voice. "They'll come crashing down into here."

"You do not think they will test the ground first?" Eglantine asked. "Even so, I will be far away. One more thing blamed on the LeClercq curse, *non*?"

"Like my great-grandmother's murder?" Cecily asked.

Eglantine darkened. "And yours," she said, stepping closer. "That is, if they ever find your body."

There was a wooden crate in Eglantine's hand. Cecily had seen it before, but it took her a moment to remember where. It was in the catacombs beneath the LeClercq abbey. The World War II–era grenades.

Eglantine followed Cecily's gaze and sighed theatrically. "It is a shame," she said, nodding to the sunken castle. "This has real historical value. It could raise the price. But if an old woman like your great-grandmother and now you yourself can pick up invisible threads and follow them to me, *alors*, one must cover one's tracks."

"You murdered her in cold blood," Cecily said, eyeing the break in the castle wall. If she had the right angle, she could get past the lawyer and escape. She had to keep her talking. "You cut her throat. Did she know you were stealing from her sister?"

Eglantine shook her head. "Oh, no. Her fear of this nonsense curse blinded her to all else," she explained. "With her it was, 'who planted these oaks, where is the castle, where is the third well, who were these massacred people?' She had gone down there, you know. Her! An old woman. When she could not find what she knew *must* be there, she asked me— *me!*—if the countess was wrong about the boundaries of the LeClercq lands."

"And you lured her to the tree one night with a promise of answers?"

Eglantine clapped her hands. "It was child's play," she said. "Once you are in the thrall of this curse, you want to believe any piece of information is a clue. That is why the countess was so easy to manipulate as well. 'You want the curse to vanish? Sign these documents.' With your great-grandmother, it was,

'You want to know the secret of the wraith? Meet me at the tree at midnight. The countess must not know!'"

"And what, you discovered this land north of the Thève was owned by the LeClercqs as well?"

"Owned yet forgotten," Eglantine admitted. "But ripe to be rediscovered following the death of the last LeClercq and, *oh la vache*—it falls into a trust only I control."

"But you got ahead of yourself," Cecily said, taking a couple of steps right. "Beauverie?"

"Ah, perhaps," Eglantine said. "Which is why I had to hasten things along. Particularly after you arrived and began snooping. Why I had to draw suspicion onto poor Bashir. Thankfully, the curse spun you in as many circles as your relatives. For a family whose fortune originated with murderers and thieves, the LeClercqs are also such fools."

"Is that how you see this?" Cecily asked. "You're avenging those wronged by the LeClercqs?"

"Precisely that," Eglantine said, as if it should be self-evident. "The history of the LeClercqs is the story of generations of vile, selfish people with no interest in atoning for their sins. They try to cheat the curse, bribe it away, or let others pay the price. What I uncovered working for the countess was contemptible. Do you think the Countess Sandrine was the first to try to sacrifice an innocent? A count in the sixteenth century paid a poor villager to impersonate him as did a countess in the eighteenth. The first Count LeClercq is hardly the only one who preyed on the innocent. The world will be much improved when there is not a single LeClercq left alive."

"But if the curse follows the fortune, aren't you afraid you'll be next?"

Laughter erupted from Eglantine. It was the most purely

joyful sound Cecily had heard in days. "How long have you been in France?" Eglantine asked. "Less than a week? And listen to you. The moment you believe in the curse you are its victim."

"You don't believe in it?" Cecily asked.

"Of course not!"

"But it possessed *you*," Cecily said. "On Nuit Blanche. In the Tuileries Garden."

Something flickered across Eglantine's face. It was the first time Cecily had seen her look uncertain. "Did it?" she asked, scoffing. "Are you so certain? Or do you mean like René getting in a horrible car accident after a night of Herculean drinking, or Madame, the countess, dying of a heart attack following days and days of intense trauma?"

Eglantine paused, eyeing Cecily closely as if to gauge the effect of her next words. "Or do you mean like your mother driven mad enough by the murder-suicide of her parents to finally walk into the sea?"

Cecily used Eglantine's amusement to break for the exit. The young lawyer was taken by surprise but recovered quickly. Cecily was maybe two steps from getting around her when Eglantine drew a dagger with a curved blade from her pocket.

"Careful," Eglantine hissed. "Or would you like to make this easy for us both? The sooner you are dead, the sooner this last bit of LeClercq land becomes mine."

Cecily tripped backward, landing near the edge of the underwater lake. She knew Eglantine was serious. She expected to see madness in Eglantine's face. Instead, there was single-minded focus, like a predator who'd cornered its prey and knew it was only a matter of time now.

Cecily's fingers reached below the loam at the bottom of the shallow lake. She touched what she knew must be bone.

Another body. Another unaccounted for, unmourned, and unburied soul dead because of the LeClercqs and their greed.

Her victims were fewer in number, but Eglantine fit right into the LeClercqs' line. She'd already proved herself willing to kill innocent people for profit. Not that Cecily was one to talk. She hadn't killed anyone, but the havoc she'd wreaked on the lives around her was monstrous on its own. To René. To the countess.

"You finally know fear," Eglantine said, advancing on Cecily. "As so many victims of your family did before you."

When Eglantine killed her, the madness would stop. Those close to Cecily would be safe. She wondered if the wraith would one day return to kill more people and claim Eglantine. Unless the rabbi was right. What if the wraith really was a physical manifestation of subconscious shame passed through generations of LeClercqs?

Would that affect Eglantine at all?

And wasn't she falling for the trap all LeClercqs fell fir anyway? Believing their sacrifice would be the final one? Thinking they could appease the past while doing nothing to confront their own culpability in the present?

The countess was right. Cecily was the Countess LeClercq. The inheritance was hers to answer for, not Eglantine. She was no sacrifice.

She rose to her feet.

And the wraith emerged from the shadows behind Eglantine.

Unaware, Eglantine continued to advance on Cecily.

"Eglantine . . . ," Cecily whispered.

Eglantine raised an eyebrow. "What is it?"

Cecily pointed behind her. Eglantine scoffed, held up one of the old grenades, and grinned. "You think I am so easily fooled?" she asked, even as she glanced back.

Cecily wondered if Eglantine would see the wraith. When the dagger slipped from the lawyer's hand and embedded itself in the loam, she had her answer.

"*Putain de merde*," Eglantine said defiantly. "What is this, Cecily?"

Cecily closed her eyes, pushed herself back into the water, and swam toward the fallen oak tree.

"Cecily!" Eglantine bellowed as the shadows drew closer.

The lake grew deeper but not by much. When Cecily kicked her legs, her toes struck the bottom. She lifted her head to take a breath and saw the wraith, her sharp, bony fingers upraised. Eglantine was pulling grenades from the crate.

There was a muffled shout, followed by the echo of metallic clicks. Cecily swam faster.

Sounds faded underwater. There was a muffled explosion. The water quaked around her. A second explosion was followed by a third. Then a fourth. The real rumbling began. The cave shook. Something heavy slammed into the lake a few yards from Cecily. More objects crashed down as if it was raining boulders.

Cecily pressed on, blocking out the commotion. She heard a scream. Something flashed over the surface of the water like sheet lightning. Light spilling down from above grew brighter as if the sun itself had slipped into the cave. The lake floor shuddered and cracked. Cecily feared she'd be swept down through some subterranean crevasse.

She finally reached the fallen tree and climbed into its tangle of roots. She looked back to the water's edge but couldn't see Eglantine. The ceiling tore itself apart. Water, chunks of fiberglass, rocks, and even trees tumbled down from above as if the cave meant to swallow up the entire earth.

Cecily pulled her legs up to her chest as she sank into the oak's broken trunk. The noise around her was so thunderous that she could hear nothing else. She waited for it to stop, but it grew louder. Earth and stone struck the tree, breaking off limbs and drilling into the trunk. Cecily made herself as small as she could, waiting for the boulder that would bury her alive.

22

Dawn came.

Cecily awoke to the ice crystals on her eyelashes melting in the morning sun. Above her, a canopy of oak limbs. Their trunks ringed her like Greek columns. She was in the forest.

Was this a dream?

No. It was far too cold for it to be a dream. Her clothes were stiff with frost. When she attempted to sit up, her hair was frozen to the ground. She gently pulled it free.

Her hands ached. Her fingernails were cracked and her fingers bloody. She remembered climbing and falling, rising again toward vanishing sunlight then to the glow of the rising moon. Of dirt filling her mouth and her hands tearing through roots and earth.

She tried to stand, but the pain shivering up her legs and torso was too severe. Her left side hurt, electric spasms of pain exploding through her body with every movement. She couldn't remember how she'd gotten hurt.

The castle, the underground lake, the disintegrating sinkhole she'd crawled out of, and even Eglantine was nowhere to be seen. It was as if the forest had grown up and over it in the night. More likely, she'd traveled some distance before collapsing, though in which direction she didn't know.

Her right leg buckled as she tried to take a step. Her jeans were torn and crusted with dried blood. She touched the wound. It stung.

She reached for her phone. It wouldn't turn on. Whether because its battery had finally died or because of the water, she didn't know. She shoved it back in her pocket, eyed the rising sun, and crawled south, lightheaded from dehydration and blood loss.

Something moved in the nearby grass. If it was the wraith or Eglantine, she didn't have a chance. She had no fight left in her. The sound of breaking twigs and bending grass drew closer. She tried to glimpse the intruder's face but saw nothing until she looked lower.

It was a herd of boar. They moved through the underbrush, snuffling in the mud, digging under roots, and breaking apart decaying bark with their hooves. A few cautiously eyed Cecily but realized right away she wasn't a threat. She tried to raise herself to her hands and knees but fell forward. Her face landed in the frosty mud with a crunch.

She lay in the mud for a long moment, gathering her strength. The boar moved on a few yards, finding another place to root. "Hold on," Cecily whispered. "I'll come with you. Don't worry."

She fought her way back up to her hands and knees. This time, she stayed upright. It wasn't easy, but she managed to crawl a few feet forward, following the boar on their hunt. A boarlet came to investigate but quickly raced back to its mother. Cecily's palms and knees became bloody and skinned until she thought to cover them with a layer of mud.

As the boar devoured acorns, Cecily realized this answered one of the questions Eglantine attributed to Marguerite. Who planted these oaks? The boar did. That was part of the symbiotic nature of the forest. Oaks dropped acorns. Boars ate the acorns and pooped out the seeds. She imagined a supernatural connection in addition. The boar and the oaks the only witnesses to the hasty covering up of the Beauverie dead, unable to do anything to stop it but mark the location.

The sun rose higher. Every time Cecily thought the boar were leaving her behind, they seemed to slow down to allow her to catch up. When she lost sight of them, their sounds traveled back to her, letting her know where they were.

At some point, she passed out. When she opened her eyes, the trees overhead were replaced by the faces of three curious horses. One sniffed her face. All three were saddled but only two had riders, both young children in helmets and riding gear who stared at her as curiously as the boar.

"*Est-elle morte?*" one child asked the other as someone spoke in rapid French nearby.

"*Tu est mort?*" the other child asked Cecily.

Cecily turned her head and saw the children's mother speaking quickly into her phone. She'd made it to the banks of the Thève, the LeClercq Forest on the other side. She felt something vibrate and took her phone from her pocket. There was a new text, this from a law firm sent the evening before confirming receipt of her renunciation of Marguerite's estate.

She scoffed. Her phone's battery died for real now. She drifted back into unconsciousness.

The next time Cecily awoke, she was in a hospital room with an IV tube running into her arm and wires twining up to electrode monitor pads on her chest. A window framed a view of Paris that included Sacré-Cœur.

A man slept in a chair in the corner. René. He wasn't as pale as the last time she'd seen him, but his skin hung loose as he'd lost a lot of weight in a short amount of time. His neck was wrapped in several colorful scarves to cover a wide white bandage.

"Ah, you are awake," said Auberon, stepping into the room with two cups of coffee.

Cecily fell back to sleep before she could answer.

She spent the next two days in the hospital. She was dehydrated but also had sustained a punctured lung that had already required surgery. She was visited by a pair of police detectives who wanted to discuss what had been discovered beneath the abbey at the LeClercq estate as well as several inconsistencies in the legal paperwork around the countess's bequeathments.

"Have you seen or been in contact with the lawyer, Eglantine Saintève?" the detectives asked.

"We were to meet up on Nuit Blanche but never connected," Cecily said. "I texted and called her several times since. There was never an answer."

"You would give us permission to check your phone records?" they asked.

"Absolutely," Cecily said. "But why?"

"In our attempt to find Mademoiselle Saintève, we tracked her phone. Its last position was near the cave-in you escaped. Her car was parked nearby. Did you plan to meet her there?"

"Not at all," Cecily said. "I read about the evergreen oaks there and I was hoping to see more."

"Are you aware that Saintève may have been in line to inherit that land herself? Whether at the countess's request or her own doing?"

"I had no clue," Cecily lied.

"Which means, they now belong to you."

"How so?"

"It would have reverted to the countess, whose sole living relative was Marguerite Varennes, your great-grandmother. You inherited her estate. This is now a part of it. There appears to be a sale pending to a group of developers, but this changes that."

Cecily looked to Thérèse, who'd come along to make sure there was nothing lost in translation. "We should talk about this," Cecily said. "For a number of reasons, I think it should be left in the hands of your friends at Temple Emanuel."

"I will let them know," Thérèse said.

Cecily had picked up on fragments of conversations between Thérèse and Auberon discussing the ongoing excavations at the abbey and in the LeClercq forest. No one was quite sure where so many bodies should finally be laid to rest. Cecily thought the land that was meant to be Beauverie might be appropriate.

When she was released from the hospital, it had been seventy-two hours since she'd seen the wraith. Every night when she'd fallen asleep, she'd looked for the specter in the shadows but somehow knew she wouldn't be there. As Auberon drove her back to Marguerite's house, she stared out passersby, waiting for them to return her gaze.

None did.

"We will pick you up at eight tomorrow?" Auberon asked as he helped her inside.

Cecily nodded. The twin funerals for Countess Aline LeClercq and Marguerite Varennes were to be held the next morning at Père Lachaise.

"One thing, though," she said. "I want to thank you for all you've done for me despite all the horrors I've visited on you and your husband. I know it's hard to believe—"

He cut her off by taking her hands in his. "You need not explain or apologize," he said. "I understand now that there are things beyond my comprehension. I do not need to see them to know they are there or true. I need only believe your words."

He embraced her and smiled. "Get some rest tonight. Call if you need anything."

"Merci," Cecily said.

"*De rien.*"

Waiting for Cecily on the kitchen counter were the countersigned documents from the arts foundation. Included was a legal letter telling her that they understood the extraordinary circumstances surrounding her recent medical emergency and would work with her to determine when it would be convenient for her to vacate the premises.

It wasn't aggressive but the meaning was clear. It was time for Cecily to go home. She washed her clothes. Packed her things. Texted the foundation's lawyers to say that she'd be out the next day and hunted for a flight back home.

When night fell, she couldn't sleep. She walked out into the Marais. It was a beautiful, cool, cloudless evening. If it was to be her last in Paris, she wanted to spend at least some of it on her feet. She walked down to the Seine, past the Louvre, and up to the wide boulevard on which she'd been attacked on Nuit Blanche. Nothing was out of the ordinary. She still stayed away from people, a habit she doubted she'd break anytime soon, but no one noticed her.

No one's faces changed. No one attacked.

She walked past a gorgeous building her app told her was an opera house, then wound her way to Montmartre. Hearing singing, she climbed the steps to Sacré-Cœur in time to listen to the choir of nuns as their voices trickled through the night.

On her way back to the Marais, she passed the spot on the road where Auberon had crashed their borrowed car. Though the car had been towed and all the shattered pieces swept up, the telltale markings on the pavement and curb from the violence of that night remained.

Père Lachaise was Paris's most famous cemetery and the final resting place of everyone from French luminaries like Balzac, Edith Piaf, and Marcel Marceau to foreigners like Oscar Wilde, Gertrude Stein, and Jim Morrison of the Doors. In short, a tourist mecca.

As Cecily wound her way to the chapel at its center for the service, she passed hundreds of people milling around or moving from grave to grave.

"Is it always this full?" she asked Auberon.

"The cemetery is closed today," he said. "All these people are here for the Sisters LeClercq."

They filed into the chapel and took their seats next to René. Before the service began, René continually nudged Auberon to get him to point out various luminaries to Cecily.

"The former Vietnamese ambassador to France," Auberon explained. "A fan of your great-grandmother's work. That woman there is an architect from Tasmania the countess helped get a college degree through one of her charities. The other lady makes hats in a village outside Loja in Ecuador specifically to match Marguerite's designs."

An elderly man, eyes red with tears, approached the coffin of the countess aided by a friend. He touched the countess's hand and then her cheek before sitting down.

"Who's that?" Cecily asked.

"A baker from Auvers-sur-Oise who was the closest the

countess came to taking a husband some sixty years ago," Auberon said. "Can you imagine carrying love in your heart for a person that long?"

René grinned and put his arm around Auberon as if in answer. Auberon kissed his husband gently on the cheek.

Afterward, the coffins were carried to a pair of open graves, a prayer was said, and a moment of silence followed. Afterward, it was announced that Pauline and her husband, Jacques, friends of Marguerite, had laid out a small feast in the nearby botanical garden. Everyone departed except Cecily. She stayed by the graves, thinking about the funeral her own mother never had and where she'd go from there.

René and Auberon came back for her a while later and drove her to the airport. They said their goodbyes, René slipped her a couple of sleeping pills for the plane, and she left for the States.

Epilogue

"Try there," Cecily said, eyeing the image on her tablet as she munched from a bag of chips on the roof of her camper. "Looks like a gap."

On-screen in the woods north of the Thève, Bash carefully dug into the soil several yards from a large oak tree.

"You were right," Bash said, holding his tablet's camera over exposed roots. "The root crown extends well past the drip line. How much farther out do you think?"

"Three feet?" Cecily suggested.

Bash marked this off and indicated the spot. "Here?"

"Turn the camera all the way around," Cecily said.

Bash did a slow 360 with the tablet. Cecily took in his surroundings. Though the birthplace of her great-grandmother's evergreen oak sapling had collapsed into the sinkhole, Bash had found a secondary site. He'd sent Cecily several photos and they'd agreed that the sapling had a real chance if planted there.

Now, they had to find the exact right spot.

"Don't kill me, but I think it should be another foot to the right," Cecily said.

"Farther from the trunk?"

"Yep."

Bash got to work digging a second hole.

It had been a month since Cecily had returned to America. In that time, Bash had landed a job as an assistant forester with the arts colony moving into the LeClercq estate. Even better, they were paying him to go to university to study dendrology. He was currently helping reestablish the garden on the estate itself while mapping out hiking and biking trails through the LeClercq Forest.

He had also worked with Temple Emanuel to determine where to inter the bodies of those recovered from the LeClercq lands. There had initially been some difficulty wriggling free from the contract to sell the land to Beauverie's developers—until they learned of the instability of the ground. Now, it would be set aside for the victims and left alone. No trails cut here. A memorial was planned for the following year.

"Good?" Bash asked, finishing the hole.

"*Parfait*," Cecily agreed. "May it grow there for a thousand years."

Bash removed the sapling from the pot and readied it to plant.

"Don't forget to take a photo and send it to René and Auberon," Cecily said.

"Will do," Bash said. "How's the job hunt, by the way?"

"Slow," Cecily admitted, angling her camera so that Bash could see the sunrise over the Sierra Nevadas. "Turns out, not a lot of people want to hire plant hunters who refuse to meet face-to-face and won't poach endangered seedlings."

"Who would have guessed?" Bash replied.

Cecily had initially returned to Charleston. But when she'd gone to the farmers market in Marion Square, the face of the woman handing back her change at the vegan fried chicken stand had begun to melt. Everyone else in the square followed suit. Cecily had fled to the wetlands for the next two days.

There, she'd caught sight of the wraith moving through the trees.

After the wraith vanished, Cecily had gone to Ina's to deliver cuttings only for it to reappear in the shadows of Ina's workroom. She'd screamed and ran, passing out on the sidewalk outside. When she came to, Ina told her she was booking her into a nearby hospital for tests. Cecily eagerly agreed to go, told Ina she would go collect her things, then left Charleston for good.

She drove west. She didn't understand why the wraith had returned. Nor why she hadn't killed Hideo or Ina or anyone in Marion Square. Whatever this new version of haunting was, Cecily would have to learn about it away from anyone else. She hoped to do this when she'd finally stopped when she reached the remote mountains above Lake Tahoe on the Nevada side.

"Will rain soon," Bash said. "Got to get back. You sure you're all right over there?"

"Definitely," Cecily said. "It's going to be a beautiful day. May drive down to the lake."

"Still planning to hit Canada?" Bash asked.

"We'll see," she said, hearing someone moving close by. "Gotta go."

She hung up as a group of five bikers, all in their twenties wearing motorcycle racing suits, came up the trail on foot. She'd heard the clamor of their dirt bikes earlier but thought they'd moved on.

"Oh, hey," one biker said, waving. "Didn't know anyone was up here."

"Let me guess," Cecily said. "Looking for Sidewinder?"

The biker grinned. "The map—"

"—*sucks*," Cecily finished. "You're almost there. Trailhead is about two hundred yards that way."

She pointed down the dirt road she'd driven the camper up. It had almost destroyed the front axle, but she kept enough tools on board for minor repairs.

"Thanks," the biker said. "Hope we're not too loud for you."

She shrugged and saw the wraith behind them. Her black, matted hair and slate-gray face disappeared into the shadows of a nearby tree. Her fingers hovered inches above the neck of the last biker in line. At that angle, she could decapitate them in a single stroke.

Cecily ignored the wraith and looked back to the lead biker.

"Nah, I had to wake up anyway," she said. "Should hit the road soon."

"Yeah, we're hoping to beat the storm, too," the biker said. "Couple of runs and then out of here."

Cecily looked west. Sure enough, low-hanging clouds billowed over the mountains on the other side of the lake like smoke pushed under a door. It would reach her within the hour.

"Stay safe out there," she said, fingering the liquid-filled vial on the string around her neck.

"You, too," the biker said.

His skin turned gray and all the capillaries in his eyes burst at once, blood first encircling the iris, then consuming it. The faces of the other bikers darkened as well, the quintet moving into a half circle around the back of Cecily's camper. Cecily searched for the wraith, but she was gone into the branches of the nearest pine.

Instead of panicking, Cecily climbed off the roof of the

camper and stood in front of the bikers. She held their gazes for a moment as if daring them to step forward.

They all did.

But only one step.

Cecily refused to run. She looked from face to face, willing them to turn back to normal. Nothing happened. Their eyes remained roiling orbs of blood. Their skin slate.

Yet they didn't attack.

She glanced down to her arm still wrapped in a bandage from where a possessed gas station attendant had stabbed her with a screwdriver the day before, driving it a full half inch into her flesh before stopping. Today's result, though terrifying, was an improvement.

She took out her keys and backed her way to the truck, never taking her eyes off the bikers. She climbed into the front seat, keyed the ignition, and released the parking brake. As she began the long drive back down the mountain, she watched the biker stare at the retreating camper in the side view mirror.

She knew they'd soon be released as the wraith was now inside the camper. If Cecily glanced into the rearview mirror, she would catch a glimpse of a passing shadow. Maybe a pair of eyes staring back at her.

So, she kept her gaze on the dirt road ahead of her as the first echo of thunder rolled up from the lake. The rain began right as she pulled off the dirt road onto something paved. The presence in the back of her truck was gone. Cecily didn't know when it left but knew it would soon return.

One day it wouldn't, she hoped. She believed.

And then she'd finally be alone.

ACKNOWLEDGMENTS

First and foremost, and as always, I'd like to thank my wife, Lauren, and my children, Eliza and Wyatt, for their encouragement and support but also for putting up with the life of a writer. Also, Lauren in particular for being a tireless sounding board, reader, and editor.

I would also like to thank my agent, Laura Dail, whose notes, ideas, and edits informed this book in particular, sending me back to the drawing board time and again to shape this into something readers might enjoy.

In addition, I'd like to thank my equally longtime editor, Lisa French, who also sent me back to the drawing board on this book years ago now, taking the time to really spell out what did and didn't work for her. As with Lauren and Laura, I can only hope I executed their notes in ways that helped the text.

Finally, I'd like to thank all those at the Royaumont Abbey in Asnières-sur-Oise, France, the Franco-American Cultural Fund, and the Ile de France Film Commission who (unwittingly) provided the research opportunity for this book while I was their guest many moons ago in the beautiful and haunted Val d'Oise while researching an unrelated film project one autumn.

Finally finally, I'd like to thank the several editors of horror anthologies with whom I've worked this past year including Samantha Kolesnik, Nico Bell, Staci Layne Wilson, Aric Sundquist, Nicole Petit, and Mitchell Lüthi. I could not appreciate their notes, revisions, opinions, conclusions, and encouragement more as their insights into the stories we worked on together have carried over into this one.

Made in the USA
Las Vegas, NV
20 February 2022

44284817R00166